BRANDED PAST

ALSO BY RANDI SAMUELSON-BROWN

On the Fringes

Dark Range Series

Brand Chaser

Branded Graves

Branded Vengeance

BRANDED PAST

DARK RANGE
BOOK FOUR

RANDI SAMUELSON-BROWN

WOLFPACK
PUBLISHING
— EST 2013 —

BRANDED PAST

DRAW 'EM IN

JUNE 1889

"Remember—the trick is to have the sun at your back, so they have to stare into it."

Most of the men checked the angle in the sky and figured it to be about two o'clock in the afternoon. The smart ones, that was.

Gunfights at high noon amounted to a sucker's bet, when the shadows flattened into nothingness, leveling the odds for all concerned. That's not how he planned on playing it—and even odds meant an even chance of losing. Hank Cross considered himself no man's sucker.

But Old Man Cooper just might be.

In fact, Hank counted on it. He had sent out his rider at noon carrying the message.

We've got your son. Ready to castrate,
and you know why.

Hank's chosen timing provided the Cross faction with two hours to get ready.

That gave the Coopers one hour to ride.

PART I

PART 1

1

FREE WHISKEY IS SELDOM TRULY "FREE"

JUNE 2023

MONTY, STILL HALF DRUNK FROM THE NIGHT BEFORE, clanked distractedly into the kitchen—single spur jangling and wearing his weird, blue-lensed hippy sunglasses. On this morning, he probably needed the protection the glasses offered beyond his throwback 1970s fashion statement. To say that he appeared disheveled amounted to an understatement—a big understatement. He didn't smell too pleasant, either.

"What are you doing here?" He threw his question over at Emory when her presence registered. His voice grumbled, rough and grating.

"I live here," she countered, snappy and spry.

Lance, seated at the table, gave his cousin a wry and amused glance. "Rough night?"

Monty groaned as he sat down. "Don't suppose a cup of coffee might be too much to ask for."

"This isn't a restaurant, and I'm busy. Get it yourself," Emory sparred, "it's in the pot."

He made no movement to rise but shot her a nasty glare before pointing his attention back to Lance and the question posed. "Hmm. In one way. In the other, maybe it turned out as the best night ever."

"Oh?" Lance snatched a slice of toast from the plate and tore into the corner. "Your parking job leaves a bit to be desired."

The criticism didn't matter, if it even registered, and Monty brightened. "Get this. A woman wandered into the Ace, and she bought my drinks! Unfortunately..." he clowned, "I chose whiskey."

Lance chuckled, wagging his head. Suspicious, Emory frowned. She refused to fall for any of this hard-drinking, hard-living, good-ol'-boy shit. "Who was she?"

"How the hell should I know?" Monty's head popped up, like a turtle poking out from its shell.

Well, he'd better pull his scrawny neck right back in. Emory paused, spatula midair. "Like that happens all the time. Didn't she give you a name or anything?"

Guilty around the eyes, he fished for the answer. "Suzanna, maybe. Hell, I don't know."

Unamused, Emory persisted. "What did she want?"

"Now, hang on, Em," her father broke in, still chuckling in defense of his errant cousin. Encouraging him, even. "Monty here used to be quite the catch. Give him a bit of respect."

She ignored both her father's words and Monty's head bobbing up and down.

"Right," she deadpanned. "Thirty years ago, he sure might have been." She lifted the eggs from the pan onto a plate, which she delivered with a clattering toss onto the table's surface. The eggs threatened to slip off the plate, but she'd made her point. "Again. What did the woman *want*?"

"Again," Monty snapped back, "why are you here?"

"Because I obviously can't leave YOU unsupervised

for long." She claimed her place at the table and grabbed the spatula first, quick on the draw. Her actions weren't lost on them.

"Shit," Monty muttered.

Lance waited to choose his moment before wading in further. His eyes sparking as he helped himself to the eggs right after his daughter. "You think this is a *ladies' first* type of outfit?"

"No." Emory grabbed a slice of toast. "I think it's an I'm-the-one-who-did-the-cooking type of outfit while you two yahoos are just sitting there, acting like high schoolers reliving their glory days."

The crow's-feet around her father's eyes deepened with unshed laughter, but his cousin suffered too deeply to appreciate the humor at his expense.

Suffering or not, Emory turned her attention to the hungover cowhand. "I have vacation days that I need to use, if you must know."

"Yeah? Well, why don't you go to Yellowstone like other people?" Monty shot back, then muttered "...keep dragging around here...need other friends..."

Now he had a point to that, although he probably didn't even realize it at that moment. Not that she would ever admit as much to him.

"Because you're always getting into something you shouldn't, that's why."

She knew she ought to find something better to do with her free time, other than hanging around with these two old codgers. And that was all she needed—for Monty to get himself a girlfriend too. Her father already had Linda and she...she had no one at all.

Taking a mouthful of eggs and chewing that notion over, she steeled her reply. No sense in acting weak. Not even among family. "Back to the woman. What did you two find to *talk* about?"

"Whiskey," he growled.

"That's it? Whiskey. Right. Unless she's a type of a cheap whiskey sales rep, you'd best try to come up with a better recollection."

The kitchen fell silent, other than the men chewing. At length, Monty rose and clanked his way over to the coffeepot, poured out a cup and took a long draw. "Better," he commented into the silence, as if any of them cared.

He clanked his way back to the table, chair scraping on the bare wood floor. "Guess we talked about the ranch."

Now *that* clarification didn't go over well. Her father's eyes turned sharp, and beneath the teasing lurked a definite edge. "You didn't pick yourself up some old, used buckle bunny, did you?"

Monty, not catching the current, chuckled and patted his own buckle won in a local rodeo one day long since passed. "What'd you take me for? No, I'd say she was about thirty."

Emory snorted.

Her father, however, retained that steely-eyed expression. "Besides plying you with liquor for the hell of it, what else did she want? You didn't mention the name of the outfit, did you?"

"The Lost Daughter? Now I can't be certain, but probably..."

Lance grumbled. "She ain't going to come around, is she?"

"She shouldn't." Monty shifted in his seat, turning a shade toward indignant. "After all, I didn't give her my number."

Emory rolled her eyes.

"And I saw that, Missy." He jabbed a fork into the air between them.

"Good. You were meant to." Their eyes locked. "Now, are you two planning on working today, or just sit around jawing?"

Her father pushed away from the table with a feigned disgust. "It sure is a good thing you don't have more vacation days. You're knocking us out of our routine—but take note that we can still manage to surprise you on occasion."

"What in the hell is that supposed to mean?"

Monty muttered under his breath, but she couldn't exactly hear it. Didn't need to, at any rate.

"You'll see," her father replied.

Yeah. And maybe next time she'd just go to Yellowstone.

———

EMORY CLEARED THE DISHES, abandoning them in the sink. As she turned away from the window above the faucet, the view caught her as it always did when she'd been away. On that morning the cloudless, soaring blue of the sky stretched forever, dwarfing the land below. Their ranch buildings, set into a sprawling green valley whose color would fade as the summer marched on, stood ringed by the guarding pale rimrocks. Beyond them the terrain ascended upward into the Never Summer Mountain Range. Flat-out, nothing compared to the views commanded by the Lost Daughter. Some other spreads nearby might come close, but the Lost Daughter would win the beauty contest, hands down.

Every single building, every single fence post, and in fact, every blade of grass framed by that one single window represented what their family fought for. What they would continue to fight for as time pressed on into the twenty-first century, for better or for worse.

Stepping away from that outdated avocado sink, she crossed the linoleum-floored ill-conceived breezeway, opened the aluminum side door, and legged it down the sagging stairs that would give way one of these days, if someone didn't attend to them. Planting her size-nine boots on the hallowed Lost Daughter ground, she inhaled and drank in the vistas her soul longed for. From the profound deep blue sky that almost hurt in its vastness, and all the way down to the scrub sage ground, they owned the land like they owned their history. Every square inch mattered. And as the sixth generation of Crosses, she could, and would, lay claim to it all.

Certain of her obligations, and she knew she'd best be making babies to pass it all down—the land, the history, the responsibility.

The grass in the hay meadow slow danced in the breeze, and the sky above whispered of freedom and promise…for those who remained vigilant. The rimrocks guarded and waited, outlasting the men who waged range wars—allies to the Lost Daughter guns wielded, but those victories came at a cost—and sometimes a heavy price paid.

Defeated or victorious, the bold and dramatic scenery meant, in time, that the entire county found itself "discovered." In hindsight, it seemed of little wonder that newcomers streamed in, and the property values soared. That didn't mean that the locals had to like it.

The Crosses weren't selling, no matter who came bounding or slithering into the area, anxious to buy themselves an honest piece of the West. No matter what stupid amount of money offered—no matter how they wheeled, bargained or cajoled—the Lost Daughter would remain intact to survive another generation.

Such troublesome mindsets and their accompanying thoughts accomplished nothing more than getting a rise. As always, ranches experienced no shortage of work to go around, and she could certainly find plenty to keep herself busy. One thing stood out—no matter how odd of a combination her father and Monty presented, their outfit, from all outward indications, appeared far better run than in the recent past. That amounted to a win right there.

Kai's whinny carried on the soft morning and snapped her out of sensing the darker current. The horses, already turned out into the pasture, hadn't a care in the world.

"Hi Kai, hi Outhouse," she sang out. In response they watched her with their large, brown eyes.

Abandoning any notion of returning to the dishes, working with the horses would be a far better use of her time. Getting to know Outhouse, to be exact. *What a name.* She chuckled with a shake of her head. *Iver's $300 Cañon City special.* That "special" grazed in the front pasture and gazed at her with curious eyes.

"Good morning, handsome," she crooned, approaching the fence and chatting to get the bay mustang used to the sound of her voice. "You're our reward for not letting Iver bleed to death when he got shot on the porch. What a start."

Jealous, Kai ambled over, and nudged his way into the conversation. "You're interrupting our conversation, but good morning to you too."

The untested mustang ambled over, uncertain but

not unwilling. Curious, more than anything, but his actions signaled a fine day to train.

Slinging a halter over her shoulder, she entered the pasture, careful to latch the gate behind. Feigning a lack of interest, she angled toward Outhouse, closing the space between them...he danced off, but remained nearby. She pretended to ignore him, all the while edging closer without making eye contact.

When within striking distance, she lobbed the lead rope over his neck and caught him.

"Let's see what you know, and what we have." Leading him into the nearby circular pen, she patted him while holding on to the lead rope, walking him around. She grabbed a saddle pad on the rail, giving him a good look at the unfamiliar object.

Her father came over to the side of the pen to watch.

"I'm not sure about trying things on his back," Emory remarked without skipping a beat, holding on to the lead rope and rubbing him with the saddle pad to get him used to the smell and the feel.

"I can see that," her father replied. "That'll go for riders too."

"No one's done anything with him recently."

"He's not my horse," Lance countered, "but you might thank me for trimming his hooves."

Emory eyed him. "Thank you to me for cleaning the bathroom."

Her father didn't fall for it, but continued on with the conversation the way he wanted it. "From what I can tell, he's a good enough horse." Lance Cross cast a practiced eye over the mustang, but they both knew that he didn't hang around the pen to simply watch her work.

Emory chose the topic that interested her. "What do

you think about that woman buying Monty's drinks? I'm hoping she was just a figment of his imagination…"

Her father snickered at that last part. "Don't know."

"Last time anyone jawed about the Lost Daughter involved Cade…and then came the gunfights. We all know how that mess ended."

"You been up to visit the graves?" Lance Cross asked, eyeing her close.

Sometimes their family history cut a little too close to the living bone.

"No. Not yet."

He jutted his chin out in response and made a great show of surveying their surroundings, eyes lingering on the rimrocks. In time, he patted the rail of the round corral. "I'll leave you to it then."

Emory again raked over those same rimrocks and swept across the vista. An uneasy feeling built in her spine. Trouble lurked on the horizon. She could feel it and worse, her father felt the same damned thing. He just didn't talk much about feelings and notions—at least not the ones he hadn't sized all the way up. And he didn't have a handle on this latest threat. Or at least, not yet.

2

FAIR PLAY IS FOR THE UNINITIATED

1889

HANK CROSS AND HIS RIDERS KILLED TIME UNDER THE burning sun at altitude, taking refuge in the scant shade if they could find it.

"Remember," Cross barked, "don't pull the trigger before you have a clear shot."

That amounted to the sum total of their conversation.

He took the measure of his surroundings for the umpteenth time. The pale sandstone rimrocks made as fine a fortress as any, far better than some. Squinting into the sky, Cross noted how the white relentless sun slanted overhead, tilting at an angle to the west. The clear cobalt sky sprawled endless and wide above man and beast over a land filled with rocks and sagebrush scrub. None of it worth much of anything, other than for the promise of the land itself.

A man of marked preferences, Hank Cross preferred to do his sharpshooting from obscured recesses and shadows. He'd eyed the specific dark crevasse he claimed for a good long time—in fact, every time he traveled along that trace. Nestled in the rimrocks, that crevasse offered a good vantage overlook and a wide enough angle for accurate shots downslope on the ravine below.

"Riders coming!" One of his men's' voice came from above.

Hank barked out his command, dead calm. "Everyone, take your positions and hold your fire until I give the signal."

He and his four men scattered along the bottom of the rimrocks, with two men already stationed on top.

Always a patient man, in him that favorable trait turned deadly. While many Sunday preachers extolled the virtue of patience, Cross held the conviction that a dark side came with damned near everything.

And he was living proof.

———

WEDGED IN THE OUTCROPPING, Hank felt hot. Uncomfortably hot. The sun blazed down on the ground below, unrelenting, and fierce—the boulders and rock surfaces radiated heat to the point they would have done some ovens proud.

Only a fool would believe an absence of clouds meant an absence of menace.

Their lookout had probably got a bit too excited and called out too early. No matter. The Cross faction would wait as long as it took for their prey to come within range—blued rifle barrels protruding through the rifts between boulders and outcroppings. No one had better dare complain about anything within his hearing.

Commanding strategic positions in the lengthening shadows and shielded from sight behind boulders and outcroppings, the men held their positions. They waited above the road, in the folds of the cliffs that guarded the route leading to the Lost Daughter Ranch.

On that day, he didn't want much of a gun*fight*—with emphasis on the word fight.

Hank Cross wanted a slaughter.

3

LEAVING A LEGACY MEANS MANY THINGS

JUNE 2023

LANCE DISPLAYED THE RANCHER BOW COMMON IN MANY men who'd spent years in the saddle. His shoulders remained wide and strong a new bend or rounding in developed, on that she hadn't noticed before. With a pang, she tore her eyes from her father and assessed Outhouse instead. Observing the mustang with a practiced eye, she figured he'd had enough for one day.

A damned twinge struck deep. Maybe her father'd had enough for a lifetime.

No sense on dwelling too long upon that loaded notion. He'd call it time when he wanted—not one minute more or less, unless death dragged him down. That damn problem of the continuance of the family line seemed increasingly difficult to guarantee.

Mood turning sour, she felt like fighting. Fighting against history, fighting against herself, or fighting against the ravages of time all played a part.

Her father expected her to do right by Hugo. She ought to go up to the cemetery to visit him...but guilt held her back. Apparently, she needed to steel herself just to face up to what never was meant to be, and that struck as a strange form of weakness. One she ought to be able to handle better, but obviously couldn't.

But damn it, vacations didn't usually involve visiting dead people. Especially not the one particular man who'd died helping her. Who had died trying to save her. That amounted to a hell of an obligation that she'd carry with her and carry with her always.

And she'd survived, all right. She'd survived.

Outhouse blew and shifted. Waiting, but not particularly bothered.

Emory inhaled and sighed. Outhouse did the same in response.

"I'll bet you've had enough for one day," she offered, but in truth she spoke about herself as the wind picked up, a cold pressing gust from the north that belied the season.

That breeze carried a message. Winds from the north usually meant a reckoning of one sort or another. The mustang lifted his head and flexed his ears, straining to hear. He let out a shrill whinny.

She led him from the round pen, across the rutted road and released him into the comparative freedom of the paddock. Typical of herd animals, he ran over and joined a completely unconcerned Kai, still contented and munching away on the tender spring grass.

Emory's attention snagged on the graves atop the rise, nestled in the long grasses that bent and waved in the wind.

A rusty hinge whined with protest and a sharp *crack!* carried.

She jumped, spooked. "Just a door," she muttered, feeling foolish. Glancing down, the fine hair on her arms and at the nape of her neck electrified.

Her phone rang, startling her again. The inopportune modern sound intruded, disrupting the haunted current flowing around her. Mercifully, the sound grounded her back into the present.

Terry came across the screen.

She took a breath and steadied her jangling nerves. "Howdy, stranger."

"Hello, Em. How's everything?"

She glanced around at the old buildings, uncertain just how to answer that question. "Fine, I guess. Earlier today I worked with the mustang, and now I'm just tromping around the ranch. It's a nice day for it."

Terry chuckled. "Bored, huh?"

"I don't know that I'd put it that way exactly…"

"Anyhow," Terry cut to the point, "how much do you like it out in Vermillion? Did you ever find yourself an apartment and get settled?"

He wants to talk about expenses. Damn. "Meaning did I sign a lease? Not yet. Things kind of took off on me, as you might recall. I got Kai settled all right, but that's about as far as all the settling went."

"Before you go signing any leases, we'd best talk."

Not strictly a social call, a note of caution entered their conversation. "We're talking now, aren't we?" Emory felt him out. "I don't understand why I shouldn't sign a lease…"

"We've hit a strange situation out here and you're just the person for the job."

Emory didn't answer right away. "I'm expected back in Vermillion on Monday, but true, I still have my apartment in Greeley. That said, I do like the job out in Vermillion." More specifically, she liked the Sand Wash Basin and its promise of the wild horse herds.

"So, as far as your job is concerned, you could drive

east, or you could drive west. There's plenty of work in both directions." In offering much of the state, it still felt like Terry didn't offer her much room.

"Ray can probably manage Vermillion for a while. What have you got?"

"Someone is stealing cattle skulls."

She blinked a few times. "When they're already dead, right?"

"What in the hell do you think?" He boomed, but his voice sounded troubled. "Of course they're already dead."

Emory shook her head, stayed silent for a moment. "But why would we get involved in something like that? It's probably a random wacko stealing the heads as trophies or souvenirs."

A loaded pause. "I'm not so sure."

And she knew he wouldn't say more until she committed to driving out there and they met face-to-face. They knew each other well, and each understood that a request for help tendered in person offered an obligation to assist.

"You want to chew that over and give me a call back?" He asked when he got tired of waiting.

"I'll come, Terry. Is Monday morning soon enough? I've got a few things I need to attend to at home."

"It sure is. I'll give Ray a call, but you might want to give him a shout also. And Emory? Thanks."

The line call clicked off, and she scanned the buildings warming in the sun, noticing how they came across as deceptively innocent—weatherworn, but innocent.

Cautious to whatever message her ancestors carried, she traced along the old wagon ruts that cut past their house, hands in her back jean pockets and wondering about her chances. Chances for her future, chances for happiness, chances for keeping the ranch intact.

The Lost Daughter, however, had needs of its own.

Stepping around rusted box spring discarded long ago, she picked her way over to the low-slung old soddy and the first permanent structure on the ranch that now served as nothing more than a storage shed. The solid brown pottery doorknob turned with an unoiled grudge, but the weathered door held firm. Offering a far stronger resistance, she hip-bumped it hard, unable to recall whether it stuck before or not. Locked outside of a damn soddy and struggling to enter drew a response from the ghosts. She felt the long reach of her ancestors come in the form of mocking laughter running down her spine.

She didn't find their laughter, their games, or the stuck door amusing in the least. Emory stood back, gathered her strength, and gave the stubborn door a swift, hard kick with her bootheel.

Jarred loose, it opened with a secret-harboring grudge—secrets that they thought she needed to work for. The door cracked open just enough for her to angle in, a tight fit. She wedged herself between the door and the jamb, but she ended up standing inside.

The interior smelled of old lumber heated by the sun and the dust of decomposing memories. Memories she almost tasted on the tip of her tongue.

Filled with listing, dusty contents, she wondered what in the hell she hoped to find. "Yeah, I'm listening."

But the ghosts, having had their fun, didn't answer.

They left her, for the moment, to her own devices.

The floor, nothing more than beaten down hardpan dirt, remained dry. Old Hank Cross or his men knew how to build. In fact, that damned soddy remained as solid as a fort. Dominance and control. And a marked refusal to throw out anything that had the remotest of chances to be pressed into later use.

The buildings' longevity came as a by-product, but their parsimony served them well through the years. The Lost Daughter remained standing, while so many other ranches had fallen.

Still, they weren't perfect.

The gap-toothed walls with chinking knocked out in places left gaps wide enough for dust, field mice, and perhaps bad spirits and memories to drift in.

Again, that zinging feeling shot up her spine. A remnant or a clue waited in there—one that she needed to find.

Stepping farther inside, she peered behind the wooden plank door, searching for the fallen or snapped hinge pin and found nothing fallen on the ground.

In front of her the old, battered, and scarred ranch desk waited. Shoved against the wall—its drawers faced the log walls, making them all but inaccessible. Old, rotting cardboard boxes waited—stacked on top of the desk for heaven only knew how long, with more boxes scattered throughout.

She peered through one of the small cutout windows, once made of mica, it now held glass. Its location provided a clear line of sight to the door leading to the tacked-on ranch office. Of course, she noted the gutters sagged and pulled away from the roof. Just another repair to tend to. Measuring the distance between the soddy and the "new" house, they stood no more than two hundred yards apart.

Yet, a story popped into mind. During a blizzard, that distance proved near fatal and almost killed her grandfather, Chuck Cross. According to family lore, he'd come out to the soddy to check on livestock—tying a rope to the house to guide himself back. Someone had untied that rope once he began his return to the house, all but sealing his fate. By the sheerest thread of luck, his shoulder had literally struck the house's corner as he staggered around.

The Coopers, through no particular thread of logic, were blamed for that untying. But her father's father had always been a bastard from what she'd heard. Maybe one of their own had untied that rope. To Emory's way of thinking, that possibility sounded the more probable of the two.

The Coopers. She'd apparently been brought into that soddy on account of the trouble with the Coopers. Driven away and vanquished, they amounted to nothing more than old news by now.

Emory moved rotting boxes from the desktop, shoving on one of the desk's corners with her full weight to move it away from the wall. It gave about six inches before refusing to budge farther.

"Dang it," she muttered, glancing down at the bottom corner of the desk caught upon a dint in the floor. If she wanted to get inside of those drawers, the desk would need lifting.

Still, the left side drawers had enough room to pull out about four inches. Knowing better than to thrust her hand into somewhere she could not see, peering inside she found various discarded papers, brittle with age and the elements. Further in an out of view hazards could await, including early rattlers. Grasping only what came clearly visible, she withdrew a stack of papers with one hand, tilting it downward toward the back of the drawer. She brushed off the dust on the desktop and set the papers down on the place she'd cleared. Flicking through the old invoices written in ink and old unlabeled tallies written in dulled pencil, she noted the embedded dirt under her ragged index fingernail with accustomed distaste. She straightened.

Horse hooves approached from the distance, the pace coming at a fast trot.

If those hooves belonged to a horse ridden by Monty, she would give him shit for the sheer hell of it, if nothing else. Talking about the Lost Daughter to strangers. He ought to know far better than that.

Dodging box corners and various other obstacles designed to trip a person up, Emory angled back out through the door ready to let him have it. An unfamiliar buckskin horse passed by. She stopped dead in her tracks. More than the horse, its rider was a strong, wide-shouldered man that she'd never seen before.

A stranger.

UPHILL ADVANTAGES— RANGE WAR

1889

COOPER'S RIDERS DREW NEARER.

Hank Cross shouted his final instructions before they could be overhead by the riders, voice carrying over the thudding of their horse's hooves.

"Don't shoot until they're square in front of us. Don't fire early, because they'll wheel around, and we'll have to fight another day. A *harder* day."

Their range war simmered on the back burner since the matter of Susan, now and again heating up to a boil and certainly never forgotten. The Coopers' latest transgression involved the disputed box canyon, fanning their past hostility into flames. Possession, as everyone out in the Colorado hinterland knew, remained more than nine-tenths of the law.

Hank Cross gripped his rifle, biding his time as he waited for the Cooper faction to ride into their sights.

Foremost in mind came the fact that while Old Man Cooper figured himself as ruthless and wily, he'd grown old over the past winter. If Cooper didn't know it, the rest of them sure as hell did. The old man only thought he pulled the strings—a fatal flaw. Cooper believed himself too old to do his own damned fighting. That failing amounted to just one of his mistakes, but a very fundamental one at that.

Hank Cross remained steadfast in his conviction. None of his family or men had better *ever* make that mistake. Not while he had a breath left in his body or he'd beat the holy hell out of them himself. And if that didn't work, he'd shoot them on the spot. Front or back, it didn't much matter. They'd be dead, or he'd die trying.

The low warning bird trill carried—their arranged signal.

A nervous electric energy sparked—the hair at the nape of Hank's neck and arms rose. With controlled and measured movements, he leaned out ever so slightly from his cover and eyed the horizon toward the thudding of the hooves. That's where men often gave the game away—as they set up for the kill. They mistakenly made their movements too big. Movements which attracted their target's eyes. Movements which gave their positions away.

There would be none of that here, and not on this day. Not if he had his way about it.

The riders' hooves thudded and approached, urgent. They sure weren't paying any social call. No, they rode, and rode hard. He'd judge by the sound that carried, at least seven riders approached.

He held his conviction that the day didn't involve any half-assed shooting match. Hank Cross pressed his back against the boulder to wait them out.

The hooves thundered closer. Their riders shared no banter.

THE FUTURE RIDES A BUCKSKIN HORSE

JUNE 2023

"Hello?" She called out, high-stepping over a pile of discarded lumber—rusted nails sticking out at angles. Good thing she'd had her tetanus shot.

The rider reined in, and his horse squared to face her like a good cow pony. "Hello."

He waited.

"Who are you?" Emory asked, trying to make it sound as nonaccusatory as possible. Intentionally, she lightened the tone of her question, liking the cut of him.

"Jace Scott," he replied, equally taken aback. "And you are…the brand inspector?"

"I am," she replied, cocking a grin. "And you are out here because…"

A quirk of his mouth. "Because I work here…"

She'd be damned. Neither man had said a blessed thing about hiring someone on. She laughed at the absurdity of it all. "Since when?"

He shifted in the saddle and chuckled in return. "Going on about three weeks now. Guess they didn't mention it."

"Nope. They did not." She sized him up. "Now I know why everything looks as kept up as it does. I shouldn't have assumed that ranch operations had changed for the better on their own. Anyhow, I heard the hooves and hoped that one of them would help me move the desk in the old soddy so I can go through the drawers."

"I can do that. Let me get my horse tied."

The cowboy rode over to the nearest hitching post and dismounted. No one, with eyes in their head, could help but notice that he fell easy on the eyes. Far more so than usual in their line of work.

Emory nodded, watching him, and taking a few steps in his direction and choosing her words not to avoid offense. "If you're from out this way, I don't think I've seen you around."

"I'm not originally. Right now, I'm bunking with Monty so I guess you could say I live here."

She stopped dead in her tracks. "I'm sorry."

He chuckled. "About which part?" Then he stopped teasing. "Monty's not that bad, but he sure snored up a storm last night."

"Uh-huh. That's because he'd had a snoutful to drink. Don't you go into the house to eat breakfast?"

"Oh, I make an appearance every now and again. Depends on the morning. Today I kind of figured I'd be intruding upon family time."

So. A cowboy with a sense of propriety.

She inclined her head in response to his manners, then returned to the soddy, leaving him to trail along behind.

"It's a tight fit squeezing in." Emory pointed at the opening. "If you can push the door open farther, that's even better. Maybe the wood shifted, because last time I went into the building, I'm pretty sure that I didn't have near as much trouble."

"No, ma'am. Is there anything behind that door that I have to worry about?"

She shook her head.

"Stand back." When she moved away, he shouldered the door hard. His efforts gained another five inches. "Is that good enough?"

"It's easier to get into," Emory said, passing into the interior, leaving the ranch hand to follow.

Inside, he glanced around at the jumble, before his eyes settled on her. "Do you want me to try to do something with that door?"

"We'll have to get it closed when I'm done, but sure. If you have time. Now, it's this desk over here, the bottom is catching against a ridge. You take that end, and I'll take this one."

Emory went to the far end and wrapped her fingers around both sides of the desktop. He did the same on his end. "Ready?" Emory met his eyes across the dusty distance.

"Yeah."

Between the pair of them, it proved a simple lift. "You're pretty strong," he offered.

"So are you." *What a ridiculous thing to say.*

He ran his eyes over her, then back to the desk curious. But once again, his good manners or common sense held, and he did not pry.

Of course, the same couldn't be said for her. "Where did you work before this?"

"Afghanistan," he replied. "But I'm originally from outside of Clayton, New Mexico."

That took her aback, and she blinked a few times. "Oh. I'm not sure what to say."

"Which part—New Mexico or Afghanistan?" He didn't wait for her to answer. "Anyhow, there's not a whole lot to say about either one, other than it's a privilege to come home."

A privilege?

She owed him at least a debt of gratitude. Hell, they all did. She shrugged, uncomfortable with undefined obligations that most certainly existed, and in plain sight. Obligations she didn't know how to address.

"Glad you're here..." she murmured, cursing the weakness behind her words, and how they fell flat. She progressed onto more solid footing. "I don't know what I'm looking for in this desk, but a long time ago, this used to be the ranch headquarters."

He considered the discards and clutter but gave no visible reaction.

"I'm on vacation," she ventured as an afterthought. Another *stupid* afterthought.

That last part surprised him. "And you go digging around old storage buildings on vacation?"

Given the direction their conversation headed, he was almost bound to assume that she had more than a few screws loose. "Now that you mention it, normally I do chores. But Dad and Monty seem to be getting along all right, and now they have you. They *are* paying you, aren't they?"

Her eyes narrowed a bit at that last part.

He threw back his head and laughed outright, showing pearly white teeth. "If they aren't, we'd all better figure that out right about now."

When she didn't laugh in return, he stopped joking around, and his expression turned a bit less certain. "They're paying."

"Good," she replied, sizing him up. "Glad to hear it."

"Why wouldn't they be?" he asked, puzzled and guarded.

Her laugh came out tinny and hollow. Their decrepit surroundings did nothing to help matters along. "Oh, sometimes there are special arrangements back here."

She dropped that line of conversation as fast as she could. Squatting down, Emory pulled out one of the desk drawers and rummaged through.

Jace Scott appeared less certain than he had only moments ago. "Need anything else from me, like to move the desk back when you're done?"

She glanced up at him, eyes about level with the desktop. Taking inventory of the mess and castoffs that surrounded them, she replied, "It doesn't matter much considering the state of things in here. What have they got you working on today?"

"Riding the fence line, although I ran into Monty doing the same."

Emory chuckled. "That's because I scared him earlier. He didn't want to stick around back here."

He gave her a strange double-take, and without saying another word, he tipped his hat and withdrew.

She'd made a bad impression, and he found her strange. Wonderful. And although she knew that she only felt it so deeply because she felt a strong attraction, that knowledge didn't help. *No, not...at...all.*

TURNING BACK INSIDE, Emory forced herself to get on with the task at hand in favor of watching him ride off, because that would have been both shameless and blatant. Having no desire to come across as desperate—which she likely already did—she halfheartedly occupied herself with rummaging through the desk's contents.

"I come from a family of pack rats," she murmured to take her mind off matters, scanning scribbled paper scraps whose meanings had long disappeared, lost to time. Discarded antique pens with nibs in place rested within—some broken, others perhaps usable if someone cared to try pen and ink for the hell of it—accompanied by pencil stubs, a ball of twine, and an old leather ledger. She removed the old ledger book as she fanned through the pages half-heartedly, thinking more about Jace Scott. Flicking through, one old sheet of paper, folded in half and stowed between two other ledger pages, felt interesting enough to deserve a look. Emory retrieved it and unfolded it with care. Written in fountain pen and ink, the wording appeared that of an old agreement of some sort.

August 18, 1889

Box Canyon near the Troublesome Creek deeded to Hank Cross. Rot in Hell.

Signed,
Victor Cooper

Agreed—Hank Cross

Witness,
Oscar Sorensen

Odd, but she got a kick out of the 'rot in hell' part.

She'd spent years believing that the Crosses and the Coopers never exchanged more than bullets and gunfire between the two of them. Who would have ever thought those warring factions had agreements written out and bothered to find a witness for a documented agreement? She slipped the paper back where she found it and moved through the rest of the ledger and found nothing but cattle tallies and other receipts. Setting that all aside, Emory resumed rifling through rusty nails, ticket stubs and yet more random delivery receipts. Finally, she found something of more interest. An old booze bottle holding remnants of ancient liquor at the bottom, which she pulled out from its resting place and set on the desk. Moving up to the next drawer, bingo. She found the anticipated old gun used for protection or company.

But it wasn't a Colt. Damn.

Carefully lifting it by its handle, she checked the chamber, and sure enough. A *loaded* old gun stowed out of sight in the middle, left drawer. Strange. Weren't top drawers the usual location for guns?

Nevertheless, its location on the left side of the desk meant that the owner shot left-handed...just like her. She emptied the old bullets, unknowing whether the gun still worked but allowed even odds that it did. Anyhow, if someone wanted to give it a try for target practice, they'd need to give it a good cleaning, no matter the case.

She'd show her dad and Monty the findings—and, more interesting to her than the gun or the liquor—she'd also hear about that new hand, Jace.

Her heart hitched sharp and clear with a stab on her conscience. Hugo's grave awaited, just up the hill and lonely.

She was lonely, too.

Sitting back on her haunches and resting on the back of her boot heels, she tried to smother any feelings of guilt. Either way, she attacked the final drawer. The contents seemed more of the same including a veritable archive of the long defunct *Range Herald*. However, underneath the stack brittle newspapers rotting over time, a corner of plain paper stuck out at an angle—a ragged hole punched at the top. She flipped it over to find a message scrawled in an ancient, dull pencil.

You think this is over, but it ain't. Not if it takes 100 years or more.

6

RANGELAND LULLABY

1889

ONE OF THE CROSS HORSES HIGHER UP ON THE FLATTOP called out, clear and shattering the silence. Hank shot a glance upward, but the offender remained out of sight. He'd told that damn fool holding their horses to keep them farther back.

The Cooper intruders caught the horse's call and turned their faces upward to the heights to scan the ridges.

"Now," Hank shouted, hefting his rifle and picking off the leader.

The man fell sideways from his horse and landed in an unmoving heap. The crack and retort of rifle fire zinged and rang, like Hell itself was a-poppin'. Bullets whined and ricocheted. Cross worked his rifle's lever, located another target, exhaled, and pulled the trigger. The man dropped with a thud.

The sulfur gunpowder smoke caught on the wind.

Another body plummeted downward from the rocks behind him. One of his men. *Damn.*

The firing died down as quickly as it all began. One

single shot followed, serving no particular purpose. *Maybe it was one of them dying shots*, Hank figured.

Hank Cross's eyes scanned the landscape as he read the killing field. He searched for the slightest sign of life and found none. No movement at all—except from the now riderless horses.

He lowered his rifle, still crouching. No need to rush. But he wanted to check if his man survived the fall. Still, experience taught him that survival, after a headfirst fall down a hundred feet, was plumb unlikely.

In the absence of the gunfire, the valley fell unnaturally quiet. Dangerous.

"Stand down," he called to his men, "but pay attention and don't get sloppy."

One by one, the men emerged from crevasses, behind boulders, or from beneath outcroppings.

Hank pushed away from his own crevasse; dusty boots pointed downhill upon the deer trail that connected the flattops to the valley below. He skidded on the dust and scree before coming to a full stop. The faint sound of the Cross faction's horses approached from the other direction. They rounded the bend in the road, led by a damned fool who would get a strong talkin' to. His son Henry rode drag in the buckboard, bringing up the rear. Polly, his dead wife, *might* have given him hell had she remained above ground—allowing the boy to view dead bodies strewn about in the road. Then again, she might have considered it a necessary and justified reminder—retribution for the loss of her only daughter, Susan.

The Cross matriarch deemed all the Coopers as murderers, and as such, Polly likely would have reveled in seeing the lifeless, bloodied bodies.

Hank, for his part, harbored no doubt in his mind—the loss of Susan had carried his wife to an early grave.

And that's how Cross Ranch became known as the Lost Daughter—on account of the mysterious loss of Susan.

Hank Cross pushed the memories from his mind. He'd made his decision, and the time for coddling the boy had passed. Twelve years old, he was near enough to a man. The time had come for him to take on those burdens.

7

THREATS COME IN MANY GUISES

JUNE 2023

RESTING IN HER HAND WAS WHAT THE GHOSTS WANTED her to find.

Emory gathered up the gun, the old whiskey bottle, stuck the discarded bullets in her shirt pocket, and held the threat out straight, carefully between two fingers.

Angling out, she left the soddy's door hanging wide, like an open invitation for more problems to enter. At first, whiskey bottle tucked under her arm, gun in her hand and a threat carried, she figured she'd just come back for it later. But then those damn warning whispers started again. Reluctantly she stuck the note in her other shirt pocket, before setting everything down in the baking dirt. Yanking hard on the door, she pulled it closed with far less of a fight than going in. Shaking her head, she stepped over the discards in the yard, and long-legged it toward the house, vindicated. Her father's pickup parked in its usual spot off to the side of the house, and his horse, Draco, ambled out in the paddock along with the other horses. Lance Cross couldn't have ventured all that far since she'd spoken with him at the round pen.

Entering through the dented aluminum side door, she angled left and stuck her head around the corner into her father's office. Seated at his desk—remarkably with the computer screen switched on—he was occupied with what appeared to be true ranch business instead of solitaire.

"Look what I found," she announced holding the castoffs. "Not to mention, I met your new hired help. Now, when were you going to tell me about him?"

Looking over at her, his eyes sparked, but he didn't bother to answer her question. "You did, did you?"

She plunked the antique whiskey bottle down on his desktop. "I thought things around here looked in pretty good order."

"You don't say." Her father humphed. "Things get done how things get done." He held the whiskey bottle up to eye level to measure the remaining contents and set it back down on his dinged-up desk.

"Something along those lines. How long has he worked out here?"

"Long enough for me to know that he's tough and knows what he's doing." He eyed the rest of her objects. "What'cha got there?"

She fished out the most important—the threat. "This."

He took it, eyes flickering over the words. "I'll be damned."

She searched his face for any traces of recognition. At times he had a noted habit of holding back on her. But this didn't appear to be one of those times. "Well?"

He shook his head, slow and deliberate, searching his memory and coming up short. "Hard to say." He eyed it longer. "Could have been aimed at us back in the day, or it could be a threat that one of ours thought about making. Interesting." He abandoned it, square in front of him on the desk. "What else you got there?"

She laid the gun down first. "An old gun, but not a Colt." Fishing around in her other pocket, she withdrew the bullets. "Still loaded and stowed away. Whoever owned it obviously shot left-handed, given the drawer where I found it. And that bottle of old booze. Don't know if it's drinkable, and I'm not even sure that you should show it to Mr. Free-Whiskey-Boozehound. At any rate, I thought you and Monty might get a kick out of it. I can put it back if you'd rather."

Relatively unbothered either way, Lance reached for the discarded gun, pointed it away from them, checked its sight, and peered inside of the crane. "There're numbers there. Chances are it's a Smith & Wesson. Not a bad find." He held it out for her, handle first. "You want it?"

She gave a disinterested shrug but took the gun all the same. "We can stick it in the gun safe for the time being. It needs a good cleaning in any case."

"Monty excels at that."

She snorted and tossed her head back knowing he probably he did.

Her father's attention, however, kept drawing back to the old threat laying on his desk—an accusation of past misdeeds. "So, you've been poking around in the outbuildings again."

"It seems to be what I do." She hesitated. "How long ago did you hire Jace?"

"Only about a month ago." Her father locked eyes with her. "We can use him for the season, and maybe into the winter then the cycle starts again. Monty and me—we ain't as young as we used to be."

"You made it through the calving season," Emory remarked.

"Yeah, and it about did us in. I'm getting too old for all this shit. *You* get up in the middle of the night to help deliver a breech calf."

"I would if I still lived here…"

He backed off a notch. "I know you would, honey. But you've got your career now. Besides, Jace needed a job. What do you think of him?"

Her father didn't miss the telltale blush that rose in her cheeks.

"Yep," he droned on when she failed to answer. "That's what I figured."

———

LATER THAT NIGHT, Monty clanked his single-spurred way over to the house, all spruced up. In other words, he took a shower and put on a clean shirt.

"Goin' into town," he crowed, hovering in the living room before settling into a calculated lean against the doorframe. She'd even bet he practiced that exact casual pose, which sure as hell wasn't casual at all.

"Nosing around for more of that free whiskey?" Lance Cross trained his eyes on his cousin, not requiring an answer.

Monty shifted, a measure of his cockiness draining. "Mebbe."

"Yeah, well don't go shooting your mouth off, whatever you do. No matter how much whiskey you put in it."

"Now, Lance…"

"*Now, Lance* nothing. I mean it. None of this operation is pillow talk. Understood?"

The locking of two sets of cold-water steel eyes. "Understood."

Emory, seated, took in the familiar slagging match.

"That's it then." Monty stuck his thumbs through two belt loops and hitched his pants skyward. He broke their stare down. "Just wanted to let you know where I planned on venturing in case you needed me."

He glanced at Emory as an afterthought, with a slight incline of his head before he clanked his way back out, the same way as he'd come in.

Neither father nor daughter said a thing as they listened to the jangle of Monty's spur until he reached his truck and climbed in, door closing and engine starting.

"Has he always worn that damned single spur?"

Her father chuckled. "Not as a teenager. Somewhere along the line he picked that up. He says it helps with his driving and his shooting."

"That's ridiculous," Emory smirked, "not to mention concerning."

"It sure would be if he drove a clutch."

Their conversation trailed off and her father fell silent, fingers drumming on the armrest. "Don't like it," he admitted at length, sounding reluctant around the edges.

"No." Her one word hung in the distance between them.

Emory calculated. From the shadows of the living room, she took the measure of her father, and by extension, the situation. Bracing herself, she ventured into dangerous territory. "How much, *exactly*, does Linda know—considering the fact that she is either your previous or current girlfriend?"

The vein in her father's jaw throbbed, as he set it into

a clench. He let that question hang there longer than comfortable.

"She probably knows more about our history than the actual operations." He offered at length. "Make that, she has an inkling based upon what can be found in public records. That's the kind of thing she *would* do— poke around in dusty old relics that don't mean shit."

His words sank in as father and daughter sat unmoving, sharing both features and a basic distrust of emotions.

Emory pressed ahead. "You know, we've never really discussed how this is all supposed to go moving forward. You and her."

Her father's posture stiffened. "Not sure there's any point in it. Where this relationship is headed, I mean."

His admission made her feel a bit hollow. She eyed him closer.

He added, "I never planned on tying the knot again. Neither did she."

"You sure about that?" Emory prompted.

Her father locked eyes with her. "Since we're on this subject, I'm more interested in you. What would you have told that Texan about us? *Really* told about us. And more to the point, what will you tell the next one?"

She'd asked herself those very same questions. Questions without any easy answers. "I would've told Hugo at least part of the truth. But he wouldn't have liked it. In the end, maybe, he would have forgiven us."

Lance Cross leaned forward. *"Forgiven us?"* She'd struck a nerve. A very fundamental nerve. "We *never* ask for forgiveness. Is that understood?"

Emory sat stock-still believing her father might be wrong on that count.

When she felt ready to answer, she chose her words

with care. "We're not always considered the pick of the litter, you know. Not unless they are like us. Cade Timmons, former ranch hand non grata, wouldn't have given any of our doings a second thought."

"Maybe so, and maybe on account of this being as big of a spread as he'll likely ever come by. He had eyes for you, but he had eyes for everyone else in town as well. Never forget that Cade has always been, and still is, a shithead. A real dyed-in-the-wool shithead." Her father ratcheted down, but only a notch. "Running drugs through the Lost Daughter of all damned things…"

"Still," Emory persisted, "doesn't Linda ask questions about why people shy away?"

"Hell, she tried in the beginning, but unlike the rest of us, she didn't really know what she was asking. That part's died down a bit."

Yeah, but curiosity always manages to rise up again.

Emory steeled herself. "Do you love her?"

He didn't rush to answer. In fact, he didn't answer at all.

At length, she dropped it. He didn't have to explain his feelings to her, any more than she did to him. Still, in truth, they only had each other and the ranch. The ranch always entered into the equation. "Do you want me to go into town to watch Monty?"

"You're not answering my original question."

She shrugged. He didn't answer hers either but poking him about his *feelings* had the distinct potential of setting him off. "I don't exactly know the answer about what to tell people that I date—not that there's that many of them. People already know there's something off about us."

And to that piece of wisdom, her father only chuckled with a pent-up irritation.

Deep down he knew that Emory merely offered a cold, hard, and factual assessment.

He accepted it as such, eyes flashing in the gathering gloom. "Yeah. Why don't you take yourself into town and check out what's going on. Monty…" He shook his head. "Guess you never can tell."

8

CARRION

1889

HANK, TAKING THE MEASURE OF HIS SON, NOTED THAT THE boy featured the same watery steel gray eyes as he did himself. And the boy had already seen his share of dead people before, just not those killed in ambush.

It hadn't played out as much of a gunfight—just as Hank planned. That's because he acted the patient man. But *patience* never meant a body couldn't fight. It just meant that battles were planned out with care. Gunfights tended to erupt from sudden anger. This mess had smoldered for quite some time.

But first things first. Tally up the dead and figure out the damages. He glanced over at his riders first. One took a shot—winged—and blood seeped through his fingers as he clutched the meat of his right arm.

"I can shoot with my left, don't worry," he'd growled when he noted where Hank's eyes traveled.

Hank hadn't worried and expected nothing less from any of the men he hired.

He walked over to his man who pitched off the cliff and plummeted, his body lay in a broken heap on the road. Obviously dead, the body listed over to one side. Hank Cross placed his Hyer boot tip on the man's shoulder and gave him a firm shove, turning the corpse onto its back. His left arm fell wide in death. Sure enough, a hole marred his cheek and his neck cricked off at an unnatural angle amounted to the obvious. *Mick Osborn. Too bad.*

Hank located his son again, staring at the dead cowboy with wide eyes and all the while edging closer. No sense in sugarcoating any of it.

Let the boy make of the scene what he would. Hank turned and walked among the Cooper dead.

A voice came from behind him, landing square between his shoulder blades. "What do you want to do with them?"

Cross stopped, glanced over his shoulder at one of his hired hands, a man called Jake. "What I want to do, and what we *will* do are two separate things."

He wanted to ride one of these corpses over to the Coopers and throw it in front of their damned door.

"Bury 'em, I guess," he barked. "It's what we brought the shovels for. Bury 'em in this hell-forsaken road. If they ever come back this way, it'll give 'em plenty to consider. Let them ride over their own damned corpses. Fools."

Of course, traveling over those same bodies on their way to town would give the Crosses the same thing to mull over themselves. They'd just planned it out better this time around. The hard truth stared right back at them all wearing the mask of death.

"Dig out two graves, or one wide enough for a pair of them. Then, Jake, you ride the third body over to where the current gets strong enough to carry it downriver to the Coopers'. We'll just consider it a calling card. Now, you two," he pointed to a couple of his men near the wagon, "load up Mick. We'll bury him up near Polly."

Hank mounted his horse and rode a length down the road just to make sure no additional wave of Coopers came riding.

A second sense or a notion itched around his stomach and across the back of his neck. The instructions he gave didn't sit right with him. He turned his horse and thundered back to his men already in the process of digging.

"Hold on there! I've changed my mind. Leave the three bodies exactly where they lay. Mount up. Everyone back to the ranch. Now."

"The animals will get 'em," another man offered.

Hank stared daggers at him. "Might be they should have thought of that afore they came riding."

"True." The man spat into the dry dirt, too late to cover his trace of sentimentality. The men heard and made note, marking the speaker as weak. Ashamed, the offender cast his gaze upward along the pale rimrocks. From that point out, he'd have to act twice as mean to live down his forming reputation.

Three of Cooper's riders remained crumpled and lifeless in the dirt. Three or four of their other ranch hands had managed to ride away.

Word would spread, and that suited Hank Cross just fine.

The Lost Daughter would be ready to fight again if needed, but for the time being, Susan's demise would be considered avenged.

9

BARFLIES AT THE ACE HIGH

JUNE 2023

Her father's words regarding the Ace High claiming that "one never could tell" flowed like a refrain in her mind. But Emory could tell all right. Same town, same sidewalks, same bar. Likely the same barflies...with a few out-of-town additions for spice.

Parking her truck one block over from the watering hole known locally as the "Ace," the summer tourist season already crept up upon them and would only gather speed as the months peeled off, ramping up further the deeper into summer they progressed. The siren's beckon of the Ace's neon, and outdated neon at that, attracted its clientele like moths to the flame and seemingly never changed. Singed wings and all, a steady stream entered through those doors, and she found herself about to join them. Reluctantly. The only thing to be counted upon when entering that establishment, remained weirdness and the ever-present lure of possibility. The possibility that gossip might prove enlightening. The possibility that the love of one's life—or perhaps just for the night—could be found within. That's usually about the time that a decided weirdness raised its head and joined in the proceedings. All of which stemmed from the lure of cheap drinks potent enough to blur the harsh realities of truth.

The hardcore day drinkers would eventually become wedged off their barstools as the rowdier crowd displaced them, the thumping music and fake cowboys on the prowl eventually penetrating their drink-induced haze, sending them tilting toward their homes, to try it all again the next day. Not that the results ever proved much different.

Tourists wanted a good time. Ranch hands, after getting off work, wanted a good time. Everyone searched for that elusive good time except for her.

Emory Cross sought information instead.

From her vantage point, she already bet that nothing about the bar had transformed for the better in her absence. What had changed, the *only thing* that changed in her opinion, was that she'd almost grown accustomed to entering bars on her own. That offered one revelation right there, and an unwelcome one at that.

She passed right in front of Monty's bug-splattered truck grill, parked in a prime spot square in front of the entrance.

That damned Coors sign still blinked on and off, *on...* and *off...*in the window. Whether it had an electrical short or a built-in flicker, it irritated all the same. Poised to leave the calm of the darkened mountain night behind, strains of music and reverberating base notes vibrated and thudded, caught and lingered on the night air.

Of course, Cade sprang into mind. Probably on account of how the Ace High amounted to a glorified shooting gallery of a sort—a gallery for the shiftless and those on the prowl. And Cade was the king of the Ace—in his own mind at least.

And she sure as hell wasn't prowling…or at least, not that kind.

Funny, how Cade had a way of tainting her mood at the mere thought of him. *Blame it on the surroundings*, she figured.

The glass door's hefty pull-handle provided a solid barrier to cross for entrance into the maw of the beast. Emory stepped inside and into an alternate world separated from the rest of Stampede. The music blared an undetermined Western singer's male voice, but the refrain *hard to love, hard to love*…couldn't have struck any truer. Carrying the same stench as she recalled—the lingering hangover smell of cigarette smoke and beer-sopped carpeting followed by countless whiskey sloshes—it all tallied up to just another night in just another year in just another decade.

And sure enough, Monty sat directly ahead in one of those battered barstools. Stranger than that, her father's girlfriend Linda sat right next to him. Downright glum in their own fashion, each stared straight ahead at the rows of the backlit liquor bottles lining the backbar shelves.

Emory's first tangled inclination involved walking straight on up to them and cracking a joke just to make sure they were breathing and alive.

"Come on in," the barman bantered when he noticed her lurking just inside of the door, offering encouragement she felt unneeded and certainly unwanted on her part. Either that, or the man really liked his job. Or he'd been drinking himself which had a history of happening in that locale.

Either way, she didn't feel like being prodded.

She nodded a measured response and took a step deeper in, testing the waters.

No two ways about it, a warning of sorts clicked in her mind and held her back. She pretended that she hadn't yet noticed Monty or Linda, just in case they spotted her. Feigning obliviousness, she scanned the assembled people without identifying any old whiskey-buying buckle bunny. No wonder Monty looked glum, but that didn't explain Linda, seated right alongside him looking like she hadn't a single friend left in the world.

As if on cue, Cade burst in through the back door like he owned the place.

No act on his part, shock rippled across his face when he spied her directly—even if Monty and Linda were oblivious, hunched over their whiskey sours or whatever poison of choice filled their glasses.

Cade navigated the pool tables and made a beeline for her, looking none too friendly. She'd deal with him later if she had to, but in the meanwhile, she decided to take shelter where she could find it.

"Hel-lo, Monty and Linda," she called all nice and friendly, startling the pair of them out of their respective trances. "Looks like I've come in time to join you for a little while."

Cade, striding toward her, hesitated, marking where her voice traveled.

Monty, for his part, expected her.

"Shit," amounted to his summation of her arrival.

Linda, on the other hand, glanced up in her direction with a surprised, yet genuine, smile. "Why, Emory! What a nice…"

Emory heard Linda, but matters beyond Linda threatened. Instead of answering, she jerked her head to the side to indicate Cade's approach. Monty picked up on her signal and fixed upon Cade's reflection in the mirror behind the bar. Those blue hippy sunglasses tracked that cowboy's every move.

Emory locked eyes with Cade, placing one hand upon Monty's shoulder. Poor Linda faded into the background. "Can I help you?" she asked their former ranch hand who, judging by his bearing, spoiled for a fight.

He certainly didn't hold back, but let his feelings fly. "You mean like you did with Dirge, getting him locked up in jail?"

As sure as hell, Monty stiffened like a coil ready to spring. Sure as hell, everyone at that end of the bar heard him.

Maybe this would be the time Cade actually swung at her...but then again, she tallied up the odds. Far too many witnesses for his liking. So, no. He wouldn't have the guts to do a damned thing about it.

In the light—or even in the dark for that matter— she could fight her own battles. That said, backup always proved a valuable asset.

"You know, *Cade*, that cousin of yours was going to run me down like roadkill. Beyond that, the way I heard it, Dirge also didn't know much about your activities up in that part of the state," Emory countered. "That means you double-crossed him. You should thank me. You could have wound up as roadkill too."

People listened, watched, and waited.

"No double-cross because I don't go up there," Cade sneered, although his words fell flat.

"Odd," she slashed back at his excuse. "But have it your way. Now, unless you have something specific to say, this is a private conversation and one that doesn't include you."

Cade's eyes narrowed, and he took a step toward her.

She stopped restraining Monty's shoulder. The older man pivoted and rose to block Cade, his timing dead bang on the money.

"You need any help, boss?" A strong, masculine voice came from behind her.

Both Crosses' eyes darted in the voice's direction. It belonged to none other than their new hire, Jace.

"No," the pair of them replied in unison.

Jace's eyes flitted from one to the other, confused by the obvious power struggle.

Emory would clear up that confusion in a moment. "Cade better leave before he gets his ass kicked."

Monty scowled at her, but they'd sort it out later.

"Linda," Emory said low, "you might want to move out of the way."

The woman grabbed her drink and dashed over to the wall. The crowd, sensing a fight, quieted down a notch but the music blared on.

Jace and Cade locked eyes. Emory knew, if given the chance, Cade would play dirty. For his part, the new hire certainly gave the impression that he'd hold his own.

"You go park yourself elsewhere, Cade, and mind your own business." She double-checked him. "In fact, outside is the best bet."

Fighting mad, the cords in his neck stuck out like wire. "Or you'll what? You'll arrest me?"

Jace took a step forward, and Emory placed a restraining hand on his chest.

"Does anyone have any missing livestock? This might be your man!" She called out to the crowd in a stronger voice.

Although she half-ass tried to make her voice sound sweet, it came out as more of a threat. As she truly intended.

Nervous laughter rippled from those listening in, and someone bleated like a sheep. Cade's eyes bugged out.

"No," she replied toying with him and softening her voice, as if giving the entire matter more consideration. "I thought not. Now leave us alone before things get out of hand."

Cade pulled himself up to his full height, attempting to make her smaller by comparison. Which never worked all that well because she stood just a shade under six feet. Nevertheless, he clenched his fists and took a step toward her.

Jace squared off and matched his movements, taking a step forward as well.

Cade weighed his options. "I'll talk to you later." Although he spoke to Emory, his eyes traveled over to Jace.

Monty, overlooked at this point, sucker punched Cade right in the gut and the cowboy gigolo folded like an accordion.

"You've gone soft," Monty sneered, reaching down to help him up. By the collar. "Now, don't make me do that again." Then playing to the crowd, Monty bellowed, "Make way for the man. He's had a bit too much to drink and needs fresh air."

More muffled laughter broke out as Cade struggled to break free, straighten his doubled-over position to stand tall, while Jace stood tense and ready. Watching his every move.

From sheer force of will, Cade made a decent show of pretending that the wind hadn't been knocked out of him, and that his gut didn't hurt like the devil.

He cleared out with a glare, slamming the door as he left. Conversations resumed, centering around Cade as the starring topic.

Linda, color drained from her face, claimed her abandoned barstool, and took a deep sip from her glass, hand trembling ever so slightly.

"Hell," Emory muttered to no one in particular. "Next time we'll have to shoot higher up than his foot."

Linda blanched even further, and Emory's mind darted back to the earlier conversation with her father.

"Can I buy you another?" Emory offered, indicating the liquor with an incline of the head. "Jace, what are you drinking?"

"What was *that* about?" Linda gasped, shocked blue eyes wide and blinking.

If the historic preservationist planned on sticking around with her father, she'd have to learn. Hugo's death should have provided a strong warning for her. A very strong warning.

Jace listened, interested in Emory's answer.

"A rotten ex-ranch hand," she replied as casually as she could make it. "One who's getting tangled up and picking fights that he really shouldn't."

10

RETRIBUTION RIDES A DARK HORSE

1889

THE MENACE OF THE DARK MOUNTAINS STRENGTHENED the unease surrounding the Cross faction as they rode back to the ranch. The birds, once singing from a distance, resumed their songs from the coyote willows along the river as if gunfire had never rung out. However, the birds, acting the part of moral harbingers, fell silent once the men and horses neared and then passed. The abrupt silencing of their trilling voices cast a deeper pall over the proceedings, responding to the violence in a saddened silence, as if the men who took part had no right to listen to the beauty of their songs.

It is unlikely that any of the men noticed anything as commonplace as the lack of birdsong to accompany their procession. Each man drew deep within himself and kept any opinions of the matter and his participation buried deep within. Silent. Although victorious, their return held nothing jubilant about it by any means, although the pride at their conduct and the fact that they won that round remained evident. Down to a man, however, they believed that the fight would follow the home and come again.

Rumors swirled about Susan, guarded notions expressed and spoken in low voices. To question such speculations aloud would provoke a fight with none other than Hank Cross himself. Such musing, or outright defiance, would certainly amount to the loss of a job at best. Likewise, it could easily land a man into an early, unmarked grave at worst. In fact, no one ever dared to discuss Susan within his hearing. The circumstances surrounding her death carried with them a bitter, poisonous taste.

The box canyon was more than just an excuse, although it provided the justification for the fight.

The Crosses never yielded land, their claims, or their children. Ever.

Hank Cross, taking the lead of their return back to headquarters, held himself taut, and ready to spring. The men's nerves transmitted into the horses who tossed their heads, some with the whites of their eyes visible as if they danced on a wire, ready to spook at the slightest provocation.

And so, the men rode in a silent procession with no immediate sound beyond the horse hooves thudding, the creaking of the wagon, and the jangling of the traces.

The corpse of Mick Osborn jostled in the wagon bed certainly did no talking.

Every rider listened for the warning sounds of danger—a danger which didn't come.

Hank Cross, although riding ahead, understood the lingering feelings of the men trailing behind him, although those opinions and beliefs held little store for him. Instead, he focused on the next move.

Cooper had multiple sons, whereas he had only the

one. All of which turned his mind toward the future. If he wanted more sons, he'd better find himself another wife to bear him some. If Cooper had any sense, he'd pack up his sons and leave.

Should that event ever come to pass, the Lost Daughter's boundaries would expand into and over the Cooper land until the name of Cooper fell, lost to memory. As that ranch fell, the Cross Ranch would stay and grow. None of them would ever leave. None of them would go anywhere at all, other than down into the very same ground.

In the ranch yard in front of the main house, the riders' progression stopped. Hank dismounted first and looped his reins over the hitching post. His men stayed in their saddles awaiting instructions, as the wagon rolled up accompanied by two cowboys riding drag.

The boy's eyes held a guarded expression, but he proved a true Cross all right. Hank figured him likely bothered, but he hid it well. That's the part that counted. One day he and his future brothers would run the Lost Daughter. And they would pass it down to their children, and the legacy would continue through the next century.

Longer, if Hank Cross had his way about it.

"Since Osborn was one of your lot," Hank called out over his men as their horses shifted and the men leaned on their saddle horns, "I'll leave the formalities up to you. Do we want to bury him now, or in the morning?"

The men exchanged glances. The unelected spokesperson of the men cleared his throat and spat. "We'll lay him out in the bunkhouse if you don't object none. He ain't coming back. We'll say a few words over him and dig the grave in the morning."

Decision made, the men dismounted, saddle leather creaking from their weight.

"One of you give me a hand with Mick." Another cowboy walked over to the wagon. Then to the boy he nodded. "Thanks, Henry. We can take it from here."

The boy hopped down from the buckboard, and, not trusting himself to speak, simply nodded in return.

"You've got chores to do," Hank told his son.

The cowboys exchanged another round of guarded glances.

"Say, boss," a different rider asked, "we ain't really going to castrate him, are we?"

Hank Cross didn't flinch from the question. "I ain't made up my mind yet. Depends upon Old Man Cooper's next move."

11

POISONED WATERING HOLES

JUNE 2023

Jace shook his head. "I just stopped in here by chance, to see what it's like. And I believe I have my answer."

"It ain't much." Emory scanned the patrons.

"Oh, I'd say it's plenty lively." He followed her eyes.

"Are you sure that I can't tempt you with a beer or something?"

"Nah," he said, a trace of humor shining through. "The morning will come plenty early." He nodded in Monty's direction. "I might take the early shift and recall the favor at a later date."

With that, he tipped his hat at Emory.

As he turned to leave, Emory stopped him. "Jace? Watch out for Cade. I'm sure he'll play dirty if given the chance."

"I'd expect nothing less, but men like that don't seem to come at me for some reason." And with that, Jace left the crowded bar, and walked into the night.

Emory watched him leave, feeling slighted that he

refused her drink, but sizing him up. He was likely right. Men like Cade preferred weaker men than Jace to fight. Weak opponents increased their winning odds substantially.

When he disappeared completely from view, Emory held up her finger for the bartender, who, like everyone else, watched and listened to the words exchanged and Cade's sucker punch.

"Hey!" Emory shot across with a grin owed to Cade's comeuppance.

Caught, the bartender offered a guilty expression followed by undivided attention. "What can I get you?"

A nod at Linda's glass. "Whatever she's drinking, a shot of whiskey for Monty, and I'll have one of those White Claw things."

"Flavor?"

"Don't care."

The drinks came straight away, with precision. "Fifteen dollars and fifty cents."

She pulled out a twenty and laid it on the bar. "Keep the change." Feeling a decided twinge at overtipping—one dollar a drink held as the going rate as far as she knew and probably most of the clientele didn't even tip that much. But it never hurt to make friends. And making friends amounted to her ulterior motive and the plan all along. Buying a favorable impression might strike as unsavory, but it surely tended to work.

Monty appeared scandalized at what he considered the waste of good, hard cash, but that didn't mean he turned down her free drink. Instead, he raised the glass in a silent toast, and took a sip.

Followed by an afterthought. "That Cade Timmons really pisses me off."

"Yeah," Emory agreed. "Trust me, he doesn't do much for me either."

Linda must have caught the wistful note, for she eyed Emory, although she didn't pry. "I'm glad I got the chance to see you, honey."

Emory smiled. "I meant to give you a call to let you know that I'd come home for a spell. I just hadn't gotten that far yet. I came back a couple of days ago." A dead pause. Emory faltered but felt obliged to continue. "It's been a bit of a learning experience out in Vermillion, but I'm sure Dad told you all about that."

She searched Linda's face, noting the woman's eyes betrayed traces of the recent turmoil.

"He told me bits and pieces. Nothing substantial..."

"Anyhow, I had a few vacation days to burn." Again, Emory paused, then switched the topic. "Do you actually come in here often?"

Linda appeared flustered at the very notion. "No. Not so much. I just didn't feel like sitting around at home tonight."

Emory felt a torn loyalty, vacillating between kindness and obtaining information.

"Say," Emory persisted, although she used a teasing voice, "there's nothing going on between you and Monty that I need to warn Dad about, is there?"

Monty's eyes narrowed, as Linda laughed outright at the mere idea.

"I actually *did* follow him in here," she admitted to everyone's mutual surprise.

Her confession resulted in Monty side-eyeing Linda with a new interest. The notion that a woman might follow him anywhere had obviously not occurred to him for quite some time. Thinking it all over, he puffed up a bit, as men tended to do.

Then he turned his attention square on Emory, turned both appraising and suspicious. "And what *are* you doing in here? Did you follow me too?"

Emory cocked a grin while looking at the Budweiser mirror on the far wall. The one cracked from either bar fights or errant pool balls—anyone could take their pick. "You don't believe that the family that drinks together, stays together?"

"That'd be a first," he grumbled.

Emory scanned the crowd and found no female of interest. In an aside to Linda, she offered a stage whisper. "We might be cramping his style."

"Really?" Linda's head snapped back a little at the notion. "Oh dear, I never thought…"

Monty cut off her apology, shoulders settling square. "She ain't in here, and I don't even know that she's coming."

Fair enough, but that really didn't produce any information. Emory, clutching at straws, eyed the clientele. Just the regular crowd—a few tourists, some ranch hands, a few town folks, and one bleary-eyed wastrel sitting down at the end of the bar.

To her dismay and surprise, the wastrel stared straight at her—which seemed the absolute last thing she needed. To break the unwanted attention, she latched upon the man working behind the bar.

"Say," Emory called out. "Were you working here last night?"

He walked over. "Yes, ma'am," he sang.

"Who bought Monty's drinks last night? He came home mighty proud of himself."

"Now," he teased, leaning over and resting his forearms on the bar, "you are asking me to divulge confidential information."

He winked at Monty.

"I told you I thought her name was Suzanna," Monty snarled.

Playacting aside, the bartender shrugged. "I thought she called herself Robin, or maybe Susie. But now, I don't believe Suzanna is right either. At any rate," he nodded in Monty's direction, "she sure hung on to his every word."

Emory shifted. No doubt, the entire situation felt off. Definitely off.

"How old is she?" Emory persisted.

Monty slapped the scarred bar's surface. "I am sitting right here..."

She held up her hand to silence his objections.

Again, the barman shrugged, eyes sparking and grin half-cocked. "Slightly older than you, I'd say. Maybe thirty. That said, I don't think she lives around here, but it sure looked like luvvvv..."

Emory laughed at his tone and the way he said it. "Buckle bunny?"

"Now what in the hell do you take me for?" Monty demanded.

"An old man with a penchant for free booze," Emory shot back, but then thought a bit better of it. Pissing Monty off would provide no real purpose, other than for entertainment value. "However, one that's pretty decent in a fight."

"Shit..." Monty replied, accepting her half-assed apology.

Linda's eyes remained wide at their exchange, and her mouth hung open a bit. *Poor, shocked Linda.* But Linda's dismay came secondary, and as such held no influence over Emory, who had her own set of problems to contend with.

The persistent question remained—what would a thirty-year-old stranger want with the likes of him?

The bartender, from his angle, had the better advantage on viewing the crowd. "Never mind all of that," he called over to the clump of them. "Guess who just walked in the door."

Predictably, all three of them craned over the bar to watch her approach, and the youngish woman made a beeline over to Monty's side.

"Line them up," she pointed with a long index finger with a perfectly manicured nail. She included all of their drinks. "Tonight, I'm having White Russians. A whole bunch of them."

The barman's eyes went a bit wide at that, and he ducked down to the refrigerator under the back counter, pulled out a carton, and took a whiff.

"I think you might want to make a different choice," he tossed over his shoulder.

His courtesy was lost on the woman. "Fine," she snapped, as if the spoiled cream amounted to a personal affront. "I'll have a gin and tonic. *If* you can *manage* that."

Her rudeness wasn't lost on any of them, other than the woman herself. She turned to Monty—all false eyelashes a-fluttering. "Now, where are my manners—aren't you going to introduce me to your...friends?"

A nerve throbbed along Monty's jaw, and for once, Emory felt better for seeing it.

"This here is my cousin's daughter, Emory, and this is his lady friend, Linda."

The blonde didn't display the least bit of interest in Linda, but she sure took stock of Emory. *Careful* stock.

"I'm Suhanna McIlroy. I'm up visiting your corner of paradise from the great state of Arizona."

"Paradise, huh? I'm not sure I'd exactly call the Ace paradise." Warning bells jangled in Emory's mind while her stomach tightened. An instinctive response with no basis in fact, other than for the shocking behavior of buying Monty drinks. Drinks, which he drank like he had a hollow leg, apparently. Maybe the woman amounted to nothing more than a lonely tourist.

Right.

"Oh, I feel a connection to it," that tourist claimed. "I'd say even say it's kind of like coming home."

That response caught her. "That's a new one. Never heard a visitor say that before." Emory studied the woman, sensing the underlying current. With careful and calculated movements, she leaned her back against the bar and faced the woman full-on. "Most people can't wait to leave."

Linda snorted, and Emory sure caught hold of that reaction. In fact, she wondered what in the hell *that* meant, but at the moment, she didn't have room on her plate for another set of problems.

Her father's girlfriend offered a strained smirk, downturned at the edges. "It took me a while to get used to life out here, and I'm not exactly sure that I ever have. Nebraska plays by a different set of rules and standards, and that's for darn sure. I'm originally from Omaha."

Linda's comments glanced off the blonde stranger in favor of staring at Emory. "For starters, my family didn't *always* live in Arizona." She turned, elaborately, and draped her arm around Monty's shoulders, whose delighted, gobsmacked expression about said it all. He sure as hell acted like he had a live one on the line. Emory figured the hook, line, and sinker went the other way around.

That's the part that bothered her.

Monty slipped off his barstool, and chivalrously offered it up to Suhanna. "I've got to hit the head."

Emory caught the flicker of distaste in the woman's eyes as Monty clanked his way to the back of the building. But she covered her feelings as she slid right onto his barstool. "Nice and toasty. I guess he warmed it up for me." She flashed a plastic, calculated smile, and tossed her blonde curls, acting for all the world like Monty amounted to the greatest prize on two legs. *Make that two legs and one spur.*

Emory frowned. "Don't you think he's kind of old and worn down for you?"

Linda, all ears at this point, appeared curious as hell.

Suhanna giggled. "I have daddy issues."

Emory's upper lip curled. "He ain't no one's daddy, as least as far as I know."

"Maybe I wanna change that." Saber rattling, hidden in those words, came through loud and clear. The question remained *why*.

Emory and Linda exchanged quick glances.

"Anyhow," Suhanna continued, "what is it that you do —work for Monty?"

"*Work for Monty?*" Emory spat. "No, I'm a brand inspector. And *no one* works for Monty."

A few puzzled blinks. The blonde turned her attention to Linda. "And what is it that you do?"

"Historical preservation," Linda replied, even enough. "That's how I met this family."

That explanation provided an opening that the tourist surprisingly found of interest. "Monty says the Lost Daughter is an old ranch. Very old, in fact."

"It probably predates 1888," Linda commented, voice warming to the subject.

Emory shrugged the date off and closely studied the stranger. "How long are you staying in these parts?"

Suhanna tossed her head, curls bouncing. "For a while. I've rented one of those kitchenettes in that old hotel on Main Street. They're opening gallery spaces, and I'm an artist." She signaled for another round of drinks. For someone so small, she apparently held her liquor. Of course, Emory didn't have any proof to back that up. For all she knew, someone would have to carry Suhanna out of the bar at evening's end.

Meanwhile, the Arizonan blathered on along the same vein. "I draw my inspiration from ranches and old Western themes. Like skulls, for example."

Monty came jangling up beside them.

Without cluing him in on their topic, the blonde turned to him. "Can I come see your ranch?"

Monty puffed up ready and anxious to answer, but Emory waded in and cut him off. "It's private property."

Monty exhaled. "Now, Em..."

"It would be in support of the arts." The woman pressed her breast into Monty's arm. "If I'm with you, I'm sure that would be OK, wouldn't it?"

And before he had a chance to answer, Emory locked eyes with the stranger. "Monty's busy riding the fence line tomorrow."

The blonde's brow furrowed, and she battered her eyes at the well-worn cowboy.

"I ain't gonna ride all day," he protested, as the next round of drinks arrived.

Emory squared her shoulders. "That's good to hear, because those tanks need cleaning out afterward."

Monty shook his head and took a deep drink of his whiskey as the blonde pouted and Linda set her mind upon a notion—and one that she wouldn't share.

"It's a liability issue," Emory claimed, as if they actually carried insurance. But it sounded good. Technically speaking, if they had insurance, she would have told the truth. Instead, she offered an easy lie on account of her rising temper and feeling pissed off in general. Monty knew the rules the same as anyone. Or at least she had assumed that he did. Either way, she'd get that straightened out right quick if she needed to.

Not to mention that he wasn't the boss. Of all of them loitering around and drinking in the Ace High, she was the closest thing to the boss of the Lost Daughter in her father's absence. And Monty damned sure knew that as well, but just wanted to make himself out as bigger and more important to their ranch operations than an honest claim would allow.

"I'd best be going," Emory said at length, with a nod toward Linda and leaving her drink on the bar, untouched. "I'm hoping we'll get a chance to catch up while I'm here."

Shit. She shouldn't have said that.

Sure enough, Suhanna perked up at that nugget—her eyes sparked, and her mouth tugged. She nestled further into Monty.

Emory felt certain that the blonde would bide her time and strike when she wasn't around to counter, and the entire scenario felt wrong. *Damn.*

She half expected Linda to leave when she did, but Linda stayed planted on her barstool. "I'll see you all later," Emory called out over her shoulder.

The bar crowd still gathered steam and grew, forcing Emory to wedge past people drinking, talking, and flirting.

Almost reaching the door and the redemption of the

clean night air, a gnarled hand threaded through the crowd and grabbed her arm. Hard.

Emory glanced down at the ragged, dirty nails, her eyes traveling over and up to find who they belonged to. None other than the wastrel at the end of the bar.

"Let go of me." She kept her voice as cold, steady, and accurate as if she drew a gun.

"I'll let go of you if you'll hear me out."

Emory gave him the coolest of nods. Taking that sign as agreement, the man unfastened her arm and his eyes now locked into hers—and strangely lit. He leaned forward, teeth rotting in his mouth and almost face-planted on the floor. "Are you that Cross girl?"

"I am, but I don't know you." She waited, eyes narrowing.

He rocked back, but those glassy eyes held hers. "I've done some shit."

Oh, hell. "Why are you telling me?"

"Real shit…"

"And you want me to know this because I'm a brand inspector?" She eyed him closely, figuring him for just another drunk, but everyone knew the trouble with assumptions.

"No. Because you might be the next lost daughter!" He started to laugh, a strange and high-pitched squeal which dissolved into a fit of coughing as he choked on his own spit.

It never did pay to talk to drunks. Emory turned on her heel, checking whether Monty noticed the man accosting her.

He didn't. Looking around, no one did.

And, out into the night she stepped, leaving the declining atmosphere of the Ace and immediately felt better in the clean, crisp night.

Not wasting any time, she headed straight for the comparative safety of her truck, hoping like hell that all the drunks had hangovers. Especially the drunk at the end of the bar because he unnerved her at a deep level. A distinct feeling built inside of her—that she just might find out something about the past. Something that she didn't want to know.

12

A STEP OR TWENTY TOO FAR

1889

THE EVENING SKY LIT UP WITH RED STREAKS LIKE A lucifer match.

Son of a bitch, Hank hoped like hell that Cooper boy hadn't heard their conversation. Hell, if the castration amounted to more than a threat and they went through with it, they'd give him plenty of whiskey to drink to deaden the pain.

Still, there was no sense in making everyone go all spooky. Not on a matter like that.

"Where's Sorensen?" Hank asked another one of the hands.

Before he had a chance to answer, another man came out from around the corner, hitching his belt after a visit to the outhouse.

"Sorenson, have you heard any sounds coming from the root cave lately?"

"No." He shot a nervous, darting glance toward the door. "It's gone quiet."

The two hands exchanged glances as Hank uncinched his horse, pulled off the saddle and hefted it over the corral rail. He turned to the unnamed man, reins in hand. "Here, take this horse to pasture and put my saddle away, will you?"

Hank and his man Sorensen stared at the door of the root cellar.

Hank nodded at the door, Sorensen went over and kicked it. "Say something so we know if you need to eat!"

"Yeah," came the one-word answer.

Yet another of the Coopers' sons, this time Christopher, had the misfortune of being in the wrong place at the wrong time. There was no helping that, not now. They'd found him on disputed land—with a strong chance that it belonged to Cooper— but any such legalities hadn't figured into Hank's calculations then, and they certainly didn't now. On the day in question, the fight amounted to three Lost Daughter riders against the one of him, and they brought him back to headquarters. They'd slapped his horse on the rump to send him, hopefully, back to the Cooper outfit. A horse returning without a rider could mean any number of things, and all of them bad.

Cooper's son had been stuffed in the cold storage along with any rotting root vegetables that had lasted the winter. Hank didn't care much about turnips and rutabagas, but he did care about thick walls to prevent escapes. The youth languished in the darkness, awaiting his fate. At least they'd left him with a bucket for his business, and a bucket of water. That was decent enough of them, to his way of thinking.

Hank chewed on the inside of his cheek. If they castrated Cooper's son, heaven only knows what they might do to Susan or her child.

"What is it about the Cooper boys that they keep getting themselves caught?" Hank lamented to Sorensen.

But there was no real answer to that. And this Cooper imprisoned in that root cellar wasn't the first to find himself detained in that particular location. That honor fell to Vern, the first prisoner they'd held in there. The prisoner who had sparked off a large portion of the problem they still clashed over. A very large portion, indeed.

13

FIVE FOOT TWO AND EYES OF
BLUE... SHIT

JUNE 2023

THE RADIO PLAYED, AND EMORY HUMMED ALONG TO AN old torch-'n-twang song whose name she never did know. She'd made an early morning run to pick up feed supplement and milk for their coffee from the general store, and the drive back to the ranch passed on near autopilot. Emory glanced at the familiar landscape—the sky framed and caught between the mountain peaks, but with clouds building behind the Never Summer Range in the distance. During the month of June, storms surely popped up.

Turning from the county pavement and onto the dirt ranch road, the crossbeam came into view, and with it the old rotting skull she once helped her father hang. Funny how she'd grown so used to it over time. She didn't really take notice of it as she once had. It amounted to all but a declaration of war against trespassers, but trouble seemed to find their doorstep with regularity, no matter what the skull had to say.

A talisman of sorts, it didn't always do its job as well they might have hoped.

Before pulling into the ranch yard, she noted Linda's Jeep parked off to the side—and not exactly at a friendly distance from her father's truck. The vehicle's disparate location appeared locked in a mechanical argument and refused proximity. Emory slipped from the driver's seat, holding the gallon of milk by the handle. Her eyes scanned the oldest ranch sections visible and found nothing all that much out of the ordinary, save for an open door that normally remained closed.

With a shrug and a slight grimace, she hopped onto the porch without benefit of using the two sagging stairs, boot heels striking the plank porch flooring.

She took in the spot where Iver almost bled out—another memorable event—and noted that no matter how hard she scrubbed, traces of his bloodstain remained embedded in the wood grain.

None of which broke her stride, being old news and all. She strode straight up to the screen door, flung it open, and let it fly with a hollow crack.

"Dad?"

"Back here," his voice called out from the office.

She stuck the milk in the refrigerator. "Is Linda here?"

"Yep."

She shut the refrigerator door and headed back to the office. Inside, she found her father seated behind his desk, alone.

"Come clean. Did you two have a fight or something?"

Her father's steely eyes peered at her from under his eyebrows. "Is that truly any of your concern?"

Without being asked, Emory grabbed a stack of papers cast off on a wooden spoke-back chair, pulled it out from the wall with the toe of her boot, and claimed the seat.

"Don't mess up my organization there," Lance Cross growled, pointing a gnarled index finger.

"Like they're in any particular order," she countered, only half teasing. "I'll set them down right here exactly as I found them."

She discarded them on the floor without a second thought. "You might as well tell me. What's going on?"

"Today?" he growled. "She's showing some girl the buildings. Haven't the faintest clue why."

Again, those damned warning bells a-jangling. "If you ask me," Emory countered, "I'd put an end to that, straight up. Personally, I don't want people poking around where there's nothing to concern them. Just my opinion, of course."

Her father's attention locked on to her. "Any particular reason?"

"Do I need one? No, other than they don't belong out here. And who's the girl, anyhow?"

"Dunno. Didn't ask. Linda left her in the car while she asked permission."

"So, she asked for your permission, and you said 'yes.'"

He frowned. "That's the size of it."

"She didn't call first?"

"Nope." Her father sat back in his chair, hands behind his head. Daring her.

Although she felt somewhat disloyal, Emory pressed on ahead. "And that's OK with you?"

"Nope," he replied again.

One-word answers didn't exactly cut it, from her perspective. She pursed her lips and glanced out the window behind him. She recognized the back of Linda's head but remained unable to see who she brought with her.

"You know," she remarked staring out the window, her focus rifle-scope sharp and offering her comment as an aside, "I found Linda in the Ace High drinking with Monty." She glanced at her father for his reaction.

A nerve throbbed in her father's cheek. "It's a free country."

"Sure is," Emory agreed. "Then Monty's tourist turned up, wanting White Russians of all damn things."

Her father offered a blank slate stare.

Emory persisted. "Are you going to let me in or keep me guessing?"

He sniffed and shifted in his chair, his eyes taking on that faraway expression as he searched for an answer.

She cut him off just as he readied himself to speak. "And tell it to me straight."

"We are experiencing a...difference of opinion." Silence.

Emory waited. Nothing further seemed forthcoming. "About?"

He scratched the back of his neck. "She's beginning to notice the...gaps."

"Ah. You mean she's noticing how we really are."

"Something like that."

"Why did you let her on the Lost Daughter with a stranger then? Strangers have caused us nothing but problems as of late."

"I suppose because I didn't want to seem like a complete bastard."

Emory laughed. "Since when has that ever mattered to you." She didn't ask a question but offered a statement. A foregone conclusion, in fact. She eyed her father more closely. "I suppose the question is not when, but who. How much does she matter to you? That's the real question."

"Well, honey," he sighed, "that's what I'm trying to figure out." Then that old familiar knife edge returned. "Not as much as this ranch, that's for damned sure."

Ah. The decades-old thread that wove them together.

Emory shifted in her seat, again catching view of Linda's blonde hair out in the ruins...before another slightly familiar blonde head entered the window-framed view.

Frowning, she got up from the chair and peered through the glass, careful to stay out of the direct line of sight.

Lance Cross noted his daughter's movements and in a single lithe move, rose and moved out from around his desk. "Problem?"

She did a double take back out the window. "Maybe. I'll be back."

"I'll come with you." Lance Cross kept his voice cold and level.

Boots thudding in unison, they emerged out the side door, and into the yard.

"I think that's Monty's free whiskey, poking around," Emory remarked, taking the measure of the woman.

Her father stiffened. "You're kidding."

"No, I don't believe I am..."

Emory and her father crossed the yard in nothing flat. She stepped over old bailing wire in the scrub cast off from the sagging buildings, her father trailing slightly behind. Neither Cross made a sound beyond that of their boots striking against the ground. Not that their mission required stealth.

Father and daughter exchanged quick glances laced with private meaning.

"Hi there," Emory called out when she caught sight of Linda.

Linda faltered upon catching sight of Lance and her guest remained hidden from view. Emory gathered that her father was disinclined to say much of anything at all.

"You didn't mention you'd be coming out," Emory offered, voice friendly. Linda didn't entirely fall for her act. "Did you bring someone out with you? I thought I saw someone else."

Looking nervous and in the wrong, Linda's eyes darted and she held her head a bit low. "You met her last night. Suhanna from Arizona."

"Did I hear my name?" A voice called out from behind one of the old outhouses. And sure enough. Monty's new Arizona pal emerged from someplace she ought not to have been.

"Are you here for Monty?" Emory asked the Arizonan, sounding stupid to her own ear but too shocked to come up with anything better.

Suhanna ignored the question, came right up to them, stepped past Emory as if she wasn't standing there, and approached Lance with her manicured hand outstretched. "Hel-lo, cowboy. My name is Suhanna McIlroy."

In her deepest of hearts, Emory wished she hadn't seen the spark her father's eyes as he reached out his roughened hand. A gnarled, work-worn hand enveloping that smooth Arizona one in his.

Linda didn't miss his reaction either.

"Lance Cross," he offered, voice strong and clear.

Suhanna hung on a moment longer than strictly necessary, and licked her lips as she did so.

This wasn't going right. Not at all.

"What are you both doing out here?" Emory asked, not particularly caring that her question might cause offense. She needed to break the spell, and her mind whirled.

Linda—crestfallen—also appeared angry. As well she should, but she brought it upon herself.

"Suhanna wanted to see the Lost Daughter, and I figured it wouldn't be a problem to bring her out here."

Emory locked eyes with the preservationist.

"The graveyard is freaky," Suhanna offered, pulling her already low-cut top a bit lower down...the swell of the tops of her breasts certainly catching the older rancher's notice. "Kind of goes along with that cute old steer skull you've left hanging off of the ranch sign."

Cute?

Not having time to deal with semantics or oddities of expression, Emory didn't give a rat's ass about the woman's boobs or her lack of language skills. She turned toward Linda, shoulders knotting and hands clenching. "You took her to the *graveyard*? That is private to this family and has absolutely nothing to do with the tax credits."

"I disagree..." Linda countered, then stopped. She'd crossed a line and bloody well knew it.

Oblivious, or at least acting that way, Suhanna flirted and swayed seductively. "We have a Susan in our family too. That's how I got my name. One great-grandmother named Susan, and the other named Hannah. Suhanna, get it? Anyhow, yours died kind of young and ours kept on going..."

Her vapid words fell away as the anger rose, and the blood rushed to Emory's head, coursing. Never mind that Linda might be about to become a victim of this

Suhanna creature, she had the preservationist in her sights. "That is *not* someplace you take people. It's *private*. In fact, Linda, you shouldn't be up there yourself. Not without one of us, and not without a reason. A *good* reason."

"But I don't see…"

"You're right. You don't see." Emory struggled to keep her temper in check and failed. "I think it's time for both of you to leave."

Emory's eyes snagged upon Linda's hand. "What is that you've got there?"

Linda opened her fingers, and in the palm of her hand an old-fashioned boot or button hook rested. Either way, Emory took it from her. "Where'd you find that?"

"In the old house back there." She pointed to Idella's house.

Out of the corner of her eye, she would have sworn that the Arizonan flinched. Even if she imagined it, the entire episode struck an odd chord, but Emory didn't have time for that now. "And did you plan to give that to us?" Emory held her voice level and near enough to expressionless. Her tone ought to have said enough right there.

Linda flushed and handed it over. "I didn't think."

Emory held it up. "Dad?"

Her father managed to tear his eyes away from the Arizonan enough to take stock of the situation. "I've got paperwork to do. I agree with Em. Time for you to go. You're getting in the way." Then he nodded at Emory and the younger woman. "Why don't you two go ahead, and I'll just have a quick word with Linda."

Emory walked Suhanna over to the car.

"Nice spread you've got here."

Emory eyed her. "Right. You're interested in old ranch buildings."

The woman's expression was cryptic, with a glint of treachery deeper down. "Some more than others."

Emory stiffened. The fact that this woman wanted something, remained patently obvious. "Did you plan on visiting Monty? He didn't mention anything about it."

"Oh, I wanted to surprise him." Her words sounded sweet, but her expression said something else altogether. "Unfortunately, I guess that just didn't happen. Say, your father is a *handsome* man."

Emory's eyes narrowed. *Bingo.* The threat she'd sensed stood right before her, five foot two and eyes of blue. *Shit.* "He's spoken for."

The blonde turned her head in the direction where the rancher spoke with his lady friend. Emory tracked along. Judging by body language, with her father gesticulating and pointing off to the side...she *knew*. Those gestures used meant he had a fundamental, nonnegotiable point to make. The ones that brokered no defiance unless someone was willing and prepared to go down swinging.

Strains of the tense conversation came across muffled, words indistinct. However, the vision and tone certainly carried.

"Oh? You sure about that?" Suhanna asked, watching the scene with interest. "Anyhow, maybe you might allow Linda to keep that boot hook. As a kind of consolation prize."

She ignored any such suggestion. Anything found on the ranch, belonged to the ranch. Nevertheless, Emory glanced across the assembled cast and decided she'd best take matters into her own hands. Immediately. Securing the hook in her shirt pocket she nodded at Suhanna, daring her to say anything further on the matter.

Watching the progression of her father's and Linda's discussion, she pretended like nothing out of the ordinary unfurled. Changing her tone to a degree friendlier, Emory offered a casual assessment of the drama unfolding. "Unless he slaps her around, I'd say nothing much of note is happening at all. Why, do you think something different?"

Suhanna's eyes went wide.

"Last time she had a shiner." Emory smirked. "I mean, haven't you *heard* about us?"

Judging by Suhanna's shocked expression, Emory'd won that round. The first round, at least.

At that exact moment, deep down, Emory felt a weight, uncertain of the course this latest wrinkle would take. No, not certain at all.

Yet, she put her hands on her hips, and stared the stranger down. "None of this is your business."

Again, the woman licked her lips, chuckled ever so briefly, and hopped into Linda's passenger seat as light and graceful as a cat. Linda hastened to her Jeep, color high and tears welling.

She avoided Emory's eyes—her entry into the vehicle hit the shocks like a ton of bricks. Starting up the engine, the preservationist backed out fast and skidded to a stop, before shifting from reverse into drive.

Suhanna gave Emory a tiny little "toodle" wave as her head snapped back from the velocity shift—still appearing as if she figured she'd won some sort of victory. A distressed Linda, by all accounts, had lost—and lost badly.

Emory stood in their dust, watching them careen

down the ranch road, headed for the highway oblivious of potholes and ruts.

Her father walked up beside her.

"Don't you even think about it," Emory snarled.

Her father knew that she referred to the Arizonan. To her horror, he simply laughed and headed back to the ranch office.

PART II

14

SUSAN—BEFORE KNOWN AS "HAPLESS"

1887 (TWO YEARS EARLIER)

THE THUDDING OF HOOVES APPROACHED—HORSES cantering at first, then slowing to a trot the nearer they came. Pulling up to a stop in front of the soddy and lingering a few yards away from the door, the unexpected, uninvited, and unknown riders portended nothing good. An unspoken threat in their arrival with a very real potential for danger—a concern shared in the silent glances exchanged between the Cross family members who hesitated inside their defenses.

The men in Hank's employ had ridden away—out of range and out of striking distance. They wouldn't know anything about the trouble faced at the homestead. That typical morning, they rode out and left behind the two women and one young boy—a woman reliant upon herself, a wispy seventeen-year-old girl, and a young boy of ten—and not for the first time. The three ranch-bound Crosses were by no means defenseless, although isolated. Any actions or responses depended upon the judgment of the matriarch.

That said, each would prove ready and able to shoot and shoot on target.

Susan, the only daughter, consulted her reflection in the cracked mirror and tucked back an errant lock of hair. Her mother investigated the arrivals through the thick and distorting mica window, nevertheless she caught her daughter's actions with disapproval.

"You both wait here," she instructed in a low voice, taking down one of the rifles from above the door, making sure it was loaded and prepared. "Susan, you be ready. Henry, you too, but stay out of sight."

Appearances now forgotten, Susan reached for the other rifle and methodically checked it as well. Henry pulled out a revolver from a bureau drawer. The gun appeared far too large for his slender young hands—none of which mattered in the least.

Survival counted. Appearances did not.

The matriarch opened the door five inches.

"What do you want?" Polly Cross asked the riders, voice cautious and noncommittal.

"Ma'am," one of the riders replied, two fingers raised to his hat brim, his glance taking in the weapon.

Susan caught the gesture through the other mica window. *Manners*, Susan thought at the time.

The other riders waited behind their leader, tense, but seated on their horses.

"What can I do for you?" the matriarch asked, opening the door wider and stepping outside, holding the rifle in both of her hands. The weapon crossed her body at an angle which required only a split second to level and pull.

"We hoped that your husband might be around," the man replied, eyeing the rifle and the woman who held it. To his credit, he tried to act as nonthreatening as possible given the circumstances. "I hoped to have a word with him."

"He's not here right now, but he's nearby."

It might have been a lie. It might have been the truth. Her claim extended the standard rangeland caution. Not that Polly and the children appeared entirely defenseless. The air menaced, and a steel-spined Polly appeared made of wire. Had she appeared as vulnerable as a nester on the plains...her husband would have taken issue and corrected that right fast. And absent or present, Hank Cross always dominated the ranch—always as the one in control and who called the shots.

Whereas Hank Cross controlled by intimidation, it seemed the Coopers used different tactics. "Ma'am, my name is Victor Cooper. Our spread is downriver about three miles."

"I know where it is," Polly replied, flinty. Then traces of long-unused manners kicked in. "Can I get you or your men a drink of water? It's warm out. Your horses are welcome to water as well."

"Yes, thank you kindly. Do you mind if we dismount?"

"Go ahead," Polly replied. Then over her shoulder she called into the soddy, "Susan, please fetch these gentlemen water."

Polly never released her grip upon the Winchester.

Susan, on the other hand, placed her rifle barrel up against the interior wall next to the door—ready and waiting if needed—but essentially discarded. Grabbing the empty bucket and ladle, she ducked outside and traced back to the stream for fresh, cool water. With covert appraisal she noted the riders, all dismounting and stretching their legs.

Five sets of eyes followed the young woman as she

slipped away down the path. A flush rose in her cheeks and she felt a thrill.

Their attention did not come as strictly unwelcome. Especially not from the one who appeared the youngest of them all. She noted his square jaw and bright blue eyes that sparked and sparkled when cast in her direction.

She didn't tarry as she made her way to the stream-bank, dipped the bucket into the strong, flowing current and turned back to the excitement of the waiting riders.

Anything that broke the monotony of ranch life...

As she returned along the worn dirt path leading to where they gathered, for the first time she noticed that their soddy came across as run-down and poor. The flush of excitement was replaced by a rising flare of shame. In comparison, she wondered about the Coopers' place and hoped that it wasn't a proper house framed by shade trees. That might prove too much to bear. Heaven knew that she missed seeing people beyond the immediate family and their ranch hands who kept their distance.

Predictably they kept their distance. A distance born from fear of Hank Cross and his temper.

Rounding the corner of the soddy, she first approached the leader and offered him the bucket and ladle.

He met her eyes. "I have a girl about your age at home. Her name's Lucinda."

"Mine is Susan," she replied.

One by one she offered water to the riders, lingering with the younger man. Although both of them bashful, it took them a moment to meet each other directly in the eyes.

"Thank you." Finished drinking from the ladle, Susan

imagined that his voice felt warm and safe. Nice and even. "My name is Christopher, but they call me Chris."

She flushed some more.

Her mother's voice seemed to come from a distance —a tether Susan didn't want.

Her conversation, however, she directed nowhere near Susan and her water bucket. "Is there any particular reason why you've come calling?"

"We seem to be short a few head," Mr. Cooper began, "and wondered if they somehow got mixed in with your herds."

When the precise nature of the question registered, Susan felt the barb. She and her mother both knew. *All* of them knew. However, the Coopers likely played the same game as did the rest of the cattle operations on the range.

"I'm sorry that he's not here to answer that question, but we can keep an eye out for them and send word if needed," Polly replied.

"I'd be obliged." The man called to his men. "Mount up!" He doffed his hat to Polly. "Please let your husband know that we came by."

True, the range was wide, but the men hadn't scattered far and wide on that day.

An hour later the Cross riders came in, and a conversation ensued. First came Polly's account of what transpired, then a later conversation held beyond earshot of the house, and back over by the barn. A second conversation handled strictly by the men.

Matters remained unresolved, although in essence, everyone in the Cross faction understood that a warning had been issued.

Likewise, and more heated, everyone knew that warnings often traveled both ways.

15

A MURDER OF RAVENS

JUNE 2023

EMORY STOOD IN THE RANCH YARD, WAITING FOR HER jangling nerves to subside and her temper to cool. Pondering her options, pondering her father's relationship with Linda, and especially pondering what in the hell that Suhanna woman wanted—none of it boded well. Still holding the boot hook in her hand, it offered a tangible link to her family's past, but true to fashion, yielded no clues. Movement in the sky drew her attention upward—dark birds flying toward the Lost Daughter. Scores of black ravens winged overhead but they did not call, several of them caught downward drafts and landed upon the old dead tree out by Idella's house. One by one they came—some circling overhead before choosing a specific branch and others gliding straight in. In silence, the leaders winged to the very tops of the highest branches and claimed their posts.

No doubt they amounted to an omen of sorts.

Years back, Emory read in a long-forgotten book, that ravens acted as messengers from the spirit world. Their arrival certainly felt ominous and true. She watched, noting their alert caution in the safety of the tree. Their black feathers, shiny eyes, and observant postures challenged her to match suit. Emory understood their message held a warning to maintain her guard and vigilance like the raven scouts.

They didn't stay long. One by one they resumed their flight, first single birds winging away and followed by twos and threes which turned into multitudes. The murder headed southwest. *Southwest*, Emory noted, *in the direction of Arizona.*

She could chide herself all she wanted for her strange, homegrown version of superstitions, but coincidentally Monty rode his horse into the yard and over to the pasture where she stood.

"Staring at them birds?" he called out to her.

"Yeah," she replied, walking toward him. "That Arizona bait came out here, poking around."

"Bait? What kind of term is that," he grumbled, leaning on his saddle horn. He knew. Hell, they all did. "What'd she want—did she ask about me?" The poor old sod held hope in his voice. Then he turned over a memory, bothered. "But I never did tell her where we were."

"Nope," Emory agreed. "Linda brought her out here, of all things. Say, Monty, you'd better tell me what you know." Her request came in a tone softened and verging on conciliatory. "No judgment against you. Promise. But something isn't right out here."

Monty sniffed as he dismounted, unbuckled the saddle cinch, and removed the saddle and pad with one lift, setting them upon the fence rail.

He led Joe by the reins over to the gate, removed the bridle, and released him into the company of the others.

"No," he replied coming back to her and taking his own sweet time about it. "Events are far from right."

Together they watched Joe run up to Kai and the rest of his herd. The four geldings nipped and raced, rough housing just to establish the herd's order yet once again.

A notion further inside bothered the old cowboy.

To get at it—Emory volunteered information. "I asked Dad about Linda, but he wouldn't say much. I get the feeling it isn't exactly working out on that front. But she took that woman to our *graveyard*!"

Monty's watery eyes scanned the distance, and in the end, he spat. "She shouldn't have done that."

"No," Emory agreed. "But she did."

Emory showed him the boot hook she held in her hand, holding it out in plain view for all. He glanced at it and shook his head. "Linda found this and forgot that she carried it," she explained. "I took it away from her. Anyhow, that Suhanna is mighty interested in this property. Unnaturally so, I would say. Dad had words with Linda, and when she drove off, she had tears in her eyes."

"Over a boot hook?"

"No, Monty. Over the fact that she got chewed out in front of everyone."

"Over a boot hook."

Emory shook her head. "Over what appeared an ended relationship. Anyhow, the Lost Daughter isn't a tomb to be raided."

Monty didn't move from her side. He just stood there watching the horses. Finally, his glance shifted in her direction as he side-eyed her. "Lance thinks he can do better than Linda."

Hearing it put so bluntly still came as a bit of a shock. "He does? He said that?"

"That was my take."

"Do you care?" Emory asked him, watching his reaction closely.

"About whether he breaks up with Linda? That'd be a shame, I'd say. Everyone ought to have somebody."

"And what about you, Monty?" Emory's voice came out soft and hesitant.

"Me? I'm a lone wolf." He tilted back his head and howled to the heavens above just to prove his point. "I just let my head get turned by the attentions of a younger woman. But she don't want me, I reckon. I just hope Lance don't get played for a fool."

Emory inhaled. "Yeah, you and me both."

LANCE, Monty, and Emory sat down to dinner that same evening. The table, covered by an old green oilcloth and lit by an outdated hobnail white glass 1950s fixture, provided the family sounding board. Emory, still bothered by events earlier, figured that the boot hook didn't amount to much—in terms of monetary value. Keeping her mouth shut on that specific matter—it symbolized another link to their past slipping away had she relinquished it. Well, she didn't.

Her father didn't say much of anything at all, leaving her to fill the spaces.

She turned to more practical matters. "Normally I'd say that we should invite Jace, but this won't likely turn out as a pleasant meal," Emory commented as the two men sat down for their dinner. "You don't just leave him sitting in the bunkhouse all the time, do you?"

The men exchanged guilty glances.

"He was headed into town anyhow." Monty picked up a slice of bread and abandoned it upon his plate with a flick of his wrist.

Emory brought the heaping bowl of spaghetti to the table. "Can't blame him there. How's he working out?"

"Fine," her father replied. "Served in Afghanistan. Marines. Pretty sure he can handle himself."

Emory nodded, helping herself to food. "What's Linda doing tonight?"

The question posed came out about as subtle as a bull in a rose garden.

Her father glared. "Don't know. And it's none of your concern."

"This is a family business meeting, and she has a bearing. A financial bearing, if nothing else," Emory replied, unwilling to back down. "First item of business, I have to go back to my job. I plan to be there on Monday, in fact."

"So, you just poke a hornet's nest and head off for cover, is that it?" Lance stared at his daughter.

Monty blinked behind those damned blue glasses. His eyes traveled from her, to Lance, then back down to his plate. He started eating. Her father did not.

Not entirely certain which way the wind blew the conversation, Emory took a bite off her plate and chewed thoroughly, waiting to respond. She swallowed. "Maybe. Depends. As far as I can tell, this is a hornet's nest of your own making with the help of single spur there."

Neither man said anything. Emory took another bite.

Lingering silence.

She forged ahead. "First of all, I assumed you and Linda had an understanding. Guess I got that wrong."

"Depends upon what understanding you're talking about." Lance offered at length.

Emory considered the best tactic in the given situation. "I figured, working together with her on the tax grant money, that you made sure she knew that certain parts of the Lost Daughter stayed off-limits."

"Like the burial ground."

"Yes. Like the burial ground. You know, Dad, it's none of her business who we freakin' have up there."

"Never said it was." His eyes locked into hers. "In fact, I told her as much, in no uncertain terms. She's taken liberties where she has no right to. Best put an end to it now." He eyed Emory closer when she offered no comment. "I've gotta tell you, I thought you'd side with her."

Emory frowned. "About what?"

"Women stuff."

Monty kept eating, doing plenty of blinking over his plate as he shoveled in the food before any disagreement turned in his direction.

"I'll tell you some *woman stuff*. And this involves you, too, Shirt Pocket," she shot over to Monty.

"First of all, that Suhanna from Arizona is no one's friend. It doesn't matter how many drinks she buys, how often she goes flashing her boobs around, or whatever else she has in that bag of tricks of hers. And likely they are *tricks* in the most fundamental sense of the word. You read me? She's using both of you, like she obviously used Linda to gain access to the Lost Daughter. You know what that makes her? A user...or worse. If you two are getting too old and senile to see through her act, I'll have to quit my job and move back down here to provide you with the obviously needed supervision. Now, do either of you really want that?"

Monty wagged his head "no" without the slightest hesitation. Her father stared at her across the expanse of the table, his mouth downturned in the corners, but it held a smile, all the same. "Don't think it's come to that yet," he drawled.

"And neither of you, and I mean *neither of you*, are going to the Ace High."

"She's getting the way she gets again," Monty said to his cousin. "Bossy."

Emory glared at him. "I'm sitting right here."

"Yep, just like I was the other night. And I'm not sure I like you telling me how to run my social life."

"Dad?"

He chewed the notion over. "It don't chap my hide any. Monty, that goes for you too."

"And what about Jace?"

The outsider card. Guarded glances telegraphed information, glances that they all read and interpreted. Neither of the men held any doubts about their new hire.

"I guess I'll go explain the situation to him then." In Emory's opinion, the very least her father could do was offer to do it himself.

He didn't. But his lack of manners provided her with an opening.

"I'll take him a plate of food which he can eat or not— as he chooses."

Lance Cross smirked, ever so pleased around the edges. An expression that said he read her attraction to Jace with nary a doubt. For her part, the truth behind his assumption got under her skin.

"What are you going to do about Linda?" She shot across at him, retaliating and rising from the table to fetch another plate.

He simply shook his head in a manner that might have meant darn near anything.

Emory held the plate of spaghetti in front of her like an offering as she crossed the ranch yard and headed for the modified boxcar that served as the Lost Daughter's bunkhouse.

Jace's truck hadn't gone anywhere but remained parked in the yard.

She knocked on the door and waited.

"Coming," he called, and her stomach did a little flip.

"It's Emory."

The door opened revealing a pair of strong, wide shoulders.

Poised to ask if a chore needed doing or if something had gone wrong, he grinned at the plate of food held in her hands. He stood back and held the door open wide. "Come on in. How'd I get so lucky?"

Emory stepped into what only could be described as a cowboy bachelor pad with two very distinct personalities. Jace's apparent belongings showed organization— stacked and gathered. Emory recognized Monty's possessions and clothing as scattered and strewn. At least the dish sink held a semblance of order, and the table stood partially cleared.

"Monty isn't exactly housebroken, if you haven't figured that out already." She held out the plate of spaghetti to him. "You don't have to eat it if you don't want it. We probably should have invited you to the house, but we had a few family matters we needed to take care of."

"Oh? No problem, and spaghetti is one of my

favorites. Would you like a beer, a Diet Coke, or... water?"

"A Diet Coke if you've got it. Provided I'm not keeping you from anything important."

"No, you're not keeping me from anything. Do you mind if I eat this while it's still warm?"

"Not at all. You might want to microwave it a minute. I also wanted to thank you for your help in the Ace High."

The cowboy put the plate in the microwave, while retrieving a Coke from the refrigerator. "Glass?"

Hmm. That meant they actually had some clean glasses. "No thanks. The can is fine."

"Monty groused around earlier in a mood. I guess your father's girlfriend and Monty's crush came by, and Monty ended up as the last to know."

"That's about the size of it," Emory replied, not overly concerned. "Monty also said he thought you went into town tonight. He, on the other hand, is confined to the ranch in the near term. Grounded, in fact."

Jace laughed. "You seriously grounded him? He's got to be what—sixty years old?"

Emory laughed in return. "At least. Well, I've tried to do what I can toward damage control. In truth, I don't actually believe Monty's groundable, but I gave it my best shot and Dad's backing me up." She eyed the ex-Marine cowboy. "Have you been up to our cemetery?"

The microwave buzzed. He shook his head. "No cattle have gone in there so far, from what I can tell. Besides, isn't that kind of...personal?"

"Yes." They both heard the shadow in her voice. "Linda, the woman my dad is, or formerly dated, is a historical preservationist. She came to the ranch one day, along with some other officials, asking to take a survey of the buildings. That's how they met. Anyhow, Linda brought that Arizona bimbo here, and into the graveyard."

Jace barely glanced up from his plate. "This is really good."

She wondered if he heard her at all. At length, he paused enough to meet her eyes across the table. "Forgive my manners, I turned out hungrier than I figured. Yeah, I might have told Monty that I planned on going into town for dinner, but as I mentioned before I'm not much one for hanging around watering holes without a reason. I just happened to be at the Ace the other night in sheer coincidence."

"Speaking of which," Emory admitted, "I'm glad that you were."

He side-eyed her, debating whether or not to pry. In the end, curiosity trumped reticence. "So, what's that guy's story?"

"Cade?" She took the measure of the bunkhouse's interior. "He used to work here. He now caters to wealthy tourists and what have you and is most likely a drug dealer. His cousin helped me out of a tight spot once a while back, but I recently had to turn him into the authorities. That's partially why we're all a bit twitchy. But as a rule, we don't like people poking around here. Especially not Cade. Now the eighty-four-dollar question is what does that Suhanna want?"

"Anything wearing pants with two legs?"

Emory laughed. "I'm afraid that about sizes it up." Turning serious, she eyed him. "This was a hard-fought-for ranch, in case you haven't figured. Also, if you haven't heard, our reputation is a bit...different. I'm just leveling with you on this."

Kindness remained in his eyes. "I've already gathered as much."

Shit. She certainly hoped he didn't feel sorry for them, or her by extension. Kindness—or worse, *sympathy*—would be unbearable.

In response, Emory jutted out her chin and took a deep breath, not fully trusting herself. "Up in the cemetery there's a recent grave. Hugo Werner. He was a good man...a Texan. While he likely wasn't as tough as the rest of us, but he was more upstanding. He died because of me."

Jace held his voice level. "Did you pull the trigger?"

"No, of course not!" Emory reared at the notion. "He ran to help me, and he got shot as a result."

"Then I don't see how you figure it your fault."

Emory started to argue, but he cut her off. "I know what I'm talking about. Combat in Afghanistan."

Emory colored. "Yes. I suppose you do. I didn't mean to imply—"

"You didn't." Again, he cut her off. "The job of the living is to go on living. I heard about this place, and frankly, I enjoy the solitude out here. I'm grateful to your father for giving me the post."

Emory nodded. "You have to bunk with Monty..."

"Hell, even that old geezer is growing on me." He joked.

"Maybe tomorrow you'd like to join us for dinner in the house," Emory said. "That is, if you want. I'll be returning to work in Vermillion on Monday."

And with that she rose to take her leave. He abandoned his food and rose, displaying decent manners. "I'll wash the plate and bring it back."

She shook her head. "Sorry that I got to talking."

"Not at all. I enjoyed it and I thank you for the food.

It's nice to meet you, Emory. *Really* meet you. And I'm sure that spaghetti tastes better than anything I'd ever find in town."

Was he flirting with her? One thing for certain, his words set off a furious blush. She could only hope that the twilight covered the rising color in her cheeks.

Another thing surely didn't escape her notice. Jace didn't drive into town that night.

16

YOUNG BLOOD SELDOM
RUNS COLD

1887

IT STOOD TO REASON THAT NATURE TOOK ITS COURSE. Susan, isolated out on the Cross Ranch with only her family and their ranch hands, found attention from someone new to gaze upon. That new someone belonged to the Cooper family—the youngest son of that brood. True, Hank Cross tended to hire more experienced men...and in this case, more experienced meant older. Additionally, had a younger ranch hand even existed within their ranks, the man would have needed nerves of steel to court someone in the Cross family. Her father would have seen to that, in nothing flat and in no uncertain terms.

Polly read the warning signs building within and around her daughter but said nothing to the patriarch about this latest development.

"I'm going down to get some water," she told her mother, grabbing the bucket.

"We don't need any right now," Polly eyed her, voice dry and brittle. "Why don't you stay put and do some mending. That's what is needed."

Susan eyed the pile. "Sure. I'll just take a few pieces outside. It's easier in the daylight."

"Uh-huh," Polly replied. "Just don't be doing anything that would bring shame upon this family, or get your father riled. Understood?"

Susan felt the flush rise, and she read her mother's eyes and expression well enough to know that the woman understood how matters stood with her as surely as the sun rose in the east.

The girl made a show of picking out a couple of her father's shirts and grabbing the sewing box.

Her mother wasn't necessarily fooled. "Stay within earshot," Polly grumbled.

Susan knew without the slightest of doubts that her mother had good hearing. *Very* good hearing.

SURROUNDED by the leafy rustle of the cottonwoods, the breeze blew a green dance against the sky and an ever-changing tune sang in the afternoon light. The stream hummed a low rushing song, and Susan located a fallen branch upon which to rest and wait. She fanned out her faded blue skirt and arranged the fabric in a pleasing drape, patted back her hair, made sure to fix a relaxed and pleasant expression upon her face, and set the contrived scene by opening the sewing box and threading a needle.

Of course, she heard his approaching horse, but took pains to appear as if she hadn't. She tried to pass off their encounter as nothing more than a lucky coincidence.

Silly, really.

The young man rode up, pausing once she came into view.

Susan, as part of the unfolding theater, pretended an absorption with the mending that she certainly did not feel.

Chris dismounted, and led his horse over in her direction, releasing the animal to graze or drink as the animal chose.

"Don't you look nice and cool," he said by way of a greeting, nice and appreciative.

Pretending a fluster, she smiled in what she hoped he'd interpret as a distracted and pleasing manner.

"Perhaps." She held up her mending. "There's always work to be done."

"Ain't that the truth." He crouched down alongside her but did not join her by sitting on the limb. "What did you tell your parents?"

"You mean my father?" Her stomach fluttered, and not in a good way.

He flexed his shoulders in response. No words forthcoming.

"My mother knows."

His blue eyes locked into hers, widening with what she thought was admiration at her bravery. His head quirking ever so slightly to the side. "That's something, I guess."

The breeze blew stronger, and the leaves danced faster overhead, rattling.

Conversation faltered as shyness took over. But the young man had something to say, something to tell her. "The boss is mad about another few head gone missing." He referred to his father. They both knew the implication, but they had no need to come out to say it.

He then gently removed the mending from her hands, and with care, laid it upon the sewing basket so that the shirt didn't brush against the dirt.

He kissed her gently.

Fluttering with an unfamiliar thrill, Susan thought her heart just might melt.

17

INVENTORY AMONG THE DEAD

JUNE 2023

The clock ticked, and time burned.

The brand inspector job waited for her in Vermillion. Her edict to Monty of no more drinking and hunting forays into the Ace High would likely fall by the wayside, forgotten once her truck's taillights disappeared over the first hill, or around that first bend.

Sunday morning broke and found her already drifting about the kitchen, waiting for the dawn. The drawn-out brightening hint of sun rested on the horizon in the east, gathering strength and fortitude as Emory sipped day-old reheated coffee. Those palest of yellow hues morphed into a strengthening blush of rose-pink delight. As the earth turned, those colors transformed from a fading rose into a gathering blue backdrop as the sun ascended farther in the sky. From her vantage point in the darkened kitchen, Emory watched the show taking place beyond the sink's window—the indistinct listing old buildings endured and persisted as dark silhouettes against the brightening landscape. Silhouettes that might fall over but wouldn't back down.

Legacy. One hard-fought legacy.

Her father stirred upstairs—his heavy footsteps and morning cough reverberated through the house, shattering the stillness.

She slipped out the side door, coffee cup in hand, and walked up the rutted road to the cemetery on the hill. In those early morning hours, the ghosts felt closest. Right at her elbow, in fact, and pushing her along.

Although late spring, the morning air danced down the slopes, mountain cold—the cleanliness undershot with the hint of danger. When it blew in from the north as it did that morning, the wind carried a sharpness that cut like a dull blade. Not deadly, but enough to remind a body that nature remained, ultimately, in charge. A jacket wouldn't have gone amiss, but in her haste for privacy, she left comforts behind.

Cresting the hill, Emory paused at the mouth of the road and considered the graves. Each and every one marked the passing of a person who had died defending the ranch. Even if those graves held the bodies of those who succumbed to old age, they had fought plenty of contests of will in their lifetimes, one way or another. Battles and fights came in different guises, but they bound the Crosses to that land. Every single one of them.

All the graves faced west per the custom of the setting sun, and each marker, wooden or stone, carried the Lost Daughter brand.

Including Hugo's.

She walked over to the newest grave and stood in front of it. Coffee cup in hand and struggling to identify exactly what she felt, and how she felt it.

"I suppose I'll tell you every time that I come home how sorry I am. I'm sorry that I dragged you into the fight, and I'm sorry I broke through the stair and called out, which I never should have done in the first place. I'm sorry for all of that and will be. I guess I'll carry all of that to my grave with me."

As she spoke those words aloud to his grave, the wind swirled and carried them off. Her guilt and apologies fell short, and he never would have wanted that for her.

"Hugo," her voice cracked, "it's best that you know…I loved you in my own way, but this place would have killed you in the end. And I guess it did. Just sooner than any of us expected."

Piece spoken, Emory stepped over to Idella's grave and felt that familiar quickening sensation. Communication with Idella came that way—a brush across the back of her shoulders, a tightening, and a ghostly whisper from the great beyond if Idella deemed the message important enough.

For the moment, she simply captured the sense that Idella wanted her to quit mooning about and to confront whatever threatened the family.

Emory laughed and tilted her head as she considered that marker and the woman below. "I know, Idella. I'm working on it."

With that, she left the dead to rest. The ghosts never felt—on the Lost Daughter Ranch—peaceful.

Nor did they hold much with resting. Not with trouble afoot.

BACK IN THE KITCHEN, her father stood in front of a sizzling frypan, poking its contents between sips of coffee. "I heard you up and about, but I figured I'd get breakfast started. Give you a break for a day, huh?"

She eyed him and for the first time became concerned with the thought. Whoever gave him a break? "You don't have to do that. But thanks. I wanted to make the rounds and look everything over. It's cold outside."

"It's still early." He flipped over the eggs in the pan. "What did you expect?"

"On my last day of vacation?"

He shot her a look. The one that said he didn't fall for it.

She smirked. "Just testing to make sure that you remembered. I figure I'll go through the old buildings a bit, and then check on the tack. Not necessarily in that order. When it gets a bit warmer, I can work with Outhouse for a while."

He nodded, concentrating on the food, but she wasn't fooled. "Guess I never asked, but what's the plan here? Does Vermillion suit you, now that you've settled in, or do you want to go back to Greeley? Hell, if you want, you can just stay here…"

Emory shrugged. "I do like the region, and especially the wild horses. You always hear the problems that I'm having no matter the location, and I'm not sure that I've settled yet at all." She cracked a grin. "Anywhere."

"Oh yes. Dead outlaw graves. It's all coming back to me now." He kind of croaked those half-sung words.

She laughed despite herself, shaking her head.

"Are you leaving Outhouse here, or taking him with?"

Emory poured herself another cup of coffee and leaned against the counter. "You two jokers aren't doing anything with him at all."

"You could ask Jace what he thinks."

She stared at her father, who didn't meet her eyes. If anything, she'd say he meddled, but of course, he'd deny it. Vehemently. "You've seen him work with horses?"

"No. But you could think about giving him a chance."

Unsure whether they still truly spoke about Outhouse, she protested. "A person knows how to work with horses, or they don't. I might think about it, but he'd really have to know what he's doing. But I'm real particular about how people handle horses—especially my horses. You know that."

"I'm just saying that you could talk to him and ask him if he likes working with them. It's one way to get the horse to handle better, especially if you don't have the time or want to pay board for the mustang."

He had a point.

"Are you sharing those eggs?" She nodded at the frying pan's contents.

He slid some on a plate, along with a couple of strips of bacon and handed it to her. "It's hardly like I'm going to eat them all myself. These are for me and my favorite girl."

"Oh?"

"Do you have a problem eating breakfast with your old man?"

No. She didn't have a problem with that at all.

AFTER CLEARING the breakfast dishes away and her father headed out for his regular chores, Emory stepped out for her own historical survey of their buildings. Truthfully, she searched for clues, but about what, she still didn't know. Beginning with Idella's house where the feelings usually came the strongest, she opened the old front door with the China doorknob. Footprints. Linda and Suhanna's damned footprints where they ought not be.

Idella never wanted strangers in her house, and

Emory shared that sentiment with her great-great-grandmother.

"They came inside and shouldn't have," Emory spoke aloud to the ghosts, and her words rattled around in the emptiness.

Not to mention, the two women had probably disturbed more than just the dust on the old plank floors. Poking around in a house and a history where neither had any right or claim amounted to a declaration of an impending struggle. The warning contained within the mere existence of their footprints on Idella's floor served as an accusation—the fact that maybe, just maybe, the latter-day Crosses had become complacent.

She rubbed out their prints with her boot and felt better. Traces might remain, but hers covered theirs. Her boot prints were the ones that counted.

The staircase and the infamous stair she bust through during the fatal gunfight remained unrepaired. Jagged splinters remained, and probably some of her blood, too —if she investigated closely. Which she didn't.

Come to think of it, she hadn't once ventured into Idella's house since that day.

In passing, she wondered where *exactly* Linda found the boot hook in the first place...common sense would place it upstairs...but no one had climbed those rickety stairs since that fatal day.

With a guilty stab, she realized she had put on the same shirt she wore yesterday, and the hook remained within the pocket. She unbuttoned the flap and withdrew it. Fancy. Uncharacteristically fancy, inlaid with sterling swirls. If she interpreted it correctly, that hook would have been a prized possession, and one of the finest things a Cross woman had ever owned.

Scanning the interior, not much in the way of possessions remained in the old house—most everything discarded over time. Yet the determination of those who lived within those walls remained and offered the subsequent generations lessons. Lessons handed down and poured over through the years—and not all of them pertaining to books. A table, spindly chairs, and the floor awaited, blanketed in dust. Ghosts lurking in the corners and awaiting the living which might, or might not, care to listen. Emory pulled one of the chairs out and set it next to the table. She removed the fancy hook from her pocket and snapped it on the table's surface. "There. What do you have to say about that?"

Emory felt the shift in the building. Presences gathered…then retreated.

As always, the distinctions between the Lost Daughter and their family history tangled. Meanings circled, taunting and elusive.

Unless the ghost of Idella felt like talking.

"Well?" Emory asked into the mocking silence and nothingness. "Fine. Don't talk. Be that way. But this hook looks pretty fancy to me."

The rising sense of a presence returning surrounded. Picking up the hook and examining it, doubts in the back of her mind told her that the hook never belonged to Idella at all.

"It's too fine, too fancy," Emory mused.

The silence in the house seemed to agree.

Then the house returned to just an old, abandoned building and Emory rose to her feet. She left the chair positioned at the table and shut the door behind her, determined to figure out what in the hell all the strangeness meant.

"I'll be back, you know I will," she sang into the emptiness.

She took care to lock the door from the outside. And as far as she knew, only she and her father held the key. Both the house and Idella knew she would return.

EMORY POKED her head in a couple of random sheds and old privies where it felt unlikely either of the two women had ventured. Probably a bit too rough around the edges for the likes of them. Emory chuckled. She'd read about outhouse archaeological digs where bottles and other artifacts were extracted.

Sometimes disposals needed to happen quickly. Something beyond bottles, like evidence.

What the heck. That might be worth a few vacation days right there.

Resuming her rounds, all the buildings carried the same scent. The old wood warming in the sun released a smell of faded memories, dust, and rust. She returned to the soddy and stuck her head inside, figuring it surely must have been one of Suhanna's targets.

But nothing was disturbed, and if the women entered, they left no evidence.

Stepping back outside, her gaze landed on an empty shanty—the last structure nearest to the graveyard. She never bothered with that building at all, and doubted anyone else did either. Still…

The morning sun warmed, but her stomach chilled. By accident she kicked an old rusty can that clattered off and careened along the ruts and dints.

The door on that shed or outbuilding didn't have a latch, but only an old, rotten rawhide strap for a handle.

She pulled it open, standing to the side in case any critters needed a clear exit. Nothing scurried.

Peering inside of the dark interior, her eyes landed square on a patch of unsullied white. A rectangular note card forced onto an old nail—the paper certainly was brand spanking new.

Be warned. The fight goes on—this valley is ours.

18

CAUTIONS OFTEN PASS UNHEEDED

1887

POLLY DIDN'T LOOK TOO KINDLY UPON HER DAUGHTER when she came traipsing back into their soddy. The dreamlike expression she wore on her face, or the way she hummed to herself with slight, fragile smiles pretty much gave the game away.

Polly knew the signs all right, and they waited right on the doorstep.

She closely watched her only girl, torn as to what she should do. The girl, coming of age, did what girls coming of age do. It was only natural that she should find a young man to court with. Pretty Susan held a place as one of the very few in that remote outpost. Nature dictated that she would attract a fair amount of attention. No, the problem wasn't so much the attention, but Hank. All fathers posed a problem to potential suitors that gazed longingly upon their daughters, ever since the beginning of time. Especially if they cared about their girls, which Hank most certainly did. The vehemence behind his feelings might have diminished if they had more girl children born to them, but as it stood, Susan remained the only daughter. As such, there could be no mistakes made, but Polly, deep down, hated to crush her daughter's dreams.

Nevertheless, caution told her that the Coopers were not the sort of folk they wanted to go mixing with.

Still, such matters remained best left between mother and daughter.

"You know how babies are made," she began the next day as a topic of not-so-general conversation.

Susan gawped as a flush shot up at the base of her throat and blossomed. "I've seen the animals, mother."

Polly appeared satisfied with her daughter's discomfort. "That's how it goes with humans too. And it only takes one time for a baby to be made. I'm telling you this for reasons twofold. First, foolish girls get their heads turned with pretty promises that don't mean squat, and you're coming of age. Second, I can't guarantee your father's actions, should you make a wrong step in that direction. Are we clear?"

The realization that her mother *knew*, hit in her heart, traveled to her stomach, and landed in her toes.

"Yes, Mother."

Polly Cross tilted her head at her daughter's apparent submission and returned to her chores.

Girls made mistakes regardless. No matter what their mothers said, thought, threatened, or believed. Youngblood ran on a course of its own making.

19

FIGHTING WORDS AND TURMOIL

JUNE 2023

She locked on to that scrawled threat a good, long minute, then tore it from the nail.

It had to be written by Suhanna.

What that Arizona floozy didn't know, came as a fundamental truth. The family that fought together, stayed together.

And the Crosses had plenty of experience on that front.

Emory scanned the visible portion of the ranch to locate her father. She brushed to the side any guilt she felt earlier in lying about his character and figured it all a lie worth telling. Especially now.

She found her father with Jace and emerging from the barn, each carrying a fifty-pound bale of hay.

Her father squinted when he saw her approaching with the note, but Jace, suspecting nothing, offered a clear, untroubled expression.

She probably failed on her return.

Flicking her fingers along the side of her jawbone—the Cross family signal asking for clearance to talk about family business in front of outsiders—she waited for his response.

Her father nodded, doing away with the standard return gesture. If she interpreted the response wrong and spoke too freely, any mistake made pointed to him.

"What have you got there?" His eyes indicated the paper with a sharp dart.

"A threat."

Her father took her words in stride. He slung the hay bale into the pickup's bed before reaching for the note— his eyes scanned over the scrawl. Jace loaded his bale as well, before joining at her father's side and raking over the offending words. His only response a firm setting of the jaw, no word uttered.

"I found it in the outbuilding closest to the grave-yard." That point hardly seemed pressing, but facts mattered. "So, unless Linda's gone rogue..." Emory's voice trailed off.

Although doubtful, one never knew. The enduring and troublesome aspect about threats was that no one and nothing remained free from scrutiny until proven innocent.

Her father cleared his throat. "What was that chickie from Arizona's last name?"

"McIlroy. Mean anything to you?"

Her father handed back the threat. "No, but I guess it does now. Maybe it's her idea of a joke of some kind, trying to get a rise."

"You feel like laughing?" Emory shot the question across.

Both men stood before her, a wall of silent wide shoulders and fighting stances. No one answered.

"I didn't think so." Emory put her hand on her hip, annoyed. "This calls for a change in business as usual. I'd planned on leaving tonight, but now I'll hold off until the morning. Later, if need be—Vermillion can wait. Right now, we'd all better figure out the next step or a response if required."

Lance Cross scoffed. "A plan? A plan for what? That ain't nothing."

"Until it's something," Emory countered. "As of late, I've seen too much shadowy shit to wander off without taking a written warning seriously."

Her father gave a brief shrug. "Good. Glad you are staying a bit longer, even if it's only a few hours. I planned on putting some steaks on the grill." He turned to face the cowboy. "Jacc, you're invited if you like. There will be some talk, however…"

"Sure," he replied. "I'd like a briefing on handling these…developments…if you don't mind."

"Dad's in charge, but if you want my vote, I'd say no lost strangers are allowed to come down that road or in through the back gate. No visitors or tourists or people who claim they want to buy the ranch. That type of thing." She aimed her next comment directly at her father. "And no one sowing or feeling any wild oats in this operation, and that includes Monty. He'll have to be told about all of this." Her piece said, she turned ready to walk away.

"I'll clue him in," her father replied.

And the wheels would set in motion.

THE SUN STRENGTHENED as it rose higher in the sky. Emory wanted to check for traces of trespass out the back gate coming in from the BLM land. Saddling up Kai for the task, a ride along familiar paths would prove pleasant if they found nothing—necessary if they discovered signs. Horse and rider threaded through the back gate onto the BLM land, tracing along the river trail that led to an old, favored watering hole. Kai, knowing the path, picked up his feet and nodded his head, straining against the bit to press forward.

Emory gave him his head, and he picked up a fast trot. "So, you're telling me that you've missed this place, is that it?"

Kai tossed his head and they switched into an easy lope—a fine pace until they reached the point where the trail narrowed down by the coyote willows. Favored by fishermen, it offered an excellent place to spook a horse. She recalled those two maverick calves they'd rounded up and she'd branded a couple of years back. What a very strange chain of events had led her to this very point. Traveling over familiar ground sure brought on the memories—some good, some...not.

The coyote willow's silky, gray, narrow leaves flickered in the sun and the wind, sparkling like newly minted dimes. Their grassy green smell combined with the running river lifted her spirits—threat or no threat. They would prevail. They had to. She slowed Kai to a trot once they reached the bend, and rounding that, the cottonwoods along the bank of the river and the water hole came into view just ahead.

Most cattle, having dispersed higher up and farther back into the mountains, allowed the grass to grow plentiful, and Kai to eat his fill.

The gelding slowed further as they reached the shaded coolness, licking and chewing as Emory dismounted. Dropping the reins onto his neck, she allowed him to wander a bit. Of course, sometimes that's exactly how riders ended up left behind...

Standing in the hollow that many hooves had carved into the land throughout the decades, she lifted her eyes to the rimrocks—the pale sandstone remained shaded in places, but mainly the cliffs glowed in the direct late-morning light.

Assessing those familiar rimrocks, conversations she'd had with her father—the one about bodies buried on the Lost Daughter and in surrounding areas—came back to mind. To hear him tell it, most of those riders once worked for the Coopers—the Cross family's fabled rivals and enemies. But they'd moved away. Defeated and with their tails between their legs, or so the dinner-table stories held.

For once, that widely believed account of triumph on the part of the Crosses felt a trifle too convenient and a trifle too distant.

Emory double-checked those rimrocks and the ledges on top and felt the history press down. With an inhale and an uncanny feeling poised to make a discovery, she reclaimed Kai.

They should take a ride over to where she felt certain an old ambush took place.

Not that the dead did much talking.

LEAVING THE BLM LAND, she decided to take a detour before returning to the Lost Daughter. Recalling her father's anecdote of a grave located at the bottom of a specific rock outcropping, the old trail into Stampede wasn't that far out of her way. Figuring that she'd give that spot a once-over, those hostilities must have dated from the 1880s or early 1890s. The rock outcropping was located along the route that traced the fork of the river split into two. One branch led into town—and that's the one she wanted. The other trail forked to mark the beginnings of the path that led into the Lost Daughter's high pasture. Heading toward the southeast, she and Kai jogged along. No need to tear up the dust...not when searching for the dead and their unmarked graves.

Two miles or so from the watering hole, the jagged rock formation overhanging the trail came into profile. The pale sandstone jutted over the trail in a shelf about two feet long and wide. Now that she'd latched on to the notion of outlaw burials—or ambush victims—she felt bound and determined to locate evidence from those violent years. Scanning the ground's surface for traces of burials, she found a few dents but had no way to be certain. Casting her gaze wide over the expanse of sagebrush scrub that never turned purple in their corner of the world—no matter what Zane Grey wrote—any bones left unburied and scoured by the wind, elements, and time would be long, long gone.

But she could *sense* the violence that lingered down through the years.

"These outcroppings are too close to this trail for comfort," Emory told Kai.

She patted his neck and shifted in the saddle as she scanned. Familiar voices calmed horses, depending upon the person's tone. The words didn't matter, but the tone surely did. Out in an unfamiliar area, it remained one of a rider's best tools. A tool, for which she felt a sudden, pressing need.

"I'll bet Dad is right, and someone is buried in this road."

Eyeing the ground for indentations, she didn't locate anything certain, and turned her attention over to the river that flowed along the curvature. Of course, the

Hapless Susan sprang to mind. Depending upon the season, the flow might be a lazy current easily crossed... or a raging torrent from the high-peak snow runoff.

According to family stories, Susan surely must have drowned, and her body carried off and lost in a heavy current. Never had another explanation been offered.

Emory gauged the rocks and overhangs, looking up along the rims and fending off a strange sensation.

Unmarked graves signaled a frontier courtesy in and of themselves—a courtesy that few range riders ever would claim.

Turned into shallow depressions scratched into rock-riddled ground, shroudless bodies would have thudded into the shallow depressions and be covered with varying degrees of care and concern. Holes filled in just enough to prevent the corpses from being chewed on by predators.

Or not.

In the Old West, to leave a body unburied displayed the mark of the greatest insult possible.

She supposed it depended upon whether the rider had friends.

The horse thieves and the outlaws who brushed shoulders alongside her ancestors were not the type of people that most would have cared two bits about, outsiders at best and threats at worst.

"Let's get out of here," she said, turning Kai and spooking herself a bit. They rode their return a few beats faster than the speed in which they arrived.

20

WARNING CLOUDS GATHER

1887

SUSAN KEPT SLIPPING FROM THE HOUSE AT ODD MOMENTS, and Polly noticed.

Of course, she noticed.

But so did Henry. The four of them lived heaped atop each other in that single-room soddy—Henry, Susan, and the two parents. And so it would remain until Hank finished that larger house, which would finally afford a measure of space and privacy. But at that moment, space and privacy didn't matter so much. In fact, living in cramped quarters made keeping tabs on each other that much easier.

Early summer burst upon the land, with the river and stream rising from the snowmelt and the rains and turning the sagebrush scrub as close as it would ever turn to green. The Coopers' youngest son's given name Polly understood to be Christopher, adding a degree of familiarity she never wanted with that boy. She told herself that she shouldn't have known that detail, but Susan let it slip by accident one day.

An unfortunate slip that meant to Polly she wouldn't

fully ignore the boy since a name had been placed upon him.

Young girls who fancied themselves in love wanted to share those feelings with any available female to listen. Poor Susan had only her mother to confide in—and had the girl considered her options carefully, she wouldn't have involved her mother at all. Apparently, bursting at the seams, the girl couldn't help herself. Common sense fell by the wayside—leaving Polly with a dilemma. The realization hit Polly hard—that she, her daughter, and her husband would never share the same outlook on the budding relationship.

In fact, it couldn't be otherwise, given the mounting animosity between the two families.

No, she'd have another talk with that girl. Before the girl forced her hand into confiding the matter with her husband. But the time fast approached. It approached with a certainty that would lead to heartbreak.

That same day, Susan slipped away yet again, and Polly'd be damned if she would go chasing after her. In her heart of hearts, she held a fear of what she might stumble upon. She certainly didn't want that.

Henry held no such compunction. He snuck up on the courting couple. Practicing his stalking skills, he crept up on the courting couple, listening intently on their conversation, which struck him as boring at best. And when they started kissing, he took off as quickly as possible, hoping to find better prey the next time to follow.

While Polly did her level best not to work herself up into a state, Susan came halfway skipping around the corner, with that dreamy expression on her face.

Polly reached out and grabbed Susan by the arm.

"Where did you go?" her mother hissed, wanting to shake that dreaminess right out of her child.

"Getting some fresh air," Susan said. Which, of course, strictly conformed to the truth—but it certainly didn't amount to the full story.

She truly wanted to slap her, but Polly didn't hold with slapping children in the face. That said, it didn't mean she was averse to a well-timed smack if sorely tested. The woman glanced around the yard for anyone lingering within earshot, or who might potentially catch the drama about to unfold.

Polly didn't let go of her daughter's arm. "You can't have nothing to do with the Coopers. They like their women fast and fancy."

Susan blinked. "I'd like to be fancy," she replied. "It sounds a far sight better than being crammed into the soddy with everyone."

"Not that kind of fancy you wouldn't," her mother replied in a tone that conveyed the matter closed and closed forever.

If only Susan had proven that smart.

———

IN OUTRIGHT DEFIANCE of her mother, Susan snuck away to meet Christopher Cooper the following day, as the two lovers had arranged earlier. Polly watched her go.

Henry sidled up beside her. "I'll bet she's going to meet that fellow."

Polly stared at her daughter's retreating back. "What fellow, Henry." It was a flat question because she already knew the answer.

"She calls him Christopher."

Giving the girl a ten-minute head start, Polly made

her way silently to the cottonwood grove, and found the two murmuring and flirting, followed by a comparatively chaste kiss or two. But it couldn't be allowed to go much further.

That night she confided in her husband, reluctant but convicted in her beliefs. She waited until they turned into bed and under the covers.

"You know," she lay her head upon her husband's chest hoping that would soften him some, "Susan is getting of the age when we should think about marriage."

"What brought this on?"

"I think her head's getting turned," Polly began, uncertain, now that she had embarked upon this course, just how far she ought to venture. "It's the youngest Cooper boy. I think he comes a-calling."

Hank put a meaty hand over his wife's and lay there silent and unmoving, thinking the prospect over. "I want her to find someone who will help us expand. While marrying into the Coopers would give us access to their land, marrying into a feud doesn't strike as advisable. They might hold it against her and punish her for our dealings."

Her husband's measured response surprised her. "I didn't know that you had thoughts or plans upon the matter," Polly replied.

"Of course I do." He patted her. "No mistakes are to be made. That's my plan. I'll send that young whelp packing—just see if I don't."

21

CUT FROM THE SAME DENIM CLOTH

JUNE 2023

LANCE SHUT THE BARN DOOR AS KAI AND EMORY CAME loping up.

"Something chasing you?" he half remarked, half asked. He did, however, bother to glance behind them.

Yeah, they cantered along a bit too fast for a trail ride. Another rule of horseback riding—don't let the horse run back to the barn or stable.

"Guess we got going a bit fast."

He eyed her. "Uh-huh. Don't get into that habit."

"Just didn't want to be late to dinner," she lied.

He didn't buy it. "Looks to me like you're spooking yourself…either that, or you want to get yourself dolled up tonight."

Not that she had any intention of admitting as much. Best offense—change the subject. "I spoke to Terry Overholzer a couple of days ago and owe him an answer."

That caught him. "You never mentioned. What did he want?"

"It's not so much what he wants, although I'm sure those two do miss me," she cracked a smile, then frowned. "Come to think of it, he didn't say anything about Dave. Anyhow, he asked if I might consider working out of Greeley for a while and leaving Ray to handle Vermillion."

Her father stopped his task and turned to face her square in the eye. "Why brought that on?"

"I don't really understand it myself. A bunch of cattle skulls apparently. I asked if the animals were dead first, and apparently, they were."

He frowned, furrowing his brow. "Then, who in the hell cares?"

"That was pretty much my question. I don't know why we'd be getting involved in all of that in the first place. There's something that he isn't saying."

His steel gray eyes turned cautious and guarded. "Terry and Dave seem pretty capable from what I've seen."

"Yes, they are. And they're the best at what they do. That's why the request is strange."

Her father clicked, like he would to a horse.

Emory tied Kai to a post and undid his cinch. In an easy movement, she flipped it over the seat of the saddle, and pulled the saddle and blanket off to return it into the tack room without clanking.

"Half of me thinks I should just drive out there to find out what he's talking about. I'll freshen up my apartment while I'm there."

"There you go, getting all domestic," Lance teased.

She snorted and threw back her head. "Yeah, right."

Walking to the tack room, she called out over her shoulder. "If I go that direction, I want to leave Kai here for a while. And I'd have to tell the Wheelers not to expect him until everything gets sorted out. That's another expense right there."

"Whatever you decide." He patted Kai along the neck before returning to his chores. "If you leave him here, at least he'd have company."

EMORY DIDN'T KNOW the best course in the given situation, but in her heart, curiosity won out.

But before she made any solid commitments, she owed Ray at least a call to find out his preferences and opinions on the matter. Who could say for certain that a whole spate of work hadn't cropped up? She scrolled through her phone and selected his number.

"Ray Thompson, brand inspector."

She wrinkled her nose at his distant, professional tone. "Don't you have my number programmed into your cell?"

"I recognized your number, but I wanted to impress you with my professionalism. Did it work?"

She rubbed her thumbnail across her forehead, scratching an itch with a chuckle. "Right. It worked. I just felt like a complete stranger there for a second. How's everything going?"

"You've only been gone a couple of days…"

"I know, I just thought…"

"I'm teasing and giving you a hard time. Let's see. Plenty's been popping off. It turns out that the formal charges against Myra have come down—tampering with a corpse and obstructing an investigation. I guess the obstruction part of that comes down to the cakewalk she led us all on."

"She knew that she strung up that dead boy..." Emory reminded him.

"Yeah, I don't have an excuse for that. But so that you know, the sheriff isn't pressing that angle too hard. Local opinion is running in the direction that drugs are a scourge, therefore no one sympathizes too much with the overdoses. None of which I suppose comes as any surprise to anyone. Myra's out on her own recognizance, and the feeling is that she'll get probation. *Provided* she promises not to do it again."

Emory shook her head at the last part. "Right. Like she's going to run across another dead body on her outfit. Still, maybe she needs a bit more help with who she hires going forward."

"Ain't that the truth. At minimum wage, pickings are slim."

Emory felt that assessment might not cover the entire issue, but then again, the rancher threw a fair amount of shade about her operations. "Say, aren't you kind of friends with Myra? I'd say she thinks highly of you..."

"Oh...she's a character, and I guess so am I," his voice rumbled.

"Anyhow, she provides room and board for her hired help besides just their wages." Emory wondered why she bothered to stand up for her. But in her heart, she knew the answer. She stuck up for Myra because of her position as a female rancher on her own.

"Be that as it may, I'm not even sure that she pays the full minimum wage, but let's not poke around under that rock right now." Ray pressed on. "Your favorite boss, Josh, has packed up his belongings and skedaddled. I have taken over his desk—if you don't want it, that is."

Emory certainly didn't care about that. "You can keep it. Has Terry Overholzer called up there?"

"Yep."

Silence. "What did he say?"

"He wanted to know if we were busy. And I said nothing too hot and heavy that I knew about. Why?"

"They've got a concern over in Greeley, plus I don't know if I ever told you, but I've got an apartment lease there that I'm still paying rent on. As for this stint, it seems like everyone is trying to spread the workload around."

"Hell, I'm fine up here." Ray sounded like he meant it. And no doubt, he did. "Normally it's quiet here, but you probably wouldn't believe me after your introduction."

Maybe, but then again, maybe not. "It was notable, I'll give everyone that much. So, you won't take it poorly if you're working on your own for a while?"

"Nope," Ray replied. "I can manage. Say, you holler if you need anything, OK?"

"It's a deal, and you do the same. I'll call Terry and let him know that I'm leaving you in charge. Bye."

THE NEXT NUMBER up belonged to Terry, and she punched in his contact.

"Hey, Em."

"Howdy. I talked to Ray, and he's not bothered to be on his own for a while. He caught me up on Myra's charges, the fact that Josh has gone on to his DEA post, and the fact that he's taken over Josh's old desk and sounds pretty damned pleased about that part. I wouldn't be surprised if he sat there with his feet on the desk as we spoke."

The older man laughed. "I love it when a plan comes together."

"Yeah, right," she countered. "I still don't really understand your issue, but come tomorrow morning, I'm
driving east."

"Glad to hear it. It's the damndest thing." His voice
held shadows and worry.

Her eyes narrowed as her instincts kicked in,
believing there was plenty he didn't say. "How's Dave?"

His chair squeaked and she imagined he sat forward.
"Sitting right here, listening in as usual. So don't you
worry on that count."

Some of the tension drained. "I've got to let Kai's
stables know that he's not returning for a while."

"That's the responsible thing to do."

"Dad said that I can keep him on the Lost Daughter
while I'm away. I've worked with the mustang over vacation, and he and Kai have bonded." She shifted her
weight, still uneasy.

"See you midmorning? Oh, and before you go start
feeling bad, we only loaned you out to Vermillion in the
first place," Terry grumbled.

Well, she wasn't exactly a library book. "So, you say."

He brightened a bit. "Yeah, if this all lasts longer, you
can bring Kai back out to us. Janet and I wouldn't mind
keeping him with ours, and it would give Jan a chance to
visit with you."

"I'd like to see her regardless of Kai, either way. I'll let
the Wheelers in Vermillion know that he won't be back
for a while. That's my next call."

"The department will pick up his boarding tab so that
you're not out any money."

"Thanks, Terry. That's unexpected, but nice. And say
hi to Dave for me."

"Will do. See you in the morning, Em. And thank
you."

Hmmm. That thanking part struck a chord with her. Normally thanks were taken a bit for granted...unless events were truly wrong and coming off the rails.

———

SHE DIDN'T HAVE TOO much time to brood upon what remained unsaid with the Greeley inspectors. She gave the Wheelers a quick call and informed them she'd still keep Kai's space and pay for it, and they took the news in stride and without concern. Next on the agenda, she had a dinner to dress for—dolling herself up a bit, as her father phrased it.

Jogging up the narrow staircase with the worn wooden floors, she jumped into the shower, blow-dried her hair, and even bothered to put makeup on—lightly. She had no reason to doll herself up like a buckle bunny pickup in a bar—which her father and Monty would certainly notice and would cause all sort of attention and speculation that she flat-out didn't want. Nevertheless, she chose a close-fitting black top with a deep neckline.

Checking the mirror, she noted that her eyes sparkled bright and surprisingly happy.

———

THE PLANNED DINNER that night amounted to a straightforward affair of steaks on the grill, potatoes, and salad. Lance Cross always handled the steaks and the spuds, but predictably left the salad to her. Smiling as she tore up the lettuce leaves, she halfway wondered why she insisted on the greens. Perhaps just to torture them. The men of her family wouldn't have minded skipping out on anything green altogether. She didn't yet know about Jace.

She chuckled to herself.

"Yeah, lettuce always does it for me too," her father deadpanned, poking fun.

"Liar."

Before long, the two bunkmates approached, easily detectable by the clanking and jingle of the elder's single spur.

"You'd think he'd realize that people can hear him coming," she muttered under her breath.

Her father chuckled. "Maybe he's giving them fair warning."

Yes, but fair warning for what? The two men came in through the front door, Monty leading the way.

In a stage whisper, he cautioned Jace, "Em can be bossy, so don't take it hard."

Lance Cross smothered a laugh, which he covered by clearing his throat unsuccessfully. He ended up coughing.

"Ain't that the truth," he called out when he'd recovered enough, the two men now standing in the kitchen, and hovering near the table.

Jace's brown hair was still damp and combed back, his beard closely trimmed, and he wore a clean shirt and jeans. Unfortunately, the same could not be said for Monty. He wore his usual blue jeans, complete with dirty thighs, those damned blue glasses, and a rumpled shirt streaked with dust.

"Ever heard of a washing machine?" Emory snarked. "Hope coming to dinner wasn't too much trouble for you."

"No," Monty replied, refusing to rise to the bait. "No trouble at all."

Jace's eyes darted over to Emory, then landed on Lance. "Can I lend a hand with anything?"

"No, I think I've got it under control. That said, I'd better check on the grill. Right after I check those potatoes."

Her father opened the oven door, grabbed a mitt and gave them a squeeze. "Pretty good. Say, Monty, why don't you come with me?"

"What for," the hippy cowboy groused.

"I want to run a couple of things by you." Lance gestured for him to get his keester out the door.

Monty launched himself away from the counter, acting as if the effort cost him. He sure dragged as he trailed behind his cousin.

Emory, uncertain whether her father tried his hand at matchmaking for her, or whether he planned on chewing his cousin out over the Suhanna creature, didn't really care. She figured Monty deserved a good chewing. But Jace appeared uneasy, bashful, and more importantly, suddenly out of place.

"Oh, Dad probably just wants to have a word with Monty about the company he's keeping."

That claim, accurate or not, eased the atmosphere as the cowboy chuckled. "Fair enough."

"There's really no cause for that woman's interest, or for her to be sticking around Stampede. Not without a reason. A *real* reason."

Jace nodded. "It's remote."

"Remoteness is what we bank on—or at least we used to. Now it's the scenery, it seems. We normally get hunters and fishermen, and there's the summer tourist crowd. But to me, this whole event feels different."

A struggle showed in his eyes. "In Afghanistan...I guess we grew a bit superstitious and all. But what I'd say is that if something doesn't feel right, it's probably not."

Emory nodded, a small nod as the wheels in her mind turned. "She certainly seems an unlikely match for Monty. By about twenty years and a few tax brackets."

Another chuckle from the cowboy. He turned the conversation. "I think it would be hard to meet a whole lot of people out here, if that's what you wanted."

"I think you're trying to turn the conversation slightly." Glancing down, he hid a grin. So, he acted true and loyal to Monty. Truth be told, loyalty was a fine quality in a man.

Hugo was loyal too.

She tried to drive his shadow from her words. "You have a point. I come and go as I can, and true, towns and cities offer restaurants and people and different possibilities. Truth be told, I miss the place and the men. Even Monty's grown on me. I didn't know him until about a year and a half ago. Dad brought him into the ranch when we needed some help."

"Yeah, I can see that this is not the easiest spread to run."

"Physically or mentally," she added. "Have they told you anything about the history of this place?"

"Oh, a bit here and there, but not a whole lot needs to be said. It's more in the way that people react when I say where I've hired on."

Salad finished, she lifted the bowl from the counter and carried it over to the dinner table. "And does that bother you?"

She measured his reaction closely.

He met her square in the eyes. "Not in the least."

22

HEARTBREAK

1887

IT DIDN'T ESCAPE POLLY CROSS'S NOTICE THAT HER husband, Hank, lingered around the ranch headquarters far more than usual. True, the reason behind his presence might pass as domestic in nature to others. The day following their conversation, Hank and three of his men hitched up the wagon and drove twenty-three miles away to the nearest sawmill. Gone two and a half days, Hank and his men returned with a large load of sawed plank boards. The day after he returned, Hank Cross started framing up a new clapboard house. Polly, of course, wasn't delusional enough to believe that he worked on it solely for her comfort. No, he kept a hawk's eye upon his daughter. Sure enough, and it didn't take long, she slipped off, she thought, without notice.

Sure enough, he caught the flicker of a long skirt rounding a corner and went following.

Polly kept to the house, awaiting the outcome, and figuring that none of it boded well. The repercussions didn't take long to arrive.

A short time later, about as long as it would take to

get to the cottonwoods and back four or five times, Susan came running toward the house, hair streaming behind her in long brown ribbons.

Polly steeled herself for the inevitable.

Susan burst through the door in tears, and threw herself upon her bed, face down and sobbing.

More importantly, in Polly's mind, she timed Hank's return. She certainly hoped that he hadn't hurt, or even killed, the Cooper boy.

Torn between waiting and watching for his return and her daughter's distress, she tore herself away from the window and had no comforting words to offer.

"I warned you." Her words, aimed like a knife at a target on her heaving daughter's back, hit their mark. "What happened?"

"He snuck up on us. Told Christopher"—sobbing interrupted the story—"he told Christopher that if he caught him anywhere near this ranch, or more specifically me, he'd cut out his innards for the buzzards to peck and leave his hide to dry."

Polly nodded, weighing the account. "Be glad he didn't kill him in front of your eyes."

"I hate him." Susan sat partially upright and glared. Glared through her tears.

"Watch what you say. He's still your father. He'd die for you, but he'd also kill for you as well."

Susan's expression turned ashamed. "He looked scared, Ma. Christopher looked scared and backed away. He mounted his horse just as fast as he could, and he rode. He rode away just as fast as his horse could take him."

Polly blinked a few times, the tightness in her body releasing.

"That tells you what you need to know right there.

Someone worthy of your affection wouldn't have run away. He would have at least tried to take a stand against your father."

"And what, get killed?" Susan demanded.

Polly understood the complication, having no real answer to her question. "All I know is that the man you end up marrying will have to be able to do better than to whimper and run away."

Not to mention that Hank Cross would have to approve of the suitor. Up front. He'd probably make the young man prove his worthiness as a test.

"Now get up off that bed before your father sees you. We don't need any more trouble in here than what's already landed."

23

CONFIDENCES EXCHANGED— ON THE KNIFE'S EDGE

JUNE 2023

"Slow elk. Rare and medium rare," her father announced as he set the platter of steaks on the table.

"Stop it. That's our meat," Emory said, although her heart did a suspicious little dance.

"Ever since you've become a brand inspector, you've lost your sense of humor some," her father countered with a spark in his eye. Laughing at her expense. In front of company too.

Sure as hell, she didn't want to pursue that conversation further.

"Did Em tell you how she got her job?" he asked Jace.

She tried to head him off at the pass. "No one cares about that now."

Jace, eyes darting around those sitting at the table, shook his head. "No," he said. "I don't believe that I've heard about that."

Monty's rapid blinking marked the only movement as the Crosses fell silent, each weighing the truth of any account they felt inclined to present.

"Dad tried to cut corners on the BLM animal unit

tally," Emory admitted. Her father started the conversation—and the less said the better, as far as she was concerned.

Lance Cross held up his hand. "Whoa. Back up a step there, hayseed."

Damn, but Emory steeled herself to answer. "All right, if the truth must be known, I came across two maverick calves which I branded with the Lost Daughter brand."

Jace frowned. "Doesn't that go against the grain, considering your job and all?"

Her father smirked, wondering just how far she was willing to go and whether she would stick on the straight and narrow.

"It does now. At the time I...knew that it was questionable. But that's not how we got busted, although that didn't help matters any. We had listing dam eighteen-oh-five down as their mother, which wasn't true in the first place. Anyhow, we did have a dam with that number, but she died giving birth to a calf. So that was one head that I couldn't account for right there. We got nailed by the BLM for underreporting more than anything."

"And the fact," her father cut in still finding the conversation a great source of amusement, "that their brands were scabbed over and fresh."

"That didn't help, I agree. Anyhow, I kept my records good and complete. I had to take a fall for the team, in other words." She glared at her father.

"How'd you make the entry for them two mavericks?" her father droned.

"Dam that died. Twins, they became. How else?"

Monty chewed that part over, tilted his head and appraised her with what appeared to be a measure of respect. "Now that we're all shooting the breeze, I'm not sure that I know the full story myself," Monty tossed into the arena. "How'd they get wind about the underre-porting in the first place?"

She pressed her lips in a firm line before speaking. Everyone waited. Her father found the developments funnier than hell.

"Well, you met Cade the other night. Cade worked for us back then, and he would go into town—to the Ace High as a matter of fact—and would start talking. Word got around. We had to pull all the cattle off their summer grazing, put them back on the ranch, and do a recount in front of the sheriff, deputies, and Terry Overholzer, my boss. But he wasn't my boss then, but just another brand inspector. We all did such a good job rounding up cattle, we gathered more than just ours —but I wasn't the one who brought those in. Anyhow, we brought in a couple of blackjacks to boot. In the sorting they discovered that I knew how to read other brands and where they belonged. That's the long and the short of it. I was offered a job with the brand inspectors."

"Now, that's not quite the entire story," her father corrected. "Em is selling herself a bit short."

Her eyes narrowed in question, wondering what he aimed at. The version she presented she found accurate enough. She shook her head and waited. Dreading what he might dredge up all for the sake of a good story.

"The long and the short of it is that now we have a member of the law enforcement in the family, all on account of recordkeeping. And we shot Cade for dealing drugs."

Jace's eyes went wide.

"Not in anywhere important," her father hastened to explain, "just his foot. But next time I'll aim up higher. Just see if I don't."

That officially killed off the conversation. Silence descended over the table.

Emory knew the signs, however. Lance Cross, in his not-so-subtle way, worked his way toward the point he planned to make. It didn't take long in coming.

"I suppose," he began, "it goes like this. As you've gathered, and I've told you, we fought to get this land and we fight to keep it to this day. The neighbors keep their distance, unless all hell is breaking loose, and then they need our help. Lately, we've noticed an uptick in the help needed."

He shot a pointed glance in her direction. So far, Emory had no quarrel with his account.

"Before Emory became a brand inspector, I'll admit it, I'd turned lazy and not much interested. It's a good thing we got busted the way we did. For some reason, that put a spark back in the operation. About that time, Linda came by, armed with preservationists and accountants. I didn't much like the idea, but there's tax credits involved, which have helped as far as repairs and improvements go. She and I took a shine to each other, but it's kind of hard to cover up the bodies. Literally and figuratively."

He took a bite of steak, acting as if this conversation fell into commonplace dinner banter.

Monty opened his mouth, then closed it a couple of times. Like a fish. He walleyed her from the side.

"Since we're playing true confessions," Monty broke in, "I might have a few warrants out under my name. Not my real name, mind you."

Emory turned on him. "What in the hell, Monty! What for?"

"None of your beeswax. I just didn't want to come across like a lightweight. Emory killed a man."

There she blew. She felt like choking him.

Jace tried to hide his shock.

"That's not exactly how I'd describe it. A card-carrying member of a biker gang, rode straight for me and a guy named Dirge—who happens to be Cade Timmons's cousin. It was either him or us. He wrecked once his tire got shot out from under him. Technically, it was the fall that killed him." A long pause. "I've got good aim."

She turned to her father. "Why are we telling Jace all of this?"

"Because," Lance Cross answered in a level voice, "we want him to know *exactly* what we are like."

The rest of the dinner passed without incident, but Jace sure didn't say much, and Emory couldn't blame him. What could he possibly say? That blunt account of their family amounted to one surefire way to run off decent help...telling him the truth like that. Especially at the Lost Daughter. In fact, if Emory extended an opinion about the entire evening, she'd say her father had the best time of all of them, and he did it on purpose. Either way, she had a job to go to in the morning.

Dishes cleared and Monty and Jace returned to the bunkhouse, Emory joined her father in the living room. He sat in the near dark, the television uncharacteristically off.

"OK, give. What was all of that about?"

She leaned against the doorframe assessing his mood. His appearance. He looked a bit older in that dim light. A bit more tired, but certainly no one to mess around with in any case.

"Linda, maybe," he admitted. "More importantly, I want to help you get a straight shot at a decent man."

"Jace?"

"You tell me. Anyhow, as far as Linda is concerned, it seems to me that after all this time that she and I have kept company, that she'd understand the deal. But this all shows that she doesn't."

A stab of guilt, regardless. "I said I'd call her when I came back, but I can call her from Greeley. I'm not back-sliding and saying what she did wasn't wrong, but I do get the feeling that she'd been played. And you didn't act very upright yourself, considering."

"Hell, that Arizonan is cute. Got a nice figure too."

"Dad..."

"I've got eyes in my head, ain't I? At any rate, we need to figure out what she wants."

Emory pushed away from the doorframe and sat down on the arm of his chair.

"I guess I'll have to leave that to you," she began. "But I don't really think you have a reason to go about being a complete asshole to Linda. If it isn't going to work between you two, well fine. Then man up. But don't go chasing that Suhanna."

"But she liked me," Lance's voice teased.

Either way, Emory decided to cut the notion off at the knees. "She likes you because you own the ranch. Don't make me go after her...or you."

He pulled her over to him, kissed her forehead, then mussed up her hair.

"I'll mind my manners," he growled. "Until you come back and tell me otherwise."

"And Jace is going to think we're insane," she grumbled.

"That's OK, pardner. Because it's the truth. Still, I saw how he looked at you. And this outfit needs babies."

"Don't press me, Dad." She headed toward the stairs.

"Wouldn't dream of it," he replied.

She slowed and turned back to face him, then took two steps toward him. "Since we're exchanging confidences all around tonight, whatever happened between you and my mother?"

He stretched his legs out and tilted his head back to stare at the ceiling. Like somehow staring into the floor above would send meaningful answers down from the sky above. Either that, or he hoped for divine intervention.

"I would tell you that it was complicated, but that's probably not the full truth. Maybe it was simple and basic."

Emory sat down in the chair nearest his and waited.

"In fact, it turned out far harder on you than it ever did on me when she left."

She struggled with her confession. "I've always wondered why she never tried to contact me. Normal mothers would—wouldn't they? Leaving an eleven-year-old child isn't normal, and don't try to tell me otherwise. For the longest time I believed I had done something wrong..."

A nerve in her father's jaw throbbed, and he avoided her eyes to gather himself. When ready, his eyes locked into hers—blazing with the protective love he felt toward her welling up and spilling over. Men like her father never cried, but they got mad, disappointed, and frustrated. But they remained steadfast and true.

"No, it never had anything to do with you...but damn it, Em, I wish you'd told me that you felt that way sooner."

She only had a lie to offer. "It doesn't matter."

"Of course it does!" Her father pulled himself upright and leaned toward her. "She came from Ohio and ventured out to Colorado and wanted to find herself a rancher. Don't know why, but that same scenario plays out around here every now and again. People fall in love with the idea of the West, and we're a symbol of that. I guess that's the explanation…anyhow, I found her truly pretty and smart and all that goes along with initial attractions. I probably added in a few qualifications that she didn't possess while at it. What I didn't realize amounted to the fundamental fact that she wasn't cut out for this life, working a ranch, or settling here permanently. I made the initial mistake of not letting her see how we really behaved and thought, and I'm talking about myself here.

"And believe it or not," his mouth twisted into a grimace approximating a smile, "I wasn't the easiest of husbands to live with. You just got caught in the middle, and for that, I'm sorry. Truly sorry. I always thought she'd come back for you, or at least make contact. Guess she couldn't bear to."

Emory sat there for a long moment, struggling. "If she doesn't want anything to do with me, I don't want anything to do with her." Her voice strangled a bit on that last part. "Remember Grandma's refrigerator advice?"

"What?" His question came out harsh.

Obviously, he hadn't listened or paid proper attention to his mother. But Emory had.

"Grandma said that most people spent more time considering the refrigerator they might buy instead of the person they might marry. They considered a refrigerator's durability, cost, and suitability far more than any potential husband or wife. She believed the basic decisions held true between the appliance and the spouse."

He bumped his forehead with the heel of his hand.

"I'll be damned! She was a card, wasn't she? Refrigerator and marital advice all wrapped into one. Good grief."

Making a wry face, Emory shook her head at the memory. "She had a point..."

When he stopped laughing, he wagged his head, bemused. "She sure did. Anything else she had to say that I need to take note of?"

"She was *your* mother," Emory scolded. "But she also said that if I had boys, they'd break my furniture."

Now he slapped his thigh with an old irritation that he found, in hindsight, funnier than hell. "I only broke the one table and maybe an old chair already falling apart. But that explains it. I can tell you she brought those misdemeanors up every chance she found." Then the hilarity drained out and he stood. "Come here a minute."

He opened his arms, and she stepped into his hug. "I'm real proud of you, girl. I miss you when you're gone. And if you need help checking out refrigerators, just you let me know. I got a vested interest that you get a good one."

"You should think of that—in light of Linda," Emory countered, breaking the tangible emotion.

"She can't ranch," he replied. "Can't ride worth a damn either."

Emory shrugged. She never asked her grandmother what she thought about stoves and that was a shame.

24

THE COLD SHOULDER

1887

Hank entered the house not that long thereafter. Still aflame after the fight, he stepped toward his sulking daughter, fists clenched. Susan saw the menace in the taut way he held his shoulders, the strain for a fight traveled down into his fists. Polly read the menace as well.

The mother hesitated beside the table, weighing out the situation. Justified in the fact that she had warned her wayward daughter didn't relieve all of Polly's worries. Hank's temper flared, interpreting her actions as willful disobedience. Perhaps Susan's wayward actions weren't entirely defiant, but those belonging to a young girl following her heart. Because of her youth and inexperience, she hadn't had time to take the message to heart—lasting mistakes could be made. And lasting mistakes held profound consequences.

Polly rounded the table and rushed up to her husband and laid a work-reddened restraining hand upon his chest, standing between him and their daughter. "You've got your point across."

The veins in his neck grew taut like leather cords running beneath the surface. "Do I? Because I sure as hell figured that any daughter of mine would have the common sense not to sneak around behind my back. Because that's what you did. You know that, right? Do you?"

She failed to answer.

"DO YOU?" he roared, taking a step closer.

"Yes, Pa," she answered, close to cowering.

But Hank hadn't finished by a long shot. "Did you see how he *ran*, Susan? Like hell a-poppin came chasing after him. Weak. And you. YOU no longer can be trusted," he snarled.

Then he turned to his wife. "And what kind of mother are you, that you can't keep tabs on your daughter?"

Remarkably, Polly didn't show the slightest trace of fear, but she noted the location of the nearby rifle just in case. "Quit your roaring. I remember what it felt like to be young and in love."

"You gonna shoot me with that thing?" Hank asked, following her eyes and softening a bit at her words.

"Not unless you make me," she replied, eyes flashing with a slight frown playing upon her lips.

"I ain't gonna make you." He unclenched his fists and ran his fingers through his hair and glared at Susan like another problem to solve. "You think you need a husband? I'll find you a husband. Hell, take your pick of any of the men on payroll."

At his suggestion, Susan recommenced to weeping.

Hank backed down. One notch. "I guess I don't blame you there."

Polly returned to preparing the meal, leaving her husband standing in the middle of the floor. He drifted over in her direction and sat down for a moment at their rough table.

Glancing over at him sitting there and looking lost, Polly drifted over to his side, and leaned down to whisper in his ear. "You know, my father wasn't too certain when you came calling as you'll recall. But I was…"

Hank winked. "I always said you were tough and smart and the apple of my eye."

"Oh, pshaw." She pushed his shoulder and drifted away.

Henry came in from chopping wood, and stared in his sister's direction and asked no questions.

Regardless, the next three weeks passed by in near silence between Susan and her parents.

THE CLIMATE within the house transformed once another dispute rose with the Coopers. Two of the Cross cowhands came galloping into the yard, pulling up to a stop in front of the framework of the clapboard house. Hank, however, did not work on its construction that day. In fact, he plotted and planned. Summonsed by the commotion, he hurried outside.

"What's happened?"

The hand they called Gip, leaned over his saddle horn, all excited. "We caught 'em stealing some cattle, but by golly we cornered one of Cooper's men!"

"No shit." Hank Cross scanned the horizon along the direction the man had galloped. "Where is he?"

"Coming. We roped and tied him."

"Good." The wheels in Hank's mind turned. "Did you recover the cattle?"

The man shrugged. "What we found of them. The rest of the men are putting the fence back up where they pulled it down. We just wanted you to know what we had coming—a prisoner."

"I'll be waiting," Hank replied.

NOT LONG THEREAFTER, the men came riding back accompanied by a prisoner with his hands tied before him and his horse led by the reins. The arrival created a commotion, and despite her heartbreak, Susan joined her mother outside in the yard. The young man astride the horse held his back ramrod straight, and his eyes flashed with defiance and anger. His capture had obviously required more than a scuffle, both he and some of the Cross riders displayed welts, bruises, and more than a few trickles of bloody badges.

"Go on, get down," her father barked.

He replied in a calm voice, "I can't. My legs are tied beneath the horse."

"Untie him."

The young man's face struck Susan as familiar. She placed him as being one of the riders with Victor Cooper about a month back. She wondered if he knew about her and Christopher and stuffed that notion back down. Older than Christopher, he appeared tougher too. More like a man instead of a boy.

As that young man dismounted, somehow one of their hands contrived to have him fall off the horse onto the ground with a sickening thud.

Two of Hank's men lifted him from the ground, one on either arm.

"Where do you want him?" they asked their boss.

"We'll put him in the root cellar," Hank directed, then turned to their prisoner. "Now, who are you and what name do you go by?"

"Vernon Cooper," he replied.

Hank took his measure before barking out further orders. "Untie his hands. We'll want him in decent shape."

Everyone watched as he was escorted to the root cellar, the door locked on the outside.

"Let me get some water and a bucket for his needs," Polly chided, unhappy that a building she considered as her preserve turned into a jail. She eyed her daughter. "You get on with your chores. There ain't nothing more for you to see."

She and Susan headed back to the house, and Hank consulted with the men who brought young Cooper in.

"He wasn't alone, was he?"

"No." Their leader's voice sounded of war. "I thought I saw at least two others."

"Just as long as someone gets back to Old Man Cooper to tell him that we've got his son."

"I've already volunteered," the leader said.

Polly returned with an empty bucket and water, which she handed off to one of the men who, covered by another man with a gun trained on the cellar door, unlocked it and set them inside.

Hank consulted his trusted man, Stuart. "Post some lookouts around, will you?"

Uneasy, everyone on the Cross Ranch settled in to wait.

25

UNCOMMON FINERY

JUNE 2023

ON THE MORNING OF HER DEPARTURE, HER FATHER ROSE an hour before his usual alarm, wanting to carve out time to spend alone with her. Together they sat at the scarred kitchen table drinking coffee as the dark sky fell away. The deep velvet of night faded and turned a blushing eastern light. That palest of pinks strengthened and shed until streaks of blue and rose crossed the sky— a vibrancy far more arresting than any painter's brush could capture.

"Ain't nothing like it." Her father admired the splendor of sky above, holding a chipped coffee mug in his hand.

"No," she agreed. "Instead of riding into the sunset, I'm heading toward the dawn." She pulled a face.

"Don't think much of that idea for some particular reason?"

Emory shrugged. "I just wonder what I'm walking into. Terry and Dave don't ask for help unless they need it."

"I'll be expecting a call, if that's the case." He only half teased. "If things turn shady, I'm your man."

While his steel eyes twinkled, they both knew that he spoke the truth.

He chuckled. "You know, I could start one of them consulting businesses. *Old West Misdeeds Inc.* What do you think?"

"I think you told Jace an awful lot last night."

"And we discussed the reason behind that."

Emory rose to her feet and stretched, acting less concerned than she felt. "All I have to say is don't blame me if you scared him off."

"Time will tell," her father droned, but he genuinely didn't seem in the least concerned.

"That's easy for you to say."

Emory snatched her bag by the door, gave her father a hug and a kiss on the cheek. "I'll let you know what I find out." He followed her to the door as she strode across the porch, stepping over Iver's indelible bloodstain and unintentionally hesitated ever so slightly as the weight she carried didn't sit right. Hell. She hoped it wasn't a bad omen.

Reaching her grandfather's pickup truck, she opened the door and slung her bag in as Jace stepped out of the bunkhouse, tucking in his shirt.

She wondered what he thought about her now in the morning light. They sure had done a number on him, unloading their secrets like that and she didn't come across like a princess, that was for damn sure. She offered a cautious, tentative wave, but remarkably he grinned as he returned the greeting. Starting up the engine she pulled around near him, rolling her window down as she paused.

"Glad to see you didn't take last night too badly," she offered, feeling somewhat foolish as she did so.

He came up to the window, put his hand on top of the roof, and leaned down a bit to peer into the cab. "Wouldn't have it any other way," he said, checking the house where her father no doubt stood in the doorway.

She refused to look over there.

"I'd say to take care of yourself on your new or old assignment, but it sounds like you can hold your own in that department. But if you need help, don't be shy in asking."

Heaven help her, she felt like kissing him. What's more, she thought he felt the same way too.

"Watch out for the Arizonan," she cautioned. "And try to keep those two old codgers on the straight and narrow."

He laughed and stepped back. "Now, what kind of fun would that be?"

EMORY TURNED on the radio once she passed underneath the crossbar and skull, happy enough about Jace, but still bothered by the Arizonan referring to their skull as *cute.* Flesh and eyeballs rotting wouldn't strike most normal people as anything other than nightmarish.

"Hell's bells," she muttered aloud.

At that moment, the pinprick that she hadn't called Linda surfaced. She thought about it, then thought about it some more. Reluctantly, she pulled out her phone hoping against hope to get Linda's message box.

"Hello?" Her voice sounded morning rough.

Half torn on whether she should speak or simply hang up, Emory told herself to get a grip. Even if she wasn't programmed into the preservationist's phone, Linda'd probably recognized her number. Not that she called her often.

"Hi, Linda, it's Emory. I hope I'm not calling too early."

Linda cleared her throat. "It's OK, Emory. How are you?"

"Feeling a bit bad about the other day, if you want to know the truth."

"I shouldn't have brought anyone out there in the first place. I knew better. And I know I shouldn't have taken Suhanna into the cemetery, but it's just that it is so unique. I was trying to be nice." She ended the sentence with a wrung-out laugh.

Emory honestly felt bad for her but found it difficult to figure out the right words to say, or where, exactly, she wanted that conversation to go. "I don't think you should have anything to do with that Arizonan—not that you asked my opinion on the matter. But it will drive a wedge between us all."

"No kidding. I'll have nothing to do with her going forward, that's for sure."

But they both knew that realization might have come too late.

The tension in Emory's shoulders lessened a notch or two. "I'm working from Greeley for the next couple of weeks. So, beyond apologizing, I'm calling to catch up. I guess the only thing else I truly have to say is that I don't know what's going on between you and Dad, but for what it's worth, I'm sorry."

The silence hung heavy between them, followed by simple words that came at length. "I don't know what he wants."

Emory shrugged. "I think he wants someone who understands him, warts and all. We are just cut from a different cloth, and that will never change."

Another dead, empty airspace that stretched over the distance.

"I'll let you go, Emory, but thank you for calling. It means a lot to me. It honestly does. Let me know when you get back into town. Maybe we can have some coffee. Oh, and Emory? About that boot hook. While I swear that I didn't mean to pick it up or keep it from you, there's something that you ought to know. I believe that Suhanna brought the hook with her."

"But why would she do that? That's a strange type of thing to be carrying around."

"That's the part I don't understand. You see, the surface where I picked it up had been empty, I'd swear, when we first investigated the building. I thought she set it down, and I picked it up, so that she wouldn't leave whatever behind. Maybe I ought not have even done that much. I really don't know where it came from, or where it belongs."

Emory shifted in the truck seat, although she did not slow her speed. "Do you remember which building you were in?"

"Not particularly. It had an indoor ledge. I guess it's near the edge of your cemetery."

Most of those old buildings had an indoor ledge used for any manner of shelving.

"Thanks for letting me know that, Linda." Emory softened her voice.

Linda, however, rallied—made of stronger stuff that morning. "Take care of yourself, and I'd love a chance to visit properly when you have the time."

And with that, the call ended. Emory pocketed her phone and turned the radio on.

That boot hook wasn't theirs.

PART III

26

DOWN TO TOWN AND THE ARTWORK OF GREELEY

JUNE 2023

THE TRUCK DROVE SMOOTHLY AT FIFTY-FIVE MILES PER hour but shuddered at sixty-three, as it had done for the last few years. Engines simply did not improve over time without a competent mechanic's help, and she never did trust those Stampede simpletons at their junk car garage surrounded by rusted-out hopeless cases. Through the pitted windshield—another hazard of the trade—the Colorado mountains slipped away along the seemingly endless ribbon of asphalt. She'd grown used to that route since becoming a brand inspector. The wide-open flattop vistas offset by the higher ranges still thrilled and soared. She drank in their vastness and longed for assurances that couldn't be given. Serene and unyielding, the mountain slopes gave way, unfurling down to the plains and beyond as they had done for countless eons. That transition from the slopes to the rolling swales and plains caused Emory's breath to hitch. Every. Single. Time.

Still, the nearer civilization loomed, those panoramas folded into themselves, constricted, and all but shut down. Buildings encroached, a scattering of houses at first, gaining in bulk and spreading wide as ranches sold off and subdivided. The traffic itself was a sight to behold. Flowing down from the foothills along I-70, the congestion through Denver on a Monday morning had to be seen to be believed. At least she didn't have a horse trailer hitched to complicate lane changes further. An hour to cross the metropolitan corridor felt more like two, and once she reached the comparative openness signaling the gateway to the plains, she pulled up at the first gas station, nerves jangling. So, she filled up the old pickup's tank and purchased a cup of coffee.

"Two dollars and thirty-nine cents," the woman at the register sang.

"That seems like a deal anymore," Emory replied.

"Doesn't it just? It's a special. We're trying to draw them in off the road. If gasoline doesn't do it for them, maybe that diesel burner will."

Emory chuckled at her description. "I'm not sure that's much of a sales pitch."

"You haven't tasted the coffee," the woman replied.

Back inside her truck, Emory took a sip and winced. Well, at least it was strong, dark, and warm. She turned the engine over and pulled out of the parking lot. The woman behind the counter watched her drive off, and Emory held up her coffee cup in a toast. The woman waved with an I-told-you-so smile.

When she rumbled into Greeley, radio playing, a sense of possibility surfaced. Taking note of the town's activity—a place alive with students, businesspeople, shops, groceries, and all the trappings of a small city— she felt a surge of excitement. Even the streetlights didn't annoy as their timing forced her to stop and wait. Once out of the main drag, the sale barn came next. On the outskirts, Emory took the familiar route winding around the cattle pens, the truck loading and unloading areas—her gaze landing on the aging catwalks which she loved out of proportion. Her heart quickened with the sense of a homecoming—especially as she pulled in and parked next to the brand inspector trucks. In a gust of enthusiasm, she hopped out, both cowboy boots on the tarmac, ready and pointed toward the double-glass doors. Long legging it over, she grasped one of the worn silver handles and flung the entrance door open wide.

"Hello, boys!" She said with a grin, greeting the black-and-white framed photographs of former officials and stepping into the hallway. "I'm back."

They probably hadn't missed her or her antics, but that was their loss.

Tracing through the darkened hallway, Emory took a left as the *BRAND INSPECTORS* arrows indicated and jogged up the stairs to the door at the sale arena's upper ring. Of course, nothing in the sale barn had changed. The office certainly hadn't moved and remained in the exact same location since the 1930s. Opening the hollow-wood door that led to the brand inspector's office, she switched on the light and ducked, expecting to be bombarded by disturbed flies. Truth be told, only a few winged insects greeted her.

Maybe the men had cleaned things up a bit without her.

At the top of the narrow flight of linoleum-covered stairs, she noted the same sagging boxes remained as when she left. A realization that caused a smirk.

It almost went without saying that the two brand inspectors, Terry and Dave, sat at their desks in the glass-walled office beyond—presumably waiting for her arrival.

Deciding to have a bit of fun, she snuck up upon them quietly. When she reached the door that separated the office from the storage, she flung it open. "Good morning!" she all but shouted.

To her amazement, they didn't react at all. Just sat there as if they hadn't heard a darn thing. That she hadn't said a thing, or in fact, even existed.

Then the two of them bust out, guffawing with laughter. "If that's how you sneak up on people, we'd better review the basics," Dave deadpanned.

"Shootfire," she responded. "I came up with the idea at the last minute."

Terry stood and came around his desk to give her a quick hug, and Dave did the same.

"So, what have you got? Really," Emory asked, once the hugging ended.

"I might have liked you better when you were trying to scare us," Dave groused.

"Right. I'll keep practicing on it, then."

"Take a seat," Terry insisted, "unless you want coffee first."

"I picked up some akin to diesel fuel at a gas station." Emory claimed the offered chair. "What have you got?"

The senior brand inspector took his time as he sat in his desk chair, rubbing his knuckles over the stubble on his jaw and looking for a place to begin.

Come to think of it, Terry was normally clean-shaven.

"Do you remember that totem thing the Pruitt's son Dustin made?"

"Yes, so what? Welded together scrap passing as art from a Denver art student. I take it they still have it."

"As far as I know." Neither man appeared in a joking mood. So, she waited them out.

Dave locked eyes with her, steely and intent. "How

are you on your regulations—the ones about slaughtering and processing meat?"

Leave it to Dave to come up with a semiacademic angle. Emory offered a slight shrug. "Isn't that USDA's territory? Shoot. Anyhow, from what I recall, there're three types of processing allowed. Own consumption, exempt custom slaughter, and the full-on deal. Is that close enough?"

Terry nodded, but Dave remained unconvinced and unsatisfied. "What are the regulations concerning the exempt custom slaughterers?"

She wrinkled her nose at Terry, who seemed disinclined to offer any assistance.

"We have one of those custom operations in Stampede. I guess it's used by hunters for processing their kills and packing the meat to go home. We've never used them, so I don't really know much about the ins and outs."

Terry and Dave appeared at least partially satisfied.

"Wait a minute. You aren't trying to loan me out to the USDA, are you?"

The two men exchanged glances which didn't make her feel any better.

"Hang with us, Em. Twenty questions are almost over. Now, if you are an exempt slaughterer or processor, who do you suppose governs you, and what are the rules?"

"Hell, Terry, I don't know. Are you tormenting me on account of the calf I skinned? I'm not going to become a butcher, so don't get any fancy ideas. I'm not kidding—I'm not going to do it."

Both brand inspectors found that funny. "Is your phone charged?"

Emory refused to dignify that question with an answer.

Terry insisted. "Show me."

Any refusal on her part would only prolong matters. She removed the phone from her pocket, took a quick glance and held it out, fully charged.

"Since you have mastered that lesson," Dave snarked, "I'll help you with the answer to the current question. Here, let me read the important parts of the guidance for slaughterers, and I quote:

"...these operators are not USDA inspected but are licensed and inspected by the Colorado Department of Agriculture to monitor compliance with the state and federal requirements. They cannot sell meat or meat products. The meat products must be returned to the original owners. The products must be marked NOT FOR SALE and are for the consumption of the owners and nonpaying guests."

Emory sat there. "That's nice."

"It would be if it worked," Dave groused.

Terry held up his hand to cut off further commentary. "The long and the short of this deal is that we have our eyes on one operation. That family displays far too many cattle skulls for them, or any private operation, to be on the level. We thought this all might be up your alley."

"Oh no," Emory started. "Just because of our skulls?"

"Of course. What else? It seems to run in your family. Now, judging by the number and age of the skulls," Terry continued, not dissuaded, "there is more going on than meets the eye. Now I'm going to take you on a drive to see an art project. Then we'll learn your feelings on the matter and what you have to say."

27

ONE DIRTY AND THIRSTY YOUNG MAN

1887

SILENCE DESCENDED UPON THE RANCH AS THE SHADOWS lengthened and the daylight grew thin, and shades of the evening sky lit up with angry salmon streaks glowing against the deepening blue.

The Coopers' son remained locked in the root cellar —a sturdy enough enclosure hacked into the rock and the clay and sand in turns.

The silence turned almost deafening when no word or riders dispatched from Old Man Cooper came in response. That lack of response forced them all to wait and consider.

Hank considered the locked plank door and pondered his next move—and the one he didn't want to make.

"Stuart!" He shouted over his shoulder for his most senior hand, the oldest among his men who never failed at holding steady of temperament while getting the job done.

Another one of his men jogged by. "I'll go round him up." The younger man never broke his stride.

Hank studied the composition of the cellar and the thickness of the door. Because steps led down deeper into the ground, it would be difficult for a man to bust through the door by kicking it, because he wouldn't be able to get his weight behind it. The door, made of three-quarter inch sawed plank boards, would hold thick and sturdy. They'd used iron hinges and a latching lock, because deep down in his soul, Hank Cross always knew that the day would come when they'd hold prisoners. It's not that he wanted it—rather that when a war was fought, prisoners were taken.

Stuart limped his way over to his boss's side.

"What happened to you?" Hank asked by way of a greeting.

"Nothin' important. It'll be good as new in a day or two." He joined Hank in staring at the roughhewn door. He nodded his head in that slow way he had—the one that said he'd go along with damned near anything that his boss told him to do.

"Guess we could let him out for a bit, just so long as no one does anything stupid." He eyed his own man. "Has anyone even fed him today?"

Stuart shook his head. "Not as far as I know. In fact, it clear slipped my mind. Maybe one of the women did."

No one died from one day's lack of food. They did die from gunshots. "Get someone to stand watch with you," he pointedly indicated Stuart's injured leg, "one that can run and chase if needed. You keep a gun at the ready and then you can let him out for a bit. I'll see what Polly's cooking or has laid by." A pause and a grudge. The dawning realization that if Henry were held by Cooper, he'd want his boy fed. "I suppose we'll feed him."

Food remained a precious commodity in that remote outpost. Still, there was mean, and then there was *mean*.

INSIDE OF THE SODDY, Polly and Susan prepared the dinner. Bustling about the moment when Hank came in through the door, he wasn't so interested in them or their activities, but upon what they hadn't done.

"Did anyone feed that Cooper in the cellar?"

"It never crossed my mind, to tell the truth," Polly replied, more worried about the chores that weren't getting done. Henry preferred to tag along with the men or would slip away to explore as boys tended to do at his age.

Susan, with another flush, thought of little else than the young man during the day—and more than just in passing. With a pang of guilt, she *had* thought about feeding him but never said a word. Horrified, if left to her, would she have let him starve? Surely not…

Hank's eyes traveled between the two women as if he found them dim, or worse, stupid. "One of you find food for him to eat, will you?"

"Yes, Pa." Susan snapped out of the confusion and fetched a tin plate.

"Not too much now," he added.

Susan ladled out beans from the pot hanging above the fire, and as an added act of kindness, she also included a slice of the morning's bread. Meal assembled, she left the soddy—rustler's plate held high—and crossed in the direction of the root cellar. Not for the first time, she felt the eyes of some of the hired hands upon her as she traversed the ranch yard. Something lingered in the way the men eyed her from the recesses and shadows that didn't feel decent or, for that matter, entirely safe.

Their eyes undressed her as they watched and waited.

Half of her liked their attention, half of her didn't.

Her father's men were a hard, cruel lot, but he'd kill any of them should one ever lay a hand upon her.

In the sunlight, just outside of the root cellar door and standing next to Stuart, the young man waited, disheveled and dirty. In fact, the closer she got, the more she smelled the musk of his sweat. Feeling shamed that her family kept him in such conditions, she handed him the plate, caught by the distinct greenish brown of his eyes framed by long lashes. Lashes which would have been the pride or envy of many a girl.

"This is fresh from this morning," she used her most melodious voice, a tone which Stuart most definitely caught. He cleared his throat.

Susan ignored him. "Do you want me to get you some water?" She handed him the plate, along with a fork and a knife.

One of the hands, whose name she did not know and never would, kept a gun pointed at their prisoner. His eyes darted over in her direction, but with a guarded care, traveled to the breasts which strained within her blouse.

"Get that knife off from there," Stuart scolded in a sharp, gravelly voice.

Susan colored at her mistake.

"A glass of water would be nice," the young prisoner remarked in a soft voice, taking a risk. "Maybe, if it's not too much trouble, some water to wash up with."

Susan nodded agreement, eyed Stuart, and turned back to the well.

"Don't you get any ideas," Stuart snarled, but whether at the rustler or their own hand remained undetermined. Regardless of the recipient, the young man emerged so dirty and miserable that it proved difficult for even Stuart to summon an adequate amount of disdain.

When Susan returned with a bucket and a ladle, the young man set the plate down and all but lunged for the bucket and ladle. He drank so deep and so fast that water streamed down his front, and he went back for another ladleful.

"They didn't leave you with water?" she asked, horrified.

When he had finished drinking his fill, he panted, sated. "I knocked it over by accident in the dark."

She handed him the bucket, and taking a measure of care on his behalf, picked up his discarded plate from the dirt to wait.

The young man, turning his back toward her, dumped the contents over his head, rubbing his hands over his face and under his arms. When he turned back toward her and Stuart, his expression turned sheepish.

"Sorry about that." That their prisoner offered an apology in the situation sealed the matter for Susan.

She signified that his actions didn't matter and indicated a felled log off to the side. "You can sit down to eat."

Stuart puffed up a bit ready to contradict her, but her expression made him think better of it.

She was a Cross after all, and he was not. End of story.

Watching the young man bolt down his food, she wondered what on earth had ever caused such a rift between the two families that her father would lock this young man with such nice eyes in a root cellar.

He handed her back the plate. "Thank you for the kindness."

She might have heard book learning and a better place in his words. She certainly noticed his manners.

She offered a shy, becoming smile, pointedly ignoring Stuart's disapproving glare.

Nor did she notice her younger brother, Henry, spying as young boys tended to do, lurking in the distance.

28

DELIVERANCE

JUNE 2023

THE RUTTED BACK ROAD RAN BEYOND GREELEY'S outskirts, belonging to a much earlier era altogether. The countryside sang with a current deep and profound—its setting wild and removed from the current decade. A few slim miles away the town sprouted in electricity's false light known as civilization. This pastoral trail traced its origins to the moccasined feet of Cheyenne or Arapahoe bands, who wore down a path through the ages. Once, the trees sheltered the local tribes camped along the banks of the flowing waters—a stream that pooled and filled a natural basin farther into the land's swales.

Although the landscape may have kept its silent secrets, a history of conquest remained written upon its features. While the earlier inhabitants measured time by the movements of stars and winter kills, they gave way to the nineteenth century and displacement by cavalry outposts. Those outposts offered tenuous safety to the veritable flood of European settlers who poured west. Settlers who traveled in wagons—their wheels and livestock trampled and wore the prairie grasses down to the point of no return.

During the twentieth century and right on into the modern twenty-first, the road, widened to accommodate motorized vehicles, kicked up dust along its length, dirt furrows shaded by the canopy of aged cottonwood trees of immense proportions. Emory's initial impression of the surrounding landscape amounted a vision of American wholesomeness. In contrast to their internet world, that remote corner retained the faint promise of summer days gone by, a place or mindset holding traditional values and a suspicion of outsiders. For better or worse, that current of wariness ran just beneath the surface as they clung to a way of life that turned elusive and faded in the modern world. This century or the last, the prairie oasis appeared like a place sheltered from the ravages of modern time.

"It's pretty," Emory remarked.

Terry side-eyed her. "Just wait."

Everyone who lived in rural America knew about the flip side; the darkness often hidden just around the bend and absent from plain view.

In that deepest of countryside, wildlife still flourished —both animal and human.

Approaching by pickup, there was no missing the very strange emblem in the distance—an emblem that guarded that road and was mounted on an old wooden fencepost. Emory squinted and sat up a bit straighter. Terry noticed her actions even before her eyes darted over to the older man. He nodded his agreement that her eyes, in fact, did not deceive her.

A few more fence posts, and a few more skulls. On and on the skull markers went, real and in varying stages of decay.

"Shit," Emory concluded at length.

"Exactly."

Shaking her head with a frown, she murmured nothing but the pain, unvarnished truth. "It puts our crossbeam to shame."

Terry tilted his head in response, which, under the circumstances, rubbed her the wrong way.

Emory rolled down the window, seeking the stench of a slaughterhouse on the wind. What she identified was nothing more sinister than the summer scent of silage, grass, and sweet animal manure carried on the breeze. Absent was any overpowering reek created by large numbers of cattle confined to holding pens.

Yet the evidence lingered. Skulls nailed to fence posts.

Even if their intent amounted to boundary markers, and while such sights weren't altogether unexpected in the West, this ran into a deeper brand of menace.

"Their wire is sagging," she remarked upon closer inspection of the posts. *Everyone tended to their wire in rural America...didn't they?*

Strange. An uneasy sense gathered in the comparative safety of the pickup's cab, and she shuddered. Terry caught that too.

"Did someone step on your grave?"

"Not yet," she replied.

A strange silence lingered beneath the birdsong. A pall that circled the rotting skulls and cast its tendrils down deep into the shadows. A road guarded by totem fence posts of lingering bone and rot drove her to lean forward and peer out the windshield.

"What do you want to do?" she asked, admitting once and for all that the Lost Daughter found herself outgored and lacking.

Terry cleared his throat. "Don't know yet. The first step, Dave and I agreed, was to have you take a gander at this. It keeps on going, farther in."

Emory sat back a little, still unnerved and marveling. "This is a public road, right?"

"Yes. There's a popular fishing spot down the road to the left about a mile or so farther."

"The fact that this road gets traffic is good, but that doesn't mean someone won't take potshots at us, all the same. Especially since we're driving a marked car."

Terry eyed the totem and house together. "Their last name is Cooper, or at least that's part of their last names. From what I've heard, it's a blended and far-flung family, or some such thing of various ties. They've got different last names is what I'm aiming at."

Emory shrugged. "Are we driving farther? I know we've received complaints, or rather Dad has, about our skull, but it's all on private property. Viewable from the county road, but not on the county road, if you catch my drift."

"I do. So, your father hasn't told you about complaints." He offered a statement instead of a question.

"Not in so many words." Despite herself, a smile tugged at her father's sheer audacity. "He just says that if people don't like it, they don't have to look at it. These fence posts are likely right on the boundary line, don't you think?"

"Who knows. Anyhow, that's someone else's battle to fight."

The brand inspectors pulled forward, taking their time about it. Drawing up level with the nearest skull—hides mostly still attached, the cattle's eyeballs withered and receded into the sockets. The next skull appeared much the same. And the one after that. And the one after that. And down the line they drove, taking it all in.

Emory, although her words and feelings remained unspoken on this topic, gave the warnings a grudging respect. "Are there any reports of problems with, or by, this family?"

"Not that I've heard, but we can check. What do you think?"

She eyed the skulls. "I'd like to see that fishing hole. It's possible that those people have had trouble and are just warning trespassers off."

Terry, unconvinced, grunted.

Farther down the dirt road they progressed until traces of a house and a steel Quonset hut came into view, shielded by the cottonwood trees. If even conceivable, Terry killed the speed, slowed, and drove along farther. "Wait till you see what comes next," Terry muttered.

The lack of speed bothered Emory, and that discomfort grew.

"We don't need to go this slow," she urged. "I get the picture."

He refused to speed up and continued along in that same ponderous pace. All the while, Emory knew.

They made perfect targets.

———

IN FRONT OF THE COMMONPLACE, low-slung, modular home stood the warning. A macabre art project of a rare type guarded the entrance to the house—an art project of a very graphic type. Five bull skulls assembled in various states of decomposition were nailed to an old, massive, delimbed, and bark-stripped, cottonwood trunk.

Each horn prominent and painted red. *Blood red.*

"This has been going on for a while," Emory muttered.

Terry grunted. "Puts Dustin Pruitt's to shame in a weird way."

And so, it did. Three of the skulls whitened with age, one showed a few years of weathering, but their attention caught decisively on one that appeared fresh.

The delimbed massive old cottonwood tree served as the base for the bloodied horn skull embellishment—the old branches dragged only about fifty feet away. The trunk's debarking still represented one hell of a project in its day. Those massive branches lay off to the side, rotting and weathering. Their house, whoever *they* truly were, kept their yard tidy, if one overlooked the massive piles of lumber gathered.

"You think they'd chop that up for firewood, or find a purpose for it," Emory groused taking closer stock of their surroundings. "They have normal decorations on their house, which is odd enough considering. Not to mention that they'll probably notice us gawking at them."

To her relief, Terry finally picked up a measure of speed. "Whatever the case, there aren't any livestock wandering around."

"No," she replied, not overly excited. "They might keep their pastures in the back."

Terry pointed with a gnarled index finger. "Their land, if they mark their territory with skulls the entire way, ends up there. So, it's narrow…"

Emory shrugged. "Not that it matters."

"We'll see," he replied.

About a quarter of a mile past the last skull, Terry took a left, and they traveled down a maintained county road that ended with a nice, maintained parking lot. A pretty enough view, the memory of what they drove past remained hard to shake. The skull alley almost felt like a haunting to Emory, but she never admitted as much.

Terry clenched and unclenched the steering wheel, taking in the comparative bucolic view. "Ready to go back?"

Emory nodded. "I still don't understand why this all has gotten so deep under your skin. I'll admit it's rough and unsavory, but most likely, nothing illegal is taking place."

"I'd like proof."

He obviously didn't plan on explaining his reasons... yet.

"OK, Terry. You tell me when you want. But sure. Let's drive back the way we came and take another pass."

Again, Terry pulled to a stop in the road, right in front of the house's picture window. Although he remained silent, he kept the engine running while they both sized up the operation.

"One thing's for damned certain," Emory concluded, staring at length. "No Girl Scouts in their right minds would go knocking on that door."

Just as the owners intended all along.

29

PROPOSITIONS OF THE ROOT CELLAR VARIETY

1887

CONVENIENTLY FORGETTING HER EARLIER HEARTBREAK dealt by her father and Christopher's youthful lack of resolve, Susan immediately settled upon the idea that she had another prospect at hand. An older, more mature, and altogether superior prospect if one overlooked his imprisonment, and the accompanying stench.

Under the circumstances, she had every intention of delivering his breakfast and stealing some forbidden conversation.

"I didn't plan on feeding him more," Polly remarked, wryoffered wryly, "nor do I know how long we are keeping him."

"You make him sound like a dog," Susan scolded, selecting one of the enamel plates with care and inspecting the edges for chips. Selection made, she dished up a portion of last night's cold stew under her mother's disapproving watch.

"You can't just open the door to feed him, you know," Polly grumbled, "and he ain't company. He'll be gone in a flash, and that'll leave you in a world of hurt when your father finds out."

Susan straightened. Her mother relented. "I'll cover you with the rifle," she said, once convinced her point found its mark.

With a quick darting glance, Susan checked her reflection in their one mirror before hastening out of the soddy, leaving her mother to trail behind. Together they crossed the yard without attracting anyone's attention but Henry's, busy piling hay.

"Next I need a couple of buckets hauled up from the river," Polly called out to her son.

Henry didn't answer because he'd reached that age where he figured he didn't need to respond to women. He yearned to be a man.

"Henry?" Polly's voice cut across the distance, sharp and would tolerate no sass. "Did you hear what I said?"

"Yes, Ma." He continued pitching hay, sullen but keeping watch on their actions.

Lord help them, Susan thought, *they all kept watch. Endless watch and endless wait.*

Casting a glance over her shoulder, she felt certain that someone else noticed all of them, but most particularly, her. No doubt, the interest belonged to one of her father's men lurking in the shadows.

"What's the matter," she asked, noticing Susan stiffen.

And Susan, with the single-mindedness of purpose, had a mission and a target. She shook her head.

"Nothing." And she would do her level best to forget about her mother who wielded a rifle as well as most men.

Susan marched straight up and knocked on the root cellar door, showing that she had manners as well. "We've brought you some food."

Susan unlatched the bolt as her mother cocked the rifle and aimed the barrel.

The young man half emerged from the dark depths. "Do you mind if I relieve myself away from your sight?"

Susan, poised to answer, was cut off by her mother. "You've got a bucket for that," Polly advised.

Every chance she found, Susan drifted by the root cellar, enticed by the young man with lovely eyes. When she felt certain no one watched or would notice, she sidled up next to the door and asked in a low voice that wouldn't carry. "My name is Susan Cross."

"We saw you when we came riding, looking for a few lost head. Don't you remember?"

Susan stared hard at that door. "I remember. I thought your pa was nice and had manners." She paused. "Why hasn't he tried to come and get you yet?"

"I guess he's thinking how he wants to go about it."

Susan focused on the mountain, unable find a suitable response. Instead, she decided to tell him something that mattered, something that held weight.

"One of your brothers, Christopher, used to come by to visit. Pa scared him off."

"Christopher *did*?" The amazement in Vern's voice rang out, unmistakable. "Anyhow, your pa scares the daylights out of most people."

She didn't need any reminders. "I don't know what you've heard—"

"That your father is a real bastard—pardon my French. I knew Christopher used to slip off somewhere, but I sure didn't know that it was here. Boy howdy, that's a good one, though."

"When Dad started raging, he couldn't get away fast enough."

Vern must have heard the pain in her voice, for his

voice gentled. "Chris's been coddled too much. Our mother died giving birth to him, so my sister kept him since he was a baby."

"But not you." Her words probed, more so than proper and she knew as much.

"Hell no. If you were my sweetheart, I'd tell your father as much. I sure as hell wouldn't turn tail and run."

Susan mulled that one over. "My father doesn't brook disobedience in most cases."

A bitter laugh. "Neither does mine."

"Vern, how old are you?" Still crouched down and hoping herself unobserved, she whispered the question near the crack in the door.

"Twenty-three." An uncertain pause. "How old are you?"

"Old enough."

Another low chuckle. "No doubt, but what does that mean?"

"Seventeen," she admitted. "Like I said. Old enough."

"Well, old-enough Susan, don't let them catch you talking to me, please. They'll only accuse me of trying to corrupt you, and it's not worth the risk. For either one of us."

She shifted defensively, yet all the while knowing him likely right. "I shouldn't have to be afraid of my own family. Do you have to worry about yours?"

"No more than usual, I'd say."

While his words didn't amount to much of an answer, they held a glimmer of promise. "What do you reckon your father is going to do?"

She felt him stiffen and grow guarded on the other side of the barrier. "Don't rightly know," he claimed, but she believed it a lie.

Still, Susan didn't blame him. Not entirely. She was, when it came right down to it, the enemy.

"I expect that they'll come and get you fairly soon... won't they?"

He shifted in the interior. "I'd expect so—but it depends upon your father and his terms, I guess. Do you know what he wants?"

If she did, she wouldn't have told him anyhow. Not until he declared his intentions and stood by her. "No, he hasn't said anything in front of me, or that I've heard otherwise."

"I would like to get out of here, that's for sure," he grumbled. "Bugs keep dropping on me in the darkness."

Susan attempted to change the drift of the conversation. "Is your family's ranch pretty?" Like her earlier probing, this question wasn't as benign as it sounded either.

"Not as pretty as yours," Vern admitted.

"You can tell that from the interior of a root cellar, can you?"

He chuckled. "We've been riding through the fringes of this ranch for quite some time. We know what you've got."

That caught her—and staying true to her family's interests, she didn't warm to it. "You admit to stealing our cattle?"

The young man must have caught the edge in her voice. "Everyone does it out here—your lot does the same as ours. Only shavetails eat their own beef when other is available."

Yeah—she knew that much held true. Whether she liked it or not, it wasn't a point to pursue.

"What's your ranch like...really like?"

Silence fell as the man considered. "Our house is

better than yours," he came up with at length. "Outbuildings too."

As she crouched beside that door, a flame of shame
certainly shot up. Feeling humiliated, out of the corner
of her eye she caught the flicker of unwelcomed human
movement.

"I've got to go," she said, fearing the watchers would
tell her father.

"You'll come back, won't you?"

Susan's eyes raked over the buildings, seeking to
locate whoever watched her. Still miffed about the cattle
stealing, she took her own sweet time in answering.
"We'll have to see."

Still, cattle thief or not, she set her seventeen-year-
old cap for him regardless of any consequences that
might follow.

30

FRIENDS LIKE THELMA AND LOUISE

JUNE 2023

TOGETHER EMORY AND TERRY DROVE BACK INTO THE sanity of Greeley's city limits. Remarkably, and probably not through any feat of city planning, many of the larger concerns colocated on that same street. The sale barn, the sheriff's office, and the region's largest hide processing plant all loomed in the distance along the town's outskirts. A short distance apart as the crow flies, but that said, the road twisted and meandered, long and circuitous—bisected by larger roads far more traveled.

In other words, the three remained away from the flow of the mainstream.

The two brand inspectors walked up to the door of the sheriff's administrative building and entered. Terry smiled at the woman behind the desk and tipped his hat.

"Hello, Maxine. Have you met Emory?"

"No, I haven't. Nice to meet you." The woman had sparkling brown eyes that probably missed very little. "We've hired a female deputy! You two might want to compare notes sometime to keep these men on their toes." With that assessment, she turned her attention back to Terry before glancing down at a light on her desk. "I expect you're here to see Frank?"

Terry nodded. "You've got it."

"You can go on back. He's not on the phone."

They headed down a nondescript hall replicated through any number of sheriff's buildings in Colorado. At the end of the corridor, his door stood open wide. Sheriff Frank Aranda sat, unusual for him, in the interior of his office when the brand inspectors arrived.

He glanced up gruffly at their approach, but that didn't mean much. "Terry Overholzer, and you brought Calamity Jane as a reinforcement."

The crow's-feet at the corners of Terry's eyes deepened, but he did his best not to laugh.

Emory quirked her mouth. "Very funny. Nice to see you too."

"Have a seat if you like." The sheriff pushed back a bit from his desk.

"We were lucky to catch you in," Terry said, claiming a seat.

Emory stayed leaning against the doorframe until Terry frowned. Reluctantly, she took the offered seat.

"She doesn't like to be called Calamity," Terry explained to the sheriff. Aranda, for his part, drew his lips into a tight line to smother any laughs before they escaped.

"I'm right here," she grumbled.

"Anyhow," Terry launched into his account, "you know the road to the fishing hole on the east side?"

"Doesn't everyone?"

"The people and outfit I'm interested in go by the name of Cooper, I believe—plus some other names thrown in for good measure. They decorate their property with cattle skulls. I'm supposing that you have noticed that."

The sheriff chuckled. "Who in the hell hasn't? Once you drive by, you're scarred for life."

Maxine's voice came through the intercom.

"Frank, line one."

He held up his index finger as he took the call. "Sheriff Aranda."

He listened. At length he said, "I'll be right there." Then he spoke into his radio. "Car number two, what is your location? Over."

A female voice came through the radio. "Just passing Harbor Freight, heading back to the station. Over."

"Meet me at the hide processing plant. Ten ninety-six. Wait for me to get there. Over."

Hanging up the phone, the sheriff rose to his feet. "Sorry, but I've got to cut this short."

Terry and Emory immediately rose, and all three left the office, the sheriff leading the way. "Some worker has apparently gone apeshit and is threatening to decapitate his coworkers, and I quote, like a steer."

Emory and Terry locked eyes.

"What?" Frank Aranda asked, halfway down the hallway.

"We're trying to check out those skulls to make sure that we don't have an issue, and that it's only Western individuality shining forth."

The sheriff shook his head, doubtful but preoccupied. "If this seems related, I'll let you know."

"We'd appreciate it." Terry strengthened his voice to carry to the sheriff's back as he hustled out the building.

Then to Emory he added in a normal speaking voice, "It's not our jurisdiction, but things have a way of inter-weaving. Let's see what we can learn."

Emory did a double take. "About the packing plant?"

"About any of it."

With the sheriff having left posthaste, the brand inspectors trailed in his wake, passing by Maxine's station for the second time. She offered them a friendly wave, placing her hand over the phone mouthing to Emory *"call her"* as they left.

"I don't even know the deputy's name," Emory groused out in the parking lot. "What am I supposed to do—call the sheriff's office and say I want to talk to the *female* deputy?"

Terry opened his truck door, pausing before he climbed in. "Actually, you know that would work. Chances are you'd be talking to Maxine, who can be a font of local information. Just give her your name. Once that woman meets someone, I'll swear that she never forgets."

Emory shrugged, loading into her side.

For a long moment, Terry just sat in the truck's interior and didn't start up the engine. "Not sure what to make of Frank's dispatch...it's probably just a coincidence. I've always assumed rendering plants offered tough jobs, and tough jobs hire tough people."

Emory waited, noticing how he appeared troubled, and she didn't truly understand the depths of his reaction.

He spoke aloud, but for his own benefit. "I'd say a portion of those workers used to be in gangs or shady dealings. Probably most are just hardworking individuals—another type of ag worker. But it takes a strong stomach to do what they do..."

He needed to toughen up a bit, she figured. "Surely everyone becomes accustomed to their job over time."

He frowned. She shrugged.

"Have you ever entered a hide processing facility?" Terry asked with a long, side-eyed glance at Emory.

Now came her turn not to squirm. "I've been around cattle all my life," she answered.

"Not in bulk like that, you haven't," he countered. "They don't let people into the facilities easily—both due to food safety and public outcry. But it's an experience you'd never forget if you're ever allowed in."

"Stands to reason. I doubt that the general public or the USDA takes kindly to contamination in any food source."

The senior brand inspector nodded his head slowly. "This plant has experienced a few problems along the years but not of that kind," he explained, providing background. "The worst, in my opinion, happened when a worker fell into a chemical vat used for processing the hides and died a few years back. Since then, it's been quiet."

"What a way to go," Emory muttered, wrinkling her nose. She stared at the outline of the large rendering plant looming in the distance and imagined any number of rough images and events within.

Terry peered through the windshield. "People want to know where their food comes from, where leather comes from—that they are ethically sourced and that type of thing. It's a balancing act as to what is communicated, I guess."

"I hadn't heard of anything amiss until you called," Emory glanced at him.

"That's what I mean," he replied. "The plant likely has nothing to do with it."

"So why are we talking about it then? Of course, it would be in their best interest to keep any difficulties quiet, wouldn't it?"

"Correct. But they can't, not if salmonella or E. coli turn up. But they don't have to report on crazy workers, any more so than does any other company. Maybe we'll just drive over there to see what Frank turns up. From a distance, as the saying goes."

True, the location stood straight ahead of them. Both noted the deputy's car approaching in the distance, which fishtailed into the plant's parking lot.

"She drives kinda fast," Terry remarked.

"That's the way it should be, I'd say," Emory watched her progress which, in truth, came hurtling in a mite fast. Still, she bristled against what she perceived as men criticizing women's driving, and that included Terry. "You don't want to call for help and wait ten minutes while they poke along, now do you?"

"I'll bet her fenders are all beaten to hell," he muttered.

Farther along the road, the brand inspectors pulled off to the side. They had a direct, unobstructed view of the door where the sheriff and his deputy entered.

"It feels kind of like we're checking up on him," Emory grumbled. "Anyhow, we never got to ask him about the Coopers...not really."

"No, we're just acting on standby, in case he needs further assistance. You know that we work closely with the sheriff's department. Anyhow, we can catch him later with questions," Terry said. "He'll probably give us a call once he gets back into his office and things settle down...or don't."

"I was impressed he has a female deputy."

Terry pursed his lips. "We hire on ability out here."

Emory smirked. "In that case, she probably had to pass a driving test, wouldn't you say? Not to mention the proven fact that women are often smarter than men—

studies have shown that for quite some time. All the same, I wonder what he calls her…"

Terry didn't exactly rise to the bait. "Hopefully her name. She looks sturdy enough from a distance."

"She'd better be, and I'm sure she is. Do you know her?"

"No," Terry admitted, appraising Emory. "But something tells me that I'm about to. Maxine's right. You should extend a hand of welcome."

Emory just stared. As he burst into laughter.

"Bite me," she said.

FIVE MINUTES LATER, the sheriff and his deputy emerged from the double-glass doors, wielding a cuffed man between them. The man hung his head, revealing dark, wavy hair and very little else in the way of distinguishing features judging from the top of his head. He wore bloodied white coveralls, as to be expected in a slaughterhouse.

"It looks like they have him handled," Emory concluded. "What's next for us to do today?"

"Guess we could always drive around to nearby ranches to see what they have to say."

That notion shocked her. "You haven't done that already?"

Terry chuckled. "Hell no. I was waiting on you for that part. You seem to bond with the women better than I do."

"Is that what you wanted me for? If that's the case, you might have just said. Truthfully, I don't understand why you need me out here in the first place."

Jace sprang to mind.

Terry held the matter in all seriousness. "People often open up to you in a way they don't do for Dave and me."

"I don't know about that," she replied. "Not to mention we have a new ranch hand that I want to keep an eye on."

"You expecting problems with him?"

"Jace? No. We're not expecting problems like we had with that asshole, Cade." She switched the conversation, fast. "But OK, let's take that drive and see who we meet. I'll trust you know their names."

"That seemed to be the least that I could do," Terry sang.

Emory held her tongue on that count. She waited for a few moments, uneasy beyond just the cowboy. "Since you have as much as admitted that you want me to go about this my way, I think we should take my truck."

"Why?"

"Because it's unmarked. Afterall, won't the Coopers notice us driving back and forth and find that suspicious?"

Terry dug in his heels against that proposal. "I don't care if they do. I want them to know that an eye is being kept on them. We'll take this truck."

Emory shrugged. "Whatever you say, boss. But you'll lose the element of surprise."

He eyed her. "I figured to save that for later."

"Uh-huh." Emory set one boot on the dashboard as she slouched down farther.

"Get that dirty foot off of there," Terry snapped, but he was glad to have her back and she knew it.

Instead of doing as he told her, Emory gave him a wink and slouched down even farther. The boot on the dashboard remained firmly in place.

THE SKULLS CAME INTO VIEW, and Terry slowed the truck. Emory, for her part, felt quite satisfied hunkered down and able to pass from ready detection.

Terry sure had plenty to learn about the element of surprise.

As they rumbled down the dirt road, Terry's phone buzzed.

"Terry Overholzer." He listened a moment. "Let me put you on speaker if you don't mind."

Another pause. Terry put his phone on the truck's dash and Sheriff Aranda's voice came through. "We picked up our man...he's in the psych ward right now. We found him waving a meat cleaver at his coworkers, threatening to chop off their heads so that, and I quote, *Creepin' Cooper* could nail them onto one of his fence posts."

Terry and Emory locked eyes. "Really? Full disclosure, Em and I took a drive over in the plant's direction for the hell of it. We watched as you and your deputy hauled him out of the plant. Is the deputy new?" Despite the drama at hand, Terry still angled to set up a play date for her.

Aranda cottoned on. "She is. Maybe the two of them could go shopping or get a beer or something. Her name's Torrie Heldenberg. She's transferred in from Nebraska. She's all right. Tough and rough around the edges, but all right."

Terry chuckled, and Emory punched him in the arm. Not as hard as she would have liked, but enough to get her point across.

"The reason we came by earlier was to find out what you knew, if anything, about the Coopers. We hoped you could tell us whether they have had any run-ins with the law—that type of thing. We're questioning their meat processing count. Some of those heads appear pretty damned fresh."

The sheriff cleared his throat. A loud keyboard pounder, the line fell silent for a moment as he searched. "Not seeing much. But I can tell you the man arrested has tattoos on his face and neck. I thought they did drug testing at that place. Who's to say that he doesn't go fishing and takes that road and noticed...their...deco-rations?"

"It's possible," Terry replied. "What happens when people get placed into the psych ward?"

"Did you want to question him?"

"More like have a conversation," Terry corrected, deadpanning. "We have a lot of conversations in this line of work. Anyhow, I have no jurisdiction about anything that happened there. Even if he did bring up the skulls."

"That guy didn't look like the conversational type to me. I guess once he's locked down in psych, he gets assessed as to what caused the episode, and then they'll let us know from there. Based upon what we saw, I'm not sure he should be let loose, mainstream. Anyhow, they have seventy-two hours to figure it out."

"Then what?"

"Then he lands in a cell here, or he can be confined for longer if that's what the doctors say. Anyhow, back to Cooper. Back in 2019 he might, and let me emphasize the word *might*, have taken a few potshots at visitors from California who filed a complaint. They admitted they didn't know what gunshots sounded like."

Emory snorted, and Terry frowned in her general direction. "Thanks. We're going to go talk to some of his neighbors to find out what they've got...or what they're willing to tell us. Hell, I don't even know if he's got cattle, horses, or absolutely nothing back there. He doesn't have a brand registered, nor does he transport animals any distance."

"Let me know if I can be of help," the sheriff said, drawing the conversation to a close.

"Will do," Terry replied, and they both hung up.

"It's the potshots that are interesting," Emory remarked.

If the man didn't shoot, he wasn't deadly. Probably.

31

DEALING WITH THE DEVIL
YOU KNOW

1887

OLD MAN COOPER'S RESPONSE CAME A FEW HOURS LATER into that morning.

One lone rider loped into the yard, pulling up short and looking wary. None other than Old Man Cooper himself and more to the point, the patriarch rode up visibly unarmed.

"Hank Cross! I want my boy!"

The lack of a gun on the part of Old Man Cooper did not assure that the situation lacked in danger. No doubt his hired guns waited, concealed from view. Anyone who assumed there weren't fighters positioned nearby and within rifle range had another thing coming. However, no warning shots sounded. Yet.

"Cross? Do you hear me?" he shouted again.

Hank emerged into the light of day, no doubt watching Cooper from a darkened recess hidden from plain sight. Unarmed himself, it remained a complete certainty that he had guns ready and waiting as well.

"I hear you." He took two paces forward.

Cooper wheeled his horse around as he pulled on the bit. "Is my boy alive?"

"He is," Hank answered, cool and decisive.

"What is it that you think you want?"

"It's not what I think—it's what I *know*. I want the land at the entrance of the box canyon and all the way back. Deeded over and written out, whether you hold it legally or not."

From the distance, Cooper's eyes appeared every bit as mean and as hard as her father's. But deep down, Susan trusted that Cooper remained the same civil man she met before. The one who told her about his daughter. She stepped out of the house and into the yard before Polly could latch on to her and drag her back inside.

"Susan, get back in the house," Hank commanded when she emerged.

However, in a breach of obedience, she lingered. At the sight of the young woman, Old Man Cooper softened.

"If she'll give her word that my boy is unharmed, we'll talk. Otherwise, I'm riding out of here and you can go to hell."

A muffled voice came from the root cellar. "I'm in here," Vern shouted.

Susan, out in the open, spoke clearly. "He has not been harmed. I promise."

"That true, Vern?"

"Yes," came the shouted reply.

"You let him out, and let me get a good look at him," Cooper challenged.

"Susan..." Hank nodded at the door.

She ran over and unfastened the lock. Vern staggered into the daylight, predictably filthy and squinting, holding up his forearm to block the bright sun from his eyes.

"Now," Cooper began. "I want him, his horse, and his guns back. You're going to let him ride away from here, and then you and I will talk terms. Deal?"

Hank wasn't quick on the answer as he eyed out the playing field.

"Deal." His agreement came with a nasty sneer. "It's no skin off of my back since I'll still have you." He sang that last part. "Of course, when the time comes, there's no guarantee that I'll let you do the same and just ride away."

Nevertheless, Hank gave a signal for his men, and within minutes Vern's saddled horse arrived, with his rifle placed in the scabbard, and his holster belt, pistol, and bullets hanging from the horn.

Vern's eyes darted over to Susan, who fought to hold back unshed tears. Yet, gathering herself with an admirable strength of will, she returned his nod, her head held high.

Old Man Cooper's son made his stiff way over to the horse, checked the girth, put his foot in the stirrup, and hefted himself over.

He locked eyes with Susan as he turned his horse and rode.

"I don't have deed to that land," Cooper began after his son rode off, "but I'll make you a deal…"

32

PUSSYFOOTIN' FOR NO GOOD REASON

JUNE 2023

THE TWO BRAND INSPECTORS PULLED INTO THE RANCH yard of a property located adjacent to the Coopers—the rancher and his son in the process of heavy business of butchering a steer. The father and son scrutinized the truck, taking in the lettering on the side. Although not exactly unfriendly, they turned instantaneously guarded at the truck's arrival.

"Let me start off," Terry instructed, alighting, "and then you chime in."

He took a few steps in the men's general direction. "Good afternoon," he called out to the pair, all jovial and hearty in his greeting.

Suspicious and confused glances followed. The pair of them stopped all movement—the son held a dismembered hock in one hand.

"Can we help you?" the elder asked, both men up to their forearms in blood and gore, wielding cleavers.

Terry held his hands up in front of him, the universal sign of an apology offered. "Please don't let us slow you down—and I realize that we've come unannounced."

The rancher and son exchanged further darting glances.

For his part, Terry shot Emory a quick glance, one that told her the next line of conversation came down to her.

"I see that the head is still attached," Emory began, and Terry cleared his throat, disapproving of her opening line.

The son shifted in his tracks, eyes darting to the head with a frown. "That's normal, isn't it?"

Emory continued with no intention of answering that question. "We all know that butchering cattle for your own consumption is well within the bounds of law, but we are curious about the Coopers' place. Are you planning on giving him the head, or anything like that?"

"Why would we?" the son flung back, earning his father's glare in return.

"Have you *seen* his place?" Emory asked with a laugh to lighten up the conversation.

The father eyed the carcass, then eyed Emory. "We don't know either of you."

"I'm Terry Overholzer, brand inspector." He walked forward with hand outstretched. "This is Emory Cross, another brand inspector."

The father wiped his hand on his coverall, but it still carried traces of blood. "I hope you understand if I don't shake," he nodded in Emory's direction for inclusion. "We don't have much to do with Creepin' Cooper. That's one crazy buster and he's only gotten worse over the years."

Emory smiled at the father. "How so?"

The older man shrugged. "He used to run cattle back in the day, but that's all done and ended. All he's got left is a passel of scary relatives that use his place as some sort of base camp. He might come across as all right—but I'd say that he's really not. All right, I mean." He eyed them both and quickly added, "But you didn't hear that from us. I don't need any of his psychopath relatives coming this direction."

"Understood," Terry agreed, as if that stabilized matters.

Emory didn't concern herself with that aspect overly much. "Any idea how he gets those skulls?"

"Probably from his crazy relatives," the son guessed, having obviously thought, or heard, talk on the matter. Nevertheless, he resumed working, but with an eye resting on Emory.

His father nodded his agreement. "One or more of them may work at the processing plant, others probably have scrub brush ranches. One thing I'll tell you, and I trust that this will go no further, is that each one of the Coopers—whatever forsaken branch of that family they lay claim to—haven't amounted to much. Sure, they claim to be artists and the like, but you've seen their handiwork. What do *you* think?"

That nugget of information might prove valuable, right there.

"You've got a point," Terry chuckled. "Well, sorry to have disturbed you, and I didn't hear anything coming from you. I'll set my card on the fence post here in case you ever have need of it. Thanks for talking to us."

Emory shot him a glance that said she hadn't finished. He caught the barb in her expression but made no comment and climbed into the truck.

"What's caught you up in a twist?" he asked once inside and out of earshot. He offered a two-fingered brim salute to the ranchers as they drove away.

"Art projects," Emory replied. "Do you suspect that the Coopers really believe they are artists, or perhaps that's just a cover? I wonder if any of those cousins' last name is McIlroy."

He side-eyed her. "So, what *is* going on at the Lost Daughter these days?"

"A tourist with an eye for either Monty or my dad, and don't you start in with that sexy senior citizen nonsense. Her last name is supposedly McIlroy and she's looking for a ranch. Our ranch, to be precise."

"I wouldn't exactly call it nonsense," he droned, "but how'd she choose your lot out from the others?"

"I'm not exactly sure, but likely it has to do with the location," Emory sighed. "But she's using sex appeal to get what she wants. And before you say anything further, any shred of encouragement on that topic earns you a one-way ticket to go sort them and their romances out. You can even stay in my room."

"Think I'll have to pass on that," he chuckled.

Emory, however, refused to laugh at all.

THE LANDSCAPE SLIPPED by through the windows as they drove, miles of road—be it paved or dirt—dissecting the prairie, the plains unfurling endlessly as far as the eye could see. The brand inspectors ventured into the land of the double-letter roads, the *AA*s and the *JJ*s creating a network of seldom-used byways that connected remote ranches, farms, and stock tanks seemingly in the middle of nowhere.

Some might claim the Colorado plains as nondescript, but that wasn't exactly the truth. Swales and creek beds interrupted wild prairie grasses, sandstone bluffs rose on occasion, along with the intermittent ravine or break. However, for an area described as "rolling plains" —to Emory—the region east of Greeley seemed remarkably flat. No wonder agriculture flourished where tended. But that didn't mean the plains didn't hold their own. Magnificent thunderheads often blew and expanded, towering thousands of feet over the earth's surface in a magnificent show that diminished the might of man. Such storms provoked a deep-held thrill at the sheer force of nature, driving its point home by the strength of the wind and the elements.

"Which outfit are we stopping at next?" Emory asked, still watching the land slip by.

"We're almost there. Now these people, I know. Their name is Jones, and they have about one hundred head. It's a legacy outfit as well...the railroad used to come through around here, but it's hard to find the traces."

"Oh?" This slim description captured Emory's interest.

"Ask them about it," Terry offered with a smirk.

"Sure." She placed weight behind her voice. "I'll do that, and that leaves you to ask about the Coopers."

"That's probably a good idea in hindsight. I sure didn't expect that you'd ask straight out whether they gave their skulls away..."

"What else should I have done? They're arm deep in butchering a cow, and we have no official reason to be poking around out there in the first place. We both know that they don't brand their livestock. But 'hey, we have questions about your neighbor even though you don't know us' would never work very well. Sheesh. It wouldn't take a brain surgeon to know that most of Cooper's neighbors would steer clear of him if possible."

"Now, when you put it like that…"

"That's exactly how I put it," she muttered. "What's Dave doing, anyhow?"

"The regular work," Terry replied, as if their labor division amounted to the most natural thing in the world.

That part bothered her—she'd never had liked shirking, and that sure felt like what they did. Dave laboring away and stuck with the real work, while she and Terry traveled around jawing. "I may be wrong, but it seems to me Dave might have gotten more out of those people at the last stop. His silence has a way of making people speak."

Terry just chuckled as they took a left onto a two-track farm road.

A LONG WINDBREAK of trees came into view, signaling the house likely stood in the middle.

"Any instruction this time around?" Emory asked.

Terry exhaled. "Not really, I suppose. Just go easy."

Emory shook her head. "Going easy," as he put it, seldom got a whole lot done.

They pulled up into the yard, met by a barking, tail-wagging dog.

"Blue!" A woman's voice called out. "You let them be." The woman belonging to the voice emerged from a back door and came out into the yard—the dog doubling back to sit down at her feet.

"Hi, Mrs. Jones. You might not remember me, but I'm Terry Overholzer and this is Emory Cross."

"I believe I recall," the woman said, offering her hand.

"This might seem a bit strange," Terry began, "but do you know a family called Cooper?"

The woman snorted and shook her head. "The skull people? I am happy to say that I do not. But do know of them, like everyone else within a fifty-mile radius."

Emory bobbed her head slightly, as if puzzled. "They call those skulls on their fence posts artwork, or at least that's what I've heard."

The woman snorted. "Artwork! It's enough to give anyone nightmares, I would say."

"They sure don't make me real happy," Emory claimed in a mournful tone.

For her theatrical efforts, she received a long side-eyed glance from Terry and persisted despite his response. "This all came about because we're trying to figure out if they are selling meat."

The woman shook her head. "I wouldn't think so. That would mean they actually raised cattle, slaughtered them, and then at least minimally processed or butchered them to sell. That would be a whole lot of work for people like them."

Emory nodded. "Their yard is clean enough, except for the lumber."

Mrs. Jones nodded. "I don't know what's going on there. Hope they don't plan on starting a bonfire for a blasphemous heathen ceremony, but I wouldn't put that past them either. Oh, here comes Mike now." She waved at her husband arriving in a battered four-wheeler.

He pulled up and parked about fifteen feet away.

"Hey, Mike," Terry sounded happy to see him, offering an extended hand. "We were just in the area and stopped by."

His wife cut to the chase. "They're asking about the Coopers."

Mr. Jones just shook his head. "They keep pretty much to themselves. Don't know 'em."

Terry nodded. "Emory here is down from Stampede, and I told her a bit about the history of the area. Specifically, I told her that I believed this is another legacy ranch."

"It sure is," he replied, puffing up a little. "Of course, they used to grow a lot of beets, which kind of did the land in. They didn't know about rotating crops back in those days. Anyhow, there's a whole story behind it, but around World War II they didn't have the manpower to bring the beets in and let the cattle feed on what they couldn't harvest. We've raised cattle ever since."

"That's interesting," Emory said, meaning it. "Did you have a railhead nearby?"

"Sure did. The Beet Shoveler's Road parallels the Union Pacific rails. They loaded whatever they wanted when the train stopped."

"That's pretty cool having your own rail stop," she admitted.

"I agree," Mike Jones replied, warming to the topic. "I can show you where that was, if you like."

"Someday I certainly would," Emory replied, meaning it. "My family has a legacy ranch outside of Stampede. I always like seeing what remains of these old spreads and try to imagine how life was like back in the day. Stampede had a railhead for shipping, but they also had a Pinkerton's office."

"Is that so?" The rancher's head bobbed up and down, interested in return.

Instead of focusing on Mrs. Jones as Terry originally planned, she felt more of a kinship with Mr. Jones, the obvious descendant of the settling family. "The reason why we are out here, as we told Mrs. Jones, is on account of the Coopers. We are checking to make sure, in a roundabout way, that they aren't butchering beef for sale. This curiosity, of course, stems from the skulls around their property lines."

"Oh, those damned things."

"We're getting ready to go straight up to their door, but common sense tells me that they might not take too kindly to company." Emory laughed.

"It's the cousins. They've got a network of family that's hard to follow where one line ends and the other picks up."

"So, we've heard. You don't know any of them we might ask, do you?"

The rancher hooked his thumbs through his belt loops. "Let's see—one of them has what they're calling a gallery, so that's public. What's it called, Ma?"

"Some nonsense about the Old West. I heard the neighbors mention that a while back—maybe even a few years back."

Terry jumped in. "Do you remember the location of that gallery?"

"The art co-op in town. I went there once. On Eighth Street. Beyond that, I don't know." The woman sniffed.

"Do you feel like taking a ride into town?" Terry asked once they reloaded and drove in the direction of town.

For her part, Emory felt they had all the information that they needed to go straight to Cooper's door. "Shouldn't we offer to help Dave?"

Terry laughed. "I'd offer to trade places with him, but I'd guess that art might be lost on poor old Dave."

Emory sighed. "Let's at least call him just to make sure everything is under control."

Terry pulled out his cell, poked it a bit and put it on

speaker. "Yo, Dave," he bellowed. "Emory's feeling a bit sorry for you and wants to know if you want to go to an art gallery with us."

A moment of dead silence. "She wants to know what?"

Emory spoke up. "Terry is messing with you. How's everything going? I can't say that I feel good with you shouldering all the work…"

"Now we're talkin'," Dave offered in that laconic way of his. "While you two have been tearing up the country-side, I went out to the Hoopers. Check this out. They're related to the Coopers but changed their name by one letter."

"Is that a fact?" Terry craned his neck to the side, eyeing both Em and the road. "I never knew that."

"Me either. But I cautioned that the skulls attracted a fair measure of attention. Paul *Hooper* said just to go up to the door and ask him straight out. It seems Creepin' Cooper doesn't like people pussyfooting around. Which is not to say that Paul Hooper likes him much. He says he's crazier 'n hell, and he's brought up his kids to be the same damn way. It might save you a bit of time to go straight to the source."

And so, it would. Emory gave Terry the stink eye.

Which he caught with a laugh. "Let's put this rest for the night. Might be that word would even reach him first, to save us some explaining. Anything Em and I can check on for you, Dave?"

"Ain't that the other way around?" he teased. "Talk at you later."

And with that, the line went dead.

Emory eyed the brand inspector. "Why don't you admit that you just missed me? You didn't need me for any of this."

"We do miss you, but this ain't over yet. Do you hear any fat lady singing?"

No, and that might be the problem. She didn't. But then again, Emory didn't hold much interest in any singing ladies. She was far more interested in a particular cowboy instead.

33

BOX CANYONS ARE GOOD FOR AMBUSHES

1887

"PLAN ON GETTING OFF OF YOUR HORSE?" HANK SNARLED at Old Man Cooper.

"No. I don't plan on staying that long." Cooper's eyes scanned the land, deliberating, and deliberating hard. "But as we both know, possession is nine-tenths of the law out here."

Hank followed the direction of his eyes. "We caught your son taking cattle off of our range."

"So?"

That drew Hank right back to Cooper. "So, I'm putting an end to it. The next son of yours we catch will be castrated. And I'll do it myself. And if you don't believe me, try me."

Old Man Cooper blanched around the edges at the threat so clearly beyond the limits of even the vigilante's code. "You're just proving what everyone is saying."

"Good." Hank waited him out.

Cooper from the height of his fine horse stared down his nose, diminishing him. Spooked, but doing his level best not to show it.

"I'll drive ten head over to balance the books, and we'll stop the practice. Agreed?"

"And the box canyon?"

"Like I said, I don't own it. Even so, you'd have to fight us for it. What do you need it for in the first place?"

"I don't need to go explaining myself to you."

"No, you don't. Come and try to take the canyon if you want it that bad. Now, do you want to accept this treaty, or should I ride, knowing I'll likely get a bullet in the back?"

Hank laughed, without a trace of humor in the sound. "Sure, I'll take the ten head."

"And you'll let the men driving them return back, unharmed."

"You have my word."

Cooper cocked an irritated scowl which conveyed the value of "his word" remained up for debate. Still, Hank Cross accepted it. "Do we have an agreement that we'll leave each other's cattle alone?"

"Cattle? Sure," Hank drawled.

The two men locked eyes and recognized the implication of what they left unsaid.

Old Man Cooper nudged his horse and rode away.

Remarkably, no bullet followed.

34

SNAKEBIT

JUNE 2023

EMORY RETURNED "HOME" TO HER APARTMENT. HER KEY still fit in the door, and the door swung open wide. Sniffing upon crossing the threshold, it smelled stale and closed—and needed a good airing. Dropping her bag by the door, she shut the door and stared at the lock.

They never really used locks much out at the ranch, but they had recently started.

After fighting with the window lock and budging the window, the scent of stockyards blew right on in. Not exactly the fresh air that she'd grown accustomed to.

"Yep...guess I'd forgotten that part."

Nevertheless, she left the window open and air circulating, as she checked each of the rooms. She rediscovered an old mascara and a discarded lip gloss on the counter. With a twist of the cap, she pushed the mascara's brush up and down a couple of times and tossed it in the trash. Old and dry.

"Don't want to turn up that way myself," she said to the mirror above the sink. Not to mention toxic. Old mascara acted as a living petri dish where bacteria multiplied and spread.

In any case, if she planned on staying for a while, that apartment needed work. Casting a glance around and taking stock, she had a cheap modern sofa, but a couple of bright pillows might help. Her sturdy, used wooden table picked up at a yard sale would last until Armageddon, but it would benefit from a vase. She laughed. A vase on a table at the Lost Daughter was about the last thing any of the Crosses would have ever considered.

The tidy kitchen appeared sterile and nondescript, but colorful towels would add cheer. All those things she never had time for at the Lost Daughter stared her in the face. A few hundred miles away, and she didn't have many good excuses. Her bedroom fared little better. She stopped in front of her dresser mirror, drawn to the pictures of the Lost Daughter tucked in around the mirror frame.

"Yeah, other than for the dust, it looks the same as it did when you left. Keep moving…"

About one hour into cleaning and in the middle of scrubbing the kitchen floor, her cell phone went off.

She didn't immediately recognize the number. "Emory Cross, brand inspector," she answered, knowing full well that ranchers didn't always abide, or couldn't abide, by the published work hours.

"Emory? It's Jace." Although thrilled to hear his voice, an icy dread brushed the nape of her neck.

"Jace." They both heard the caution creep into her voice. "Is this a social call, or did something happen?"

She imagined the warmth in his eyes.

"A bit of both." His voice came through strong and firm and a bit…uncomfortable.

"All right then…where do you want to start?" She squirmed, finding the small talk hard to navigate.

"Where I want to start and where I will start are two different things."

"Understood." Her voice likely struck both as impatient and growing restive.

"That Suhanna came out here, and we found her hanging around Kai."

"What?"

"Your dad reached her before I did. And get this—he's formally charging her with trespassing. Before he even got to that part, I would swear that I heard him tell her that people got their legs broken back this way—meaning on the Lost Daughter."

She felt her eyebrows lift. "Do I need to come home? I can leave right now."

"No," Jace said, calm and level. "Your father handled it —a bit more ironclad than I expected, but he got his point across. Trust me, she didn't hang around long after that. Of course she tried to sweet-talk her way out of it first, but your father didn't fall for her bullshit."

Good. "Glad to hear it. Seriously, I can come home. To be honest, I don't even know why I'm out here."

A noticeable pause on the other end of the call. "Why'd they call for you then?"

"I'm not certain. Probably marking territory so that I don't stay up in Vermillion, but still. They're not the type who overreact without a good reason…and something's going on over here. Everyone can feel it, and no one knows exactly what it is, but then again, neither do I. Anyhow, Kai is OK, isn't he?"

"Yes, he's just fine. Probably missing you, but that's another matter." A long pause. "I went into town and picked up a few spare parts for the yard light, and I installed a few motion detectors while I was at it. I already fixed it once…"

"Thank you. That's bugged me for a while now. So, backing up a bit, Dad actually filed a real report with Sheriff Preston?"

"He said he did." She heard the question in his voice.

"He might be bluffing on that count."

Jace had a few things to learn about her father.

"He likes to handle things himself," Emory explained. "Fewer formalities leave more room to scare people."

He chuckled. "Like I said, she did leave pretty quick."

Emory nodded, figuring that she'd just call the sheriff herself. "Perhaps I should move Kai off the Lost Daughter for a time. Even though I just brought him home, maybe Vermillion would be the best place for him after all."

"Whatever you decide. As far as that is concerned, I can haul him to wherever you want him. You don't have to drive back here unless you want. Hey, Em?"

"Yes?"

"What would you say if I gave you a call every now and then?" Space fell dead while her heart did a funny lurch for joy. "Just to keep you up to speed on what is going on back here and so that you know I'm earning my keep."

Whoa.

Any joy came crashing down, and his words came out cold and businesslike. Had she formed the wrong impression? Maybe she should have jumped in when she had the chance…

"Call whenever you like, and I have no doubts about…you…" She blinked a few times, her thoughts scrambled. "I'll be getting a few days off soon. I'll probably come home for those."

He sounded closed off. "Looks like your father needs me. He's coming this way."

"Tell him that I'm going to call him, will you?"

"Sure thing, boss."

With that, the line went dead.

She sat there for a few moments, tapping the edge of her cell against her lower lip. I-70 and the route back home stood miles away, and she'd sure stepped in it. The Lost Daughter took three hours to reach. At least he recognized her as a boss...a hollow victory this time around.

Any action felt better than inaction. She'd take concrete steps. Hell, she'd call Sheriff Preston first. She still had his number in her contacts.

"Sheriff Preston," he answered.

"Emory Cross," she replied, feigning a playfulness that she certainly didn't feel at that exact moment.

"Emory! How in the heck are you—and where are you?"

"I am in Greeley helping out Terry and Dave for a while, but officially I'm supposed to still be in Vermillion. I'm fine all things considered. How is everything in your world?"

Humor crept in. "Just trying to keep up with you."

"Very funny. Say, I hate to ask but did my dad file a trespassing complaint?"

A cautious silence filled the distance. "No..."

Damn it. "I figured as much. Jace, our new hand, said Dad said he would file...but that didn't sound right considering how Dad is, so I win that round. Anyhow, there's this woman kicking around Stampede named Suhanna McIlroy. She says she's from Arizona."

"Yeah, I've heard. I've also heard that she spends a lot of time in the Ace High buying free drinks and asking questions. Questions mainly about the Lost Daughter."

That took her a bit by surprise. Then again, overly familiar outsiders stood out in the Stampede crowd, as limited as that crowd numbered. "That's not so good," she edged into the conversation. "Linda Paulson, one of the Colorado preservationists, brought her out to the ranch for some unknown reason. Perhaps to make matters worse, I was there at the time they came out uninvited." She struggled with how much to reveal.

"Go on."

"I don't know how much of all of this you want to know, but it ended poorly. Dad told Linda basically not to come around anymore, and that caution certainly included Suhanna. Who, and I just received a call from Jace, was not only out at the ranch again *today*, but they found her near Kai and the mustang. Look, Sheriff Preston, I don't want that woman anywhere near my horses, and especially not Kai. Dad told Jace he would file a complaint, probably to placate him. In the meantime, I guess he changed his mind."

A dry laugh from the sheriff. "Your father *never* turns to the law unless there is no other recourse, and most likely, not even then."

Truth often concealed a few stingers—in this case the stinger concerned the old history versus the new. Emory wanted to operate on the straight and narrow—when possible—yet her father had other ideas. "That's precisely why I decided to call you first. Can you run her name through a database or similar?"

"Sure, I can run her name, but you know, it just so happens that I wrote her license plate number down."

"Any particular reason?"

"Expired *Colorado* tags provided the superficial

reason. That, and curiosity. Give me a little while, and I'll call you back with what I find."

Colorado. Not Arizona. As she had figured all along, the parts didn't add up.

———

THIRTY-FIVE MINUTES LATER, Emory's phone buzzed.

Sheriff Preston flashed across the screen.

She didn't even say hello. "That was quick."

His voice cut across the distance. "The car isn't registered to her."

"Oh?"

"No, it's registered to Orran Cooper out in rural Colorado, on the plains."

Emory belted out the most unladylike guffaw. "No shit."

"You know him?" the sheriff asked, surprised.

"Of him," she admitted. "He's out in this general direction and we are trying to figure him and his habits out. He, check this out since you've fielded complaints on behalf of our ranch, nails cattle skulls to his fence posts. If that isn't enough to spook you, he also has a totem pole with the horns painted blood read. Puts our two skulls completely to shame."

"Oh? So, he's one of your kind, is that it?" He didn't even leave her space to answer. "I typed in the name Suhanna McIlroy into the database, and it came back kind of interesting. Nothing major, but a string of low-level activity. Bounced checks, failed marriages, and minor infractions that might be her fault, or might come down to relationship breakups. Nothing stands out in particular...but I don't like that car business. All of which points to another question—and the same one I started out with—where is her bar money coming from?"

Emory stared at the ceiling hoping for a lightning-bolt answer. "She said she rented a gallery space in the old motel they're turning into artist studios, or whatever they're claiming along those lines."

Of course, everyone in town knew the place she referred to. Another attempt to revitalize the downtown area bound for certain failure. "I'll go pay her a visit and welcome her into town. Or I can serve her a notice. The choice is yours how I go about it."

It wasn't the time to waver. "That's the twenty-four-dollar question. What would trespass charges involve?"

"It depends upon what she is truly up to. Any trespass charges in your case would be considered second-degree trespassing unless she enters a house or a vehicle and camps out. In this case, messing or tampering with your horse can be charged as a class four felony because she trespassed on agricultural land with intent to commit a possible felony. You honestly don't know what she was doing?"

"No, I'd tell if I knew. Promise. I don't think the men know. But let's say arson for the hell of it."

"Arson's a big deal." He didn't really buy into that possibility—nevertheless, he would answer her question. "If she's convicted of a class four felony, she might be sentenced to a lengthy prison term as well as a fine of up to five hundred thousand dollars. Arson is usually class three and incurs a minimum fine of three thousand dollars but it carries four to twelve years in jail. Do you want to charge her, knowing those penalties, because she trespassed on the Lost Daughter?"

His tone provided the precise reason why her father

seldom turned to him as "the law." Sheriff Preston entertained the distinct reluctance to go for broke.

"Sure. I don't care," she answered, no matter how harsh that might come across.

"Well," he hesitated and drew the matter out, "your father might."

Emory shook her head. "No—he won't, unless we need to hire a lawyer and it will cost money. Do we?"

"Right now, it's one party's word against another. Pictures tend to help that type of thing along."

She doubted anyone of their crew took a picture—but she would ask. With luck, Jace might have snapped a photo for proof. "What about a written warning?"

"Sure, I can do that, but your lot caught her red-handed, and you have two witnesses. Those written notices are usually made when no one's caught them in the act of trespassing, although suspicion remains probable and high. Did your father speak to her? Times are changing. He needs to learn to try to take the easy way out."

"You mean instead of shooting someone in the foot?" She joked, but in truth, she found precious little to laugh about in the matter. "Anyhow, there never was any complaint filed."

"That's because Cade feared what would happen if he did."

Emory remained ever quick to defend. "But yes, that's the general idea. And Cade better never set foot on the Lost Daughter again, if he knows what is good for him."

Ending the call on that shadowy note, Emory tried her father next.

"Yes?" His voice came across as unusually cautious toward her. "Now before you get going, I'm not sure I like to conduct ranch business on the phone."

Bingo. He knew why she called and didn't want to deal with it. For her part, she certainly didn't want to land Jace in hot water. "Why not, are you turning paranoid?"

"Mebbe."

"Look, Dad. I've already spoken to Jace, and I've called the sheriff on your behalf."

"Damn it, Em…"

Em's blood pressure rose hot and high. "Jace found her near Kai. That ain't gonna work and I'm not playing around. I know you think she's cute and all, but this is a nonstarter."

Humor crept into his voice. "Listen to you…"

"Yes. *Listen to me.* I called Sheriff Preston—"

"You mean Bob? I knew him back—"

"*Dad.* For starters, she's driving a car that doesn't belong to her. Then she's had a string of husbands, so there's no reason for you to go adding your name to that list of losers. Besides. Monty will head out and now when we truly need him and his damn-assed single spur."

Lance sounded laconic. "I'll tell him you said as much, but I don't know—"

"I'm not finished yet. Get this. The car is registered to Orran Cooper, the man with the skulls on the fence posts."

Dead silence. "Dad?"

"I heard you."

"And?"

"If you must know," the words strung out as if they cost him, "I'm getting a strange feeling."

"Good. Because I've had one for some time now. So can we file that trespassing report?"

"I suppose," he sighed, reluctant. "I might tell Jace—"

She snapped right on in. "You tell him nothing. He did the right thing."

Her father chuckled. "My, my. Aren't you getting territorial?"

Then he hung up.

Once again, the man had a definite point. What struck her as even worse—Jace probably wouldn't have felt too favorably about her getting territorial over him. Damn.

35

GET YOUR WOMEN UNDER CONTROL

1887

VERN'S RETURN HOME FORCED SUSAN BACK TO LIFE ON the straight and narrow, and made her lonely.

If her parents noticed her moping about, they didn't say. Understandably, to their family's way of thinking, they believed they had more important things to consider such as the valuable box canyon, and whether or not Old Man Cooper would stay true to his word. Therein rested a fundamental difference between the two families—while smart enough on both sides, Hank set up a spy to watch the Cooper headquarters.

Old Man Cooper proved smart enough to involve the law—and the land registry office.

Such fundamentally different approaches led to fundamentally different results. Old Man Cooper and his hired guns left a few people at their headquarters to protect the property, but mainly they rode. They rode for the nearest town which also served as the county seat. Of course, Hank Cross's man rode to notify his boss that a contingent of the Coopers rode east.

"Perfect time to check out the box canyon," Hank stated with a grin.

MEANWHILE, another rider rode for the Cross Ranch—this one from a small homestead nearby, a legal, by-the-book homestead holding, the size of something that would never amount to much. Tommy Engler almost took a bullet for his efforts, but no such misfortune happened. The Cross lookouts figured he posed little threat by the quality of his horse, and the way he flopped around in his saddle.

He certainly wasn't a range rider, so they allowed him to come riding right into their midst.

He addressed the first man he found, which happened to be Hank. "We need Mrs. Cross, if you don't mind, sir. My wife's time has come, and she sent me to ask for help."

If the woman's husband in labor noticed he had ridden into an armed camp, he hid it well. In fact, showed no recognition of it—a curious oversight that Hank put down to his firstborn's impending birth.

"Polly!" Hank shouted, "Tommy Engler's wife is having a baby and needs you."

Then he turned to one of his men. "Has that wagon been unharnessed? Give 'em a team of two so that they can make decent time." Then he turned to Engler. "You can leave your horse here with us, or tie him on the back of the wagon, but whatever the case, you don't want him to give out on the way back to your missus."

Inside the house, Polly grabbed her coat and her nursing bag. In her haste, she never gave Susan a second thought.

One of the cowhands pulled up with a double-teamed wagon, and the settler and Polly climbed onto the box and sped off leaving the tired horse behind.

"One of you put him in a corral and see to him." Hank spoke his command, and a new hire jogged on up and did as bid.

Far more interested in his newest land acquisition, Hank mounted up, and so did a selection of his men. His attention focused on the task at hand—the box canyon.

"Let's go see what we've got," he called out to his accompanying men. "Let Cooper ride for the sheriff—it don't matter. He's only one sheriff with a lame-ass deputy and nothing more."

As was their custom, the men laughed, harsh and low.

Everyone thundered off. Everyone except Susan and the few hands left behind with plenty of chores to see them through.

Susan had a decision and a couple of choices to make, and she had to make them quick.

In a blink of an eye, she ran into the barn to get the rickety second wagon, collected the traces and tack, and then captured her father's big bay and the sorrel. If any of the men noticed her frantic speed, no remark passed forth.

Out in the yard, Susan backed them into their traces, one by one. Once she fastened their harnesses and made sure she had them harnessed correctly, she ran into the soddy to gather her things—running for all the world like hell a-blazing chased after her. She didn't own much when it came right down to it, but she grabbed what clothes she had, and she tied them into a smallish bundle. She also picked up her hairbrush and the two books her mother had given her on various birthdays over the years.

Setting the bundle down on the wagon box beside her, she drove off at a fair clip, down the road and back over toward the Coopers' spread.

She knew just the spot she wanted. She drove, searing the riverbanks until she located the well-used ford crossing the river. Eyeing the swollen current, it ran fast and deep from the late spring runoff.

Slapping the reins on the horse's rumps, she pointed them into the current. The horses didn't want to cross. Susan slapped the reins and yelled.

"Ha! Get going. MOVE!"

Restless in their traces, they tossed their heads defiantly, but one started forward so the other did as well.

They stalled midstream.

Susan gauged the water as well, fully realizing that if she got out of the wagon, she could be swept away. If she stayed and waited, it was even-odds who found her first —her father and his men or the Coopers.

Panic rising, she urged them forward. "Yah! Yah! Yah!"

The horses, unhappy themselves, moved forward, deeper in. The water level against the buckboard rose.

She prayed. She tried again. "Go!" she screamed, slapping the reins.

The horses pulled the wagon through.

She made it to the other side. Knees shaking and heart racing, she climbed down and practically heaved. Nevertheless, she turned the wagon, removed her possessions, and again slapped the horse's rumps so that they crossed back over, the way they came.

Having just crossed, they made the return crossing without hesitation, instinctively understanding of which side of the river they belonged.

She had every hope that they would return to the

ranch, but they were in no hurry. Instead, they stared at her from the opposite bank, dripping wet, and content to dry in the sun.

But her work hadn't finished, and her getaway remained incomplete. Susan scouted the cottonwood stand until she found a fallen branch with leaves intact. Brushing the leaves over the dry ground, she obliterated any traces of her footprints. She continued the sweeping for at least an eighth of a mile. She'd swept enough in that damned soddy, she certainly would sweep for her freedom.

When finished, she tossed away the branch and faced down the Coopers' home road and her new life. Butterflies in her stomach, she walked down that road, hoping for a welcome.

36

JOSE CUERVO AIN'T NO FRIEND OF MINE

JUNE 2023

EMORY'S CELL PHONE RANG, THE SCREEN DISPLAYING another unknown number. "Emory Cross, brand inspector."

"Hi, Emory. My name is Torrie Heldenberg, and Maxine said I should give you a call."

Emory laughed. "Maxine told me the exact same thing about *you*."

"The difference being I work with her every day. And I get the distinct feeling that we've been matchmade. Say, I don't know what your schedule's like, but maybe sometime we could get lunch or a beer."

Emory cast a glance around her apartment, and her stomach rumbled. "I've just been cleaning and don't really have any food in the house. Don't suppose that now might be a good time?"

Another friendly laugh came through. "I haven't eaten, although I've got reserves. Where do you want to meet?"

Emory cast a glance around. "I don't really know of

anywhere other than McDonalds or the dance hall place, and they don't serve food."

"Not that I have anything against dancing, but I don't really feel like getting all dolled up. One place that has decent food is called El Rincon. It's Mexican…"

"Mexican sounds great. I live near to the sale barn—can I make it there in, twenty minutes?"

Torrie obviously knew the town and its layout without hesitation or second-guessing. "It's not far from there at all. Now the only detail that is missing, is that I don't know what you look like."

It did feel almost like a blind date. "I'm tall with long brown hair and a nose that's been busted. Beyond that, I'm sturdy."

Another chuckle. "I'm tall and blonde, no busted nose, but I have shoulders like a linebacker. If anyone tries to give us any trouble, we sure as hell can handle them."

"Dust the floor with them, even." Emory added, liking her "date" from what she could tell. Best of all, the entire call lasted no more than two minutes. Fairly concise, and just how she liked it.

EL RINCON AWAITED, not that far away at all, and unremarkably, didn't seem like much from the outside. It wasn't exactly what she'd consider a drinking establishment, but songs in Spanish played in the background, and they carried more of a dance beat than the traditional ballads, so it stood to reason things turned livelier at a certain point in the evening.

Standing inside of the door and scanning the patrons, she noted a blonde woman seated by herself. Glances meeting and contact made, they waved to each other, and Emory joined her at the table. Torrie rose to meet her.

"I saw you at a distance before," Emory admitted, "when you arrested that man from the hide processing plant. Terry and I were keeping tabs at a distance it seems."

"Why?" The deputy asked, taken aback.

"If you want the honest answer, I think Terry wanted to get the chance to go inside. I guess it's hard to obtain clearance to enter."

Torrie grimaced. "I could have done without it, that's for sure. And trust me, that visit provided an experience all the way around." She advanced, hand outstretched and scanning Emory's face. "That nose isn't too busted up. I've seen worse. Far worse."

With a startled laugh at the brutal honesty, Emory shook her hand, noting the firm grasp in return. "Since you put it that way, I suppose so. No wonder Maxine thought we should meet."

Torrie smirked. "That woman knows more on a Sunday than a lot of the deputies know all week."

The waitress dropped off the menus, and they ordered two house margaritas.

"What's Maxine's story? She seems pretty sharp."

"I don't really know many details about Maxine, but she sure as hell knows all of mine. And you're right—I ought to ask her. It's only the polite thing to do. So, how long have you been a brand inspector?"

"About two years now."

The margaritas appeared.

Taking a sip, Torrie winced. "Strong. This'll get smoother on out from here, trust me." She set her glass down, put her elbows on the table and peered at Emory.

"Maxine told me that they call you Calamity Jane and the stories behind it, and I thought to myself, 'now there is a woman I need to meet.' From what I've heard, no one is going to f-around with you when you have a rifle in your hands."

With a long inhale at the reminder, Emory shook her head, struggling to find a suitable response. Before she had a chance to answer, Torrie cut in.

"She's proud of you, you know."

"Who is?"

"Maxine."

Emory narrowed her eyes at that piece of information. "But I just met her. She doesn't know me."

"She says you can hold your own. Like I said, and that's why I called you. I don't always seem to find much in common with...frilly girls."

Emory burst out with a gut laugh. "I've never been accused of that." She lifted her glass in a toast.

Clinking glasses, Emory ventured further. "The reason why Terry and I came to your offices the other day to see Sheriff Aranda was to find out about the Cooper family. You've seen the skulls on their fences?"

She signaled to the waitress to bring another round, although Emory had barely touched hers. "Who hasn't. Anyhow, what did you want to know?"

Emory took a sip to catch up. "Essentially, if there have been any complaints, or if you've had trouble with them in the past. Odd events, or anything notable that comes to mind."

The waitress returned with their next round and took their orders, twisting off as she left.

Torrie watched her walk away. "Now there's a frilly girl who probably can handle herself when push came to shove."

"I can't say that being a waitress is an easy job without any built-in hazards. But back to the Coopers."

The deputy pursed her lips off to the side, considering. "I'd say it appeared more like trouble accumulating *around* them. Since you're a branch of law enforcement yourself, I guess I'm not breeching any protocols. Take that guy from the plant. True, he ended up in the psych ward and is still there, but he's the ex-husband of one of the granddaughters. He calls the old man Creepin' Cooper."

"Oh yeah? You don't know the name of the woman he married by chance, do you?"

Torrie searched her memory but ended up shaking her head. Truthfully, she couldn't have cared less about the mysterious woman's identity, but the deputy remained professional enough to hide her disinterest. "Not off the top of my head. I'll see if I can look that up for you. Anyhow, enough talk of cleaver-wielding lunatics. Do you have a special someone, or what's the story there?"

Emory shifted in her chair, and the deputy caught it. "I had hopes about a fellow, but I turned out mistaken. What about you?"

"Oh, I've got a fling named Leroy. It's casual and nothing serious. He ain't the keeping kind, but he's fun in the meanwhile."

Slightly shocked, Emory managed a cautious smile, more at the deputy's sheer rambunctiousness than anything else. "Umm, I found someone I like, and who I thought liked me…but apparently my wires got crossed."

The deputy leaned forward and stared into Emory's eyes. "Spill."

Emory took a deeper drink. "He's a ranch hand at the Lost Daughter—that's my family's outfit. He's good-looking and a combat vet. He seemed interested...but then he turned cold. He asked if he could call me—and then said the reason why was not so much to hear my voice, but so that he could keep me informed of the happenings in my absence."

"Sometimes men need an excuse," Torrie swaggered.

"I wouldn't know," Em admitted, and instantly wished that she hadn't.

"Don't have a lot of notches on your bedpost, is that it?" Torrie asked, already knowing the answer. "Hell, we can take care of that if you want. Just say the word."

Emory shook her head, finding that the very last thing that she needed. "I've had a few boyfriends, but pickings are slim out in our direction. The last one died."

"Damn, girl. Well, I have dated plenty—or at least what I count as a date and let me tell you. They buy me a beer or a shot, and I consider it a date. That's a parameter. After that, those who don't cut it get kicked to the curb with a smile on their face and bite marks on their butt. If you want my advice, some men like to have the woman calling the shots."

"I can't imagine that happening with Jace. That's half of the problem. Jace knows I'm the boss. I made that point crystal clear all by myself. Now I wish that maybe I hadn't."

"I'd say good for you, no matter how it ends." Torrie concluded, "If he doesn't work out, I'd say a night out dancing is in order. We can find you a man in nothing flat...if you're not too particular."

"Sure, why not? Exercise, right? Anyhow..." And the rest of their meal passed with laughter.

Emory, remarkably to her way of thinking, had found herself a friend.

LATER THAT NIGHT, blame it on the booze, but tequila and Emory had never mixed with good results. Feeling those two margaritas and completely ignoring any common sense which she possessed, Emory called Jace.

The phone rang through. "Hi, Em!"

"Hi, Jace." Gosh, she tried to make sure she didn't slur. "I hope you don't mind that I'm calling this late."

"Not at all, and it's only eight thirty. What's up?"

"Following up on our interrupted conversation, I asked the sheriff to go ahead and to file those trespassing charges after talking to him and understanding the implications. I called Dad after I spoke with you, and he hadn't exactly reached the point of going through with the filing yet."

Although he made no sound, Emory sensed his confusion.

"Oh, don't be surprised," she droned. "Law is always the last resort in his mind. However, I did bother to inform him of my plan beforehand, so he can't say that he doesn't know about it."

"OK. I don't exactly have a horse in this race. But would you have gone ahead anyhow, even if he said 'no' to the charges?"

"That's a good question," Emory replied, bristling a bit. He didn't take her side on the matter, and frankly, she didn't have to explain herself to a hired hand. "I don't have a certain answer for that, but maybe."

The tequila talking told her that his exhale proved his disgust with her actions.

Then the tequila started talking and taking over. "I went out to dinner tonight with a female deputy named Torrie. She's lively all right. She seems to have the idea that her boyfriends ought to fall in line with her wishes. I'd bet she probably thinks they ought to follow the rule of law. Then she asked me about my old boyfriends. One turned out about as crooked as they come, although I didn't know that at the time, and he and I weren't all that involved. Then came Hugo who felt the need to protect me. That ended up poorly, as you already know."

"Emory…"

"I am ready, waiting, and willing to take over the reins at the Lost Daughter. Dad and Monty are getting older and slower, but they still have their wits about them. And they like you. I thought I did also for that matter, but I can tell that you don't approve of my methods."

"I never said that—"

"I've got to go, Jace. Even if you don't approve of me and how I go about things, the trespassing citation is moving forward. I shall leave you out of the details going forward if you like, but make sure that you understand that Suhanna McIlroy or whatever her name is, is not allowed on the property. In fact, you ought to check with Dad about who is allowed entrance. Then I'll thank you to email that list to me. Good night."

"Em—"

Emory clicked off the phone. Then she burst into tears.

She and tequila had never been on speaking terms. And now they never would be.

37

TREACHEROUS DROWNING CURRENTS RUN DEEP

1887

HANK CROSS AND HIS MEN'S RECONNAISSANCE OF THE BOX canyon confirmed the impressions he held all along, and a few others besides. The entire ride back, Hank considered the myriad of possibilities presented from a holding pen for pilfered cattle, a mustanger's pit, and perhaps the aspect most crucial of all—the canyon provided a natural defense—an easily guarded enclave where the entire outfit could hole up in the canyon fortress.

Hell, it might even be worth it to build a house back there, along with some stock pens.

No wonder Cooper claimed he would go down swinging for that holding, rather than to simply surrender it over to the Cross faction.

Hank was willing to take up that gauntlet and fight for it too.

As soon as he and his men arrived in the ranch yard, met by two of the less experienced ranch hands, everyone dismounted and busied themselves unsaddling and caring for the horses. Henry hurried over to his father's side, breathless before anyone had the chance to go much of anywhere.

"I can't find Susan."

The pronouncement gained Hank's immediate and undivided attention. He held up his hand, and his men stopped moving. "What do you mean, you can't find Susan?"

"When I came back from the higher pastures, I looked for her, and she's gone. So is the wagon and Jimmy and Buster, besides."

Hank's watery blue eyes scanned the surroundings and landed upon the two hands who had stayed behind on the ranch. "Did either one of you prairie turnips see anything?"

The two men exchanged worried glances, with deeper thoughts left unsaid. "We mucked out the stalls, and then rode the fence line. She didn't leave while we were mucking. Nor did we notice anything out of the ordinary as we rode the fences. We did, however, stop to work to free a bogged down cow…"

Henry fidgeted and squirmed at that account, and the truth came out in a gush. "I had to ask them to help me. I couldn't get that cow unstuck on my own. I guess while we worked on that, Susan…um, left for some reason."

A vein in Hank's jaw throbbed, a sure sign of pure displeasure. He said nothing in response to his son's confessed lack of ability, and again scanned the land. "We didn't pass her on the way back in." He addressed everyone assembled. "That only leaves the road into town."

The men shifted, feeling uneasy.

"Stuart, you and Bill mount up. We're going to go search for her. Henry, you come along too. Go get your horse and your rifle and make it fast. And Henry?

Make sure the rifle is loaded. This ain't no Sunday cakewalk."

THE MEN, accompanied by Henry, all rode with a silent determination that precluded any voiced speculations. Half an hour later, they located the team from the distance, standing unconcerned and peacefully on the bank. The pair of horses waited in their traces, drying and warming in the sun as if they hadn't a care in the world. Which, perhaps, they didn't. But Hank Cross sure did.

Approaching with caution, the riders scanned the rimrocks for any traces of an ambush, then commenced to searching for traces of Susan. Which they didn't find.

"Susan!" Henry wailed, but his call went unanswered.

A family of unknown prairie busters traveled along the road and predictably slowed, as they noted the search party.

The husband called out. "Is there a problem here?"

Hank approached their wagon, and the travelers came to a full stop. "You haven't seen a young woman, have you? It's my daughter. Her name is Susan. Susan Cross."

"No." The woman eyed the swift river with the obvious conclusion. "But we're happy to stop and help you look."

Nerves jumping like they never had before, Hank swallowed. "There's no trace of her. But that is our team and wagon."

One of his rider's returned from downstream. "Not a trace," he told them all.

The woman and man exchanged glances. "We'll keep

an eye open for her. Is there anything else that we can do for you?"

"No," Hank answered, and it cost him. "But I'm much obliged."

The Cross faction turned away after more searching, that yielded nothing. Of course, they knew that the Coopers lived nearby. Unwilling to ride into their territory, the Cross faction returned to the ranch. From that day forward, the Cross Ranch became referred to as the Lost Daughter, and Susan picked up the designation of "hapless."

PART IV

PART IV

38

DECAPITATED HISTORY— WHERE THE SKULL DOESN'T FALL TOO FAR FROM THE BODY

JUNE 2023

THE FOLLOWING DAY, A HUNGOVER AND MISERABLE EMORY dragged her way into work. On time, but certainly not bright-eyed and in desperate need of a cup of black coffee—coffee of a strength that allowed the spoon to stand up of its own accord. Dave and Terry sat positioned at their desks, ready to start the day without a trace of the headache that stabbed behind her eyes. Nothing amiss where those two old codgers were concerned, each poked around shuffling paperwork on their desks and consulted the mysteries within their computers. Whatever form their research took, both sorted out their workloads for that particular day and week.

Since Emory didn't have her own workload assigned, she felt at a disadvantage in more ways than one.

The sagging cardboard boxes gathering dust in the hallway got on her nerves, and she gave one a kick with her boot tip for the sheer hell of it.

"Someone really ought to clear out those boxes, and

don't think it's going to be me," Emory snarled, coming in through the door. "Do you even know what's in them? Probably whatever it is has been chewed to pieces by rats or mice."

Dave and Terry exchanged glances. "It's possible," Dave said, taking her measure, "but it's nothing that we've missed but as sure as anything, once we take them to the dump, that's the time we'll discover their importance."

"You'd have extra space if you got rid of them," Emory argued, sitting down. "What do we have going on today?"

"That depends on you." Terry eyed her suspiciously close.

"Yeah, I feel rough. I met that Torrie the deputy last night. We had dinner and more than a couple of margaritas. She's a lively one…"

Curiosity satisfied, Terry offered a wry glance. "Dave and I had a powwow. Dave has volunteered to go with you to meet Cooper himself. That is, if he's at home."

"You've found something better to do?" Emory snarked, no matter that deep down, she felt certain that Dave would prove the right man for the job. Terry came across as a mite one-track on the subject of the skulls.

"I don't think they're butchering an excess of beef at all," Emory commented. "Before you tell me what's really bothering you about those skulls, I learned more from Stampede. You remember Sheriff Preston?"

"How could I ever forget? Underreporting on the Lost Daughter. Wasn't that the charge?" He chuckled at her expense.

Emory stared daggers at him and didn't bother to grace his question with an answer. An answer that they all knew. Dave just smiled down into his mustache and waited the tussle out.

"The *sheriff* ran Suhanna McIlroy's name through a database because the car she's driving had expired tags. Get this—the car isn't registered to her. It's registered to none other than Orran Cooper." There. A turn of events or an association that neither one of them knew or even suspected.

Dave's eyes sparked as he leaned back in his chair, mulling over that information.

Terry rubbed the top of his head like he might have the beginnings of a headache himself about now. "There you have it then. A motive beyond those damned skulls. Which I just don't like. They bother me, all right? And I can't figure out where they're coming from."

"That's what we aim to find out," Dave replied. "Remember?"

"Yeah, Dave. I remember. I've haven't lost my mind yet."

"If you had," Dave countered with mock concern, "you might not even know."

"Thanks. I take it that you'll be around to tell me."

"That I will," Dave intoned.

Having had enough of the brand inspectors' tango, Emory waded back into the deep. "You know, back when the Lost Daughter was known as the Cross Ranch, our rivals for the land were called Cooper. I figured it all amounted to nothing more than a mere coincidence. But now, coupled with the car registered to Orran, I'd say it's looking of more concern all the time where our ranch is involved."

"Coincidence, huh?" Dave didn't appear convinced. "I checked the records, you know. He hasn't raised cattle since 2012 according to the records. And your Sheriff Preston is right. Orran Cooper is his name." Chewing on the ends of his mustache, he came up with an angle. "You know, my cousin is all into that genealogy stuff. Let's find out what we can, and then we'll set her loose on it."

"Good one." Emory nodded. "Do you think she'd mind?"

"Mind?" He shook his head. "There's nothing she'd like better. Crime fighting and genealogy rolled into one. She'll have bragging rights for the next five years."

Emory nodded, casting her mind back. "You know, it's possible they're related if they've been in Colorado for a long time. There didn't used to be that many people out here."

Terry followed the conversation, nodding his way through. "Don't let me slow you two supersleuths down."

"Come on, Emory, he's getting testy." Dave rose from his desk and moved toward the door.

"Do you want us to do anything for you while we're out that way?" Emory paused before joining Dave.

The senior brand inspector shook his head. "I'll do the inspections today. If I need anything, I'll be in touch. You two do the same."

Dave tipped the brim of his hat as he long legged it out the door, leaving Emory to follow in his wake.

———

"WE'LL TAKE MY TRUCK." Dave loaded into the driver's seat without a second thought. Nor did he say a whole lot as he navigated. Emory eyed him once or twice, but he didn't appear overly concerned or bothered about a damned thing. Normally Western taciturn herself, the silence following the previous night's blunder with Jace weighed heavily upon her.

"What are you thinking, Dave?"

He took his time in answering. "I'm thinking how I don't really believe in coincidences."

Emory shrugged. "The more I think about it, one of our family's stories bothers me. The daughter of the ranch's originating family drowned. They claimed to have never found her body. Ever. That is beyond rare that she vanished without a trace. No body, no article of clothes, absolutely nothing. Now, this Suhanna McIlroy woman has turned up and is asking questions around town about the Lost Daughter. As I said, she wormed her way into my dad's ex-girlfriend's good graces and for some unknown reason, Linda brought her up into our cemetery. Which, as we all know, she shouldn't have done. Anyhow, the Arizonan noticed Hapless Susan's grave. She said her family had a Susan as well, but that, and I quote, 'their Susan lasted much longer.'"

Dave frowned. "You're going to have to fill in the blanks for me, pard."

"Since our Susan's body was never found, what if…?"

He side-eyed her. "What if, indeed."

FIFTEEN SILENT MINUTES LATER, the two brand inspectors rattled down the road guarded by the grim fence-posted skulls.

"I'm almost getting used to them," Emory cracked, "and I even have a few favorites picked out."

Dave just chuckled.

"Last time we ventured down this path, Terry had me

attempt to gather information, but it didn't work out the way he wanted. Beyond that, no one much seems to like this outfit. In fact, they think Cooper is nuts."

"No…" Dave appeared completely unbothered by any of her account, or the prospect presented.

Emory persisted. "Do you have a plan of attack?"

Of course he did. "We're going to go to the door and straight out ask. Beyond that, we'll play it by ear."

"Pull over a second, Dave. Where they won't see us from the house. I want to call Torrie first."

"Your new partner in crime?"

"More like a drinking buddy," Emory replied.

Dave guffawed. "Shoot. That's a good one."

Pulling over in a tree-sheltered place and away from the direct line of view, Emory placed the call.

"Hey, Torrie, it's Emory and Dave, one of the other brand inspectors. I know I haven't given you much time, but we're headed over to Orran Cooper's place. I just want to make certain that they don't have a history of taking potshots at people."

A firm voice responded. "I already looked first thing." Apparently, her head didn't hurt as much as Emory's. "There have been complaints filed with animal control about those skulls, the Dumb Friends League went out there and, I quote, 'got run off.' They claimed the man menaced them with a gun…but the report says nothing about shots fired. Cooper did tell them that the skulls symbolized his religion."

"What religion is that?"

"Damned if I know," the deputy replied. "That's out of our jurisdiction and we're keeping it that way."

Emory rubbed her forehead, but it didn't help the throbbing all that much. "Anything else we should know before he tries to run us off?"

"Not that I can think of unless you want backup. Do you two want me to drive out and give you a hand? I sure can."

Dave whistled low to grab Emory's attention and shook his head.

"Thanks, but not yet. We're keeping this low-keyed."

"If you change your mind, you know where to find me. Over and out," the deputy concluded, and the line went dead.

"Do you figure that's how they all talk in Nebraska?"

"Very funny, Dave."

"Yeah, I sure thought so," he replied.

Dave pulled back out into the road and drove at a maddeningly slow speed. "Just so that he has plenty of time to see that we're coming."

The truck advanced into Cooper's yard at a crawl. Sure enough, before they even came to a full stop, the front door opened, and revealed a man wearing a clean white shirt and crisp unfaded overalls. Hair combed and face washed, his well-tended appearance came as a surprise.

"Mr. Cooper?" Dave asked, hand outstretched as he advanced. "My name is Dave Worrell, and this is Emory Cross."

Cooper's eyes turned shifty at the name Cross.

Still, he stepped out of the house and shook Dave's hand, and Emory's for that matter. "Can I help you?" he asked, not even rude. Standing there, hands on hips, he was missing the half of his right index finger. Emory took it as another reminder of the hazards of agriculture —machinery.

Dave flicked his head back toward the road. "Have you been having some trouble out here?"

"Not anymore," Cooper crowed, proud of himself.

Dave nodded as if giving the matter deep considera-tion. "Actually, the trouble aspect came from Emory's take on the situation. For my part, I wondered about the skulls."

"Nothing says 'keep the hell off my land' like rotting skulls," Orran Cooper claimed, and despite herself, Emory laughed.

"My family kind of thinks the same way," she explained. "I'm from up Stampede way."

At that admission, Cooper's eyes turned both beady and wary. "You don't say."

Emory encouraged. "So, if one skull is good, fifty are better?"

"Something like that."

Dave cut in, sensing a shift in the current. "We don't have a beef with you—sorry, brand inspector's joke—but you don't raise livestock any longer, do you?"

Cooper shook his head warily. "Not for the last decade or so, and those weren't even mine. I ain't no damned cowpusher, and I was a miner by trade until they closed the mine—assholes. A bunch of men's jobs went right down the toilet on account of the EPA who don't know their asses from their elbows. If you ask me, they owe the lot of us big-time. But I can't say what any of this has to do with you."

The other brand inspector didn't appear to take offense but filed all that information away in the files of his mind. An odd and unexpected tirade that had nothing to do with cattle—and whether Creepin' Cooper came across as clean and kept or not—Emory sensed the man played them.

"Fine then, that's the first matter of business covered," Emory countered. "The second matter is that there is a car registered to you driving around Stampede with expired tags. Do you have any idea why that might be?"

"Is that a brand inspector concern? You know," he said, eyes narrowing and telegraphing threat, "that's just the problem with Stampede and the government. And that's why I don't go up there myself anymore. Just a bunch of yokels who think they're the backbone of the state because their property values shot up. Come to think of it, I'll bet that not *all* those ranches hold clear title. What do *you* say about *that*?"

Emory sized up the red-horned cattle totem and chose her words, refusing to be intimidated. "I'll take your bet. I'll bet you that they do possess clear titles. Besides, when those ranches sell, they do go through title insurance. Heard of it?"

The man spat off to the side and glared at her.

Emory persisted. "So, we've got a reasonable idea that either Suhanna McIlroy is related to you, or you know her. If that is not the case, you might want to consider filing a stolen car report to reduce your liability. You see, that's the woman driving around up there in a car registered to you. Of course, there will be fines and tickets to pay on account of those expired tags, and who knows what else, unless you report it stolen. Technically speaking, you will be the one that's on the hook for everything as the responsible party."

For his part, at the mention of paying for tickets and fines, Creepin' Cooper transformed into a shifty and enigmatic threat.

"*Did* you loan her that car?" Emory asked flat out.

"Not that it's any of your business, but she's my cousin's niece. Sure, I loaned her that car because she's on the side of right and doing the good work. She's addressing a past wrong. Now, I'm tiring of this conversation. Are you writing me up or just jawin'?"

Dave smiled. "No, that's not our purpose at all. I guess we got sidetracked. For right now, we just wanted to make sure that those skulls weren't the result of commercial meat sales. As to whether or not the Stampede sheriff's office sends you tickets and fines, I couldn't possibly say."

Cooper, a tall man standing over six feet, pulled himself up to the tallest height possible, to make himself bigger and even more threatening. Dave, also tall, matched his stance. For that matter, so did Emory.

If Cooper noticed the posturing in return, he didn't show it. "I'm not producing meat of any kind. If anything, I'm thinking of changing careers and moving into real estate. And, speaking of real estate, those skulls just keep people away from mine. Now, take the hint."

"SOMETIMES YOU AIN'T much in the charm department," Dave offered as they pulled out.

Emory peered through the rear window to find Orran Cooper watching their departure. "He pissed me off."

"I could tell," Dave said, as placid as usual.

"And?" Emory demanded.

Once again, the downturn of his mouth meant he hid his smile behind his mustache. "I'd say your fight is up in Stampede, and there's no mass butchering of animals taking place. He sure don't think much of the government."

Emory brushed some errant hair back from her face.

"Whatever. You can see some of those skulls are pretty old."

"Yeah, and Terry can see that as well. Hell, we all can."

"So, where's Cooper getting the money to live— Social Security?"

"Maybe, if he's of the age," Dave replied. "Or maybe his relatives help him out. Maybe he's got some sort of mining pension, but I think that'd be rare. Anyhow, those topics are definitely off-limits in this line of work —unless they volunteer the information by telling us. And that old boy ain't going to tell us shit."

"Then what gives? Why am I down here?" It wasn't an idle question, and she heard the traces of exasperation edging in.

"One of Terry's hunches. Anyhow, let's call my cousin Elsa. Now that we know Orran is related to Suhanna who has a fixation on your ranch, it would be best to gather whatever information possible."

Emory stared out the side window weighing the odds. "They have to be *those* Coopers."

"I'd say. But I'd also say they have a bead on something you don't."

The imagery struck a spooky note. As typical, he chose his words with care, and said exactly what he meant.

"What?" he asked, catching her eyeballing him.

"That's an old shooting term, you know."

"Yep," he replied, turning the steering wheel to pull off the road. "I know."

Coming to a stop, Dave fished in his pocket for his cell, scrolled for the number, and selected it. He put the cell on speaker mode and placed it on the dash. An older woman's voice answered.

"Hello?"

"Hello! This is your cousin Dave. How have you been?" He mouthed the words over to Emory—*she still has a land line.* "I've put you on speakerphone, so watch what you say." He winked at Emory.

The woman giggled at the notion.

"I have a nice young lady with me named Emory Cross from Stampede."

"Oh my." The woman's voice held the hint of scandal. "That's real outlaw country."

Truer words were seldom spoken. "Yes, ma'am," Emory replied.

"Emory here needs some information that would help with an investigation, and I said there's no one better for the job than you."

The older woman giggled again, flattered. "That all certainly sounds exciting. I've got a pen and paper ready to take notes."

"I don't know how you go about it," Emory began, "but we're looking into a man named Orran Cooper who lives in this county. He's got a grandniece, or so he claims, named Suhanna McIlroy."

"How old would you guess they were?" Dave's cousin asked, efficient and professional.

"I'd say Suhanna is about thirty-five or forty, as to Orran, I have no idea. Dave?"

"Fifty to sixty-five, I'd guess."

"That's quite the range," Emory groused.

"Some folks stay better preserved then others. Hard to tell." He spoke to himself more than to either one of the women. "He looked surprisingly clean. Probably hasn't really worked for a while. Says he used to be a miner, but the mine shut down or something like that."

"I'll get back to you both later today." Another giggle from Elsa, and she hung up.

"See?" Dave asked. "That is the sound of a hap-py woman. We just made her week."

Emory shook her head and widened her eyes.

"Just wait until you get a few years on you," Dave cautioned.

"I hope to find something I like doing as much as she does." All the same, Emory didn't figure that she'd be doing much genealogy. But she guessed he had a point. One never could tell.

39

THE DEMISE OF A WAYWARD DAUGHTER

1887

THEIR RETURN TO THE RANCH AMOUNTED TO A DEATHLY silent affair. The horse's hooves thudded against the dirt at nothing more than a disheartened walking pace. Saddles creaked as the men shifted in their seats uneasily. Meanwhile, the birds chirped and called, unheeding of the unfolding tragedy.

No one, least of all Hank Cross, wanted to return empty-handed, but empty-handed they returned.

He scanned the ranch yard for the wagon, which hadn't yet returned. That absence gave him a measure of time to figure out how to tell Polly. Completely out of character, after Hank dismounted and handed over his reins, he returned into the soddy and sat down to wait. Idle, other than for his thoughts. Henry joined him, doing his best to hold back the tears that his father, despite his stoicism, most certainly and painfully felt.

Henry struggled. He wanted to offer comfort, but there was no true comfort to give. He also knew better than to involve his mother in this. "I think she was lonely," the boy offered at length.

Hank turned his face away.

A heavy and oppressive silence fell over the Cross Ranch. Their hired hands did all the work and chores that needed doing, but in as near silence as humanly possible. No conversations carried, and single words and grunted replies sufficed.

Finally, within the soddy, Hank broke the silence. "Henry, I need to tell you something. I need to tell you that I'm proud of you, even when I come across as hard. Do you understand?"

Judging from the boy's shocked expression, he hadn't been certain in the slightest. And that uncertainty amounted to a failing on Hank's part. He would own up to that.

"Your ma and me, you see, we don't come from much. Whatever we have or had, we had to take or build. That's the size of it. This ranch holds promise. Pure unadulterated promise. But that's the thing, boy, and I need you to take this to heart. There will always be others who grasp the promise it holds as well. They will try take what we've built. And you will have to be ready to fight for it. You always must be ready for the fight, because it is a-coming."

Miserable, Henry nodded, eyes brimming and struggling to hold back the tears. He most certainly didn't want to appear weak before his father. Not if he was expected to fight. Fighters didn't cry. "Yes, Pa."

Hank nodded, and they fell silent, straining to hear the dreaded sound of wagon wheels returning.

———

THE WHEELS CAME CREAKING up in the dark of the night, the moon the only source of light.

The Crosses didn't own a clock or a watch to judge the passage of time. Just the moon, the stars, and the sun overhead. It didn't much matter anyhow. Exhausted, Polly entered the soddy, and stopped dead in her tracks when she noted Hank sitting by the fire's ashes.

"None of the men challenged my arrival," she griped. "I drove straight on in. Henry?" She called over to him lying in bed. "Put those horses away for me, will you? The girl had a hard time of it, but now she has a healthy baby b—"

Hank rose to his feet like it cost him...and it did. "Polly..."

"What's happened?" Her eyes burned, and her spine stiffened.

"It's Susan..."

That information caused her eyes to narrow with suspicion. "Did she run off with that Cooper boy?"

Hank partially reared back. "We found the team and the wagon across by the river, with nary a sign of her. I don't think she ran away with any Cooper...I think she drowned!"

He took a clumsy step toward his wife. Her eyes darted and blinked. She didn't turn into his outstretched arms but sank into a heap on the rough floor instead.

"Damn, damn, damn," she uttered through clenched teeth. Then she burst into hot, angry tears, the sound of her wail rose from her diaphragm and escaped from the soddy and reverberated through the ranch yard.

Hank lifted her from the floor and held her. "I'm sorry." He spoke over the top of her head, into the room. Henry, pulling on his pants, stood stock-still by the blanket that marked off his bed, eyes large and worried.

"Go see to the horses," Hank told him.

"I want my girl!" Polly sobbed.

"She drowned," he said as gentle as he could make it. "She drowned, we couldn't find her body, and she's not coming back."

"I won't rest until she does," Polly insisted.

"She can't come back now." He stroked her hair. "She's gone."

And so, she was. Gone. Gone for good.

40

SHAPED BY THE STORM

JUNE 2023

EMORY HAD JUST PULLED UP INTO A RANCH YARD TO CHECK the paperwork for a shipment. *Jace* flashed across the screen.

Figuring, based upon where they'd left matters earlier, whatever he wanted would likely not be anything that she wanted to hear. Whatever the reason for his call, it couldn't be anything good.

"Hi, Jace," Emory answered, struggling to hold her voice dead even.

"I'm trying to beat your dad to the punch line," he said. "That Suhanna came out here again, and she was near the horses. *Your* horses to be exact."

Her blood ran a bit cold, and she sat up straighter. She quirked her head to the side, much as she would if listening for a rattlesnake. "What happened?"

"I fired a warning shot, what else?"

Impressive. Emory felt a smile forming.

Jace continued his account. "She may have been trying to lure Outhouse, so…"

Emory stiffened. "Then what?"

"Once they heard the shot, I've got to give those old boys credit. They came running and Monty, get this, tackled her flat out like a linebacker!"

"No shit," she laughed. "I'd say it doesn't pay to get Monty riled. Then what?"

"I got a rope, they tied her, and we called the sheriff. Right now, to the best of my knowledge, she is sitting in a Stampede cell."

"They've got only the one."

"Then she'll be sharing it with drunks or whatever loose change is rattling about. Anyhow, your father will no doubt be calling you." He paused. "I felt bad how our last conversation ended. I didn't mean for it to go that way."

"I didn't either." Her voice came out both regretful and soft.

"Can I call you later?" Jace asked. "To talk...not to report."

"I'd like that. But, Jace? I bet I'll be coming home soon to help. I'm discovering things down here that can't be considered exactly good for us. The main thing would be to keep Suhanna McIlroy locked up for as long as possible."

"Your father followed the sheriff's car into town. Don't know what will come of that, but he hasn't returned yet."

"Where's Monty?"

Jace chuckled. "Patrolling. What's with the single spur, anyhow?"

Emory sighed and shook her head, thinking how crazy they all sounded. "He claims it helps him aim better. But I'm interested in what Dad learns. He certainly doesn't make a habit of going into the sheriff's office if he can help it."

No sooner had Emory ended that phone call than her cell lit up again. This time the call came from Dave.

She didn't even bother to say hello. "That Suhanna woman was just arrested out on the Lost Daughter. I'm trying to figure out what's coming next, but apparently, she doesn't take the warning not to trespass seriously."

"Is that a fact," Dave commented, not sounding terribly surprised.

"It is. Monty tackled her to the ground."

His direct response amounted to a bemused chuckle. "I don't know if that's good or bad. Anyhow, my cousin called back. I think I'd better sit you down in person. I'd rather go through this face to face if you don't mind."

"What is it, Dave? I need to try to get a handle on what's going on at home."

"Trust me, it's all related."

Emory scanned the horizon, eyeing the cattle in the pen. "I just need to sign off on this shipment, then I can meet you back in the office. Does that work?"

"It does," he replied.

———

Twelve butts with identical brands and numeric tags checked out later, Emory drove back toward the sale barn when her father rang through. Truth be told, all the phone conversations on that day wore a bit thin.

"Did Jace call you?" His voice didn't sound irritated per se, but more curious about how the land might lay in their budding relationship.

"Yes, he did. But he didn't know the whole story. So, to cut to the chase, you all let her back on the ranch."

A ripple of irritation flowed. "Now, I wouldn't exactly phrase it that way. She snuck on."

"By driving in on the ranch road? That doesn't sound too covert to me." Emory didn't feel like letting any of them off easy.

Her father understood her angle and started hemming and hawing. "Yeah, she came down that way." His voice growled. "What did you want us to do—shoot out her tires?"

"Sure. Why not? So, just to make sure I understand... she drove down the road, and no one saw her coming. Is that your version of events?"

"You sound kinda like a lawyer there. I wouldn't say 'no one saw her coming' exactly either. We were all scattered about doing chores. Anyhow, Jace found her first and fired a warning shot into the air when he cottoned on to her presence. Had he aimed somewhere that splintered like a fence post, that would have been the icing on the cake..."

Emory shook her head, eyes narrowing. "He might have hit one of the horses."

"Actually, his aim is much better than that. Do you figure they still train snipers?"

Did that mean her father thought Jace capable of being one?

"I don't know, Dad. Is Suhanna still in jail?"

She heard the relief in his voice. Not so much due to the Arizonan languishing in her cell, but rather that she had changed the topic of the conversation. "She is."

"What's the plan, and when does she get out?"

"I guess when she posts bail. Bob is dragging out the procedures as best as he can. We don't exactly have a plan yet. Any ideas?"

That caught her. "So, it's Bob now, is that it? Apparently, your opinion about him has changed as of late."

"I never didn't approve of him exactly...we're just on two different sides of the river."

Emory's impatience grew. "OK, but never mind all of that. Suhanna's got ties down here, and Dave has called a meeting in person. He has something that he wants to tell me—something that he thinks is going to upset me. Depending upon what that might cover, I may come home for a spell. One more set of eyes and one more person to keep watch on the ranch."

"Because of this?"

"Damn straight because of this. Suhanna McIlroy didn't come onto the Lost Daughter for the *second* time during my watch. More than that, I don't want people messing with my horses. I'm even more seriously considering driving them over to Vermillion to keep them safe at this point."

"What did you say they call you over there—Calamity Jane?"

"I don't like to be called that," she argued.

"I know," her father agreed, and upon that note, he terminated the call by the single press of a button.

Manners never had been their family's strong point.

BACK AT THE SALE BARN, Emory pulled her marked brand inspector truck right next to the others. Both Terry and Dave waited within, and that didn't bode well for whatever message or intel awaited. Sitting in the driver's seat a few moments longer than necessary, gripping the steering wheel and staring straight ahead, she chided herself.

"To hell with it," she muttered, placing one cowboy boot onto the ground, followed by the other.

Purposefully clamping her hat on her head, she strode forward, flung open one of the glass doors wide, and failed to greet the boys on the wall. All business and determination, she strode into the arena, and directly up the stairs to the office. From the darkened hallway she noted their postures—the stiff ways they held their spines and shoulders. Neither man appeared happy.

"Here she is," Dave announced as she stepped through the door, like a cheerful comment and voice might make things better.

"If you want to know, I feel kind of spooky."

"And you should," Dave agreed. "You'll feel definitely spooky once this is done."

Terry sat rubbing his chin with his knuckles and pointedly failed to discredit Dave's ominous warning. Distracted or disturbed by worry, he wouldn't give voice to his concerns.

"To cut to the chase, the way Elsa sees it, Suhanna McIlroy is your..." Dave consulted his notes, "third cousin."

She blinked in rapid succession. "Excuse me?"

"Elsa emailed me one of those chart things." He pointed to his computer. "You ought to take a look at its."

He swung his chair around and typed on the keyboard.

Emory shot Terry a worried glance, but he remained stock-still, watching her. For her part, she felt like a deer in the headlights.

Nevertheless, she sidled over to stand near Dave, staring at the computer screen from over his shoulder.

Nervous, he pointed a gnarled finger toward the computer screen. "See here? That's you, and there's your father Lance and mother, Barbara. Then comes your father's parents, Charles Cross and Verna Jean, then their parents, Asa Cross and his wife Hannah, then comes Hank Cross and his first wife, Polly. His second wife was Idella."

Emory shook her head. "I don't get it. So what? Anyhow, I'm Emory Idella Cross."

"Exactly." Dave clicked around a bit more. "Here is Suhanna McIlroy's chart or tree. Whatever. Here's Suhanna McIlroy, who is the daughter of Dotty Cooper Larson. Going back along the Cooper line, Dotty's parents were Max Cooper and Erma his wife. Max Cooper is Orran's younger brother. Elsa also sent some article about the mine Orran worked for, but I didn't pay too much attention to it. Up in Leadville. Seems like they had some problems keeping control of their dynamite."

Dave continued. "Max and Orran's father is George Cooper, that goes back into Fred Cooper and his wife Hannah, and they came from Vern Cooper and Christopher Cooper—both of whom were married at one point to *Susan Cross*. And there you have it."

"*Suhanna*. Damn. Now I understand her lame-ass weird comment."

"Which was?" At the sound of Terry's voice, she flinched completely having forgotten that he sat there listening.

"She said 'our Susan didn't last long.' That they had a Susan, and I quote, 'who lasted much longer.' And then she said she had a great-grandmother or some such thing, and a combination of their names made her Suhanna. Damn, damn, damn." Emory claimed a seat, mind whirling. "This is not good news by any stretch."

"No," both Terry and Dave replied in unison.

"And that fourth cousin or whatever the hell she is, is sitting in the Stampede jail charged with trespassing."

Terry eyed her closely. "Do you need to go home and help sort things out a bit?"

"I believe that I do."

Terry glanced at his watch. "Well, if you start driving now, you might make it home by six."

Emory hesitated. "I'm really sorry."

Terry shook his head. "It's the other way around. I have the distinct feeling that I should be apologizing to you."

A strangled laugh from Emory followed. "Not at all. But now we know that Dad comes by his penchant for skulls honestly. He's not going to like this. He's not going to like this one bit."

41

THE LIES WE TELL OURSELVES

1887

POLLY DID A STRANGE THING. SHE TOOK TO HER BED.

No one slept much during the night following Susan's disappearance. When the morning light broke low upon the horizon, for the first time in living memory Polly Cross remained in bed. The fire amounted to nothing more than last night's ashes and the stove remained unlit. Never before in their married life had Hank Cross, confronted by the absence of coffee brewing or food warming, roused himself to light the fire.

"How are you doing, Polly?" He prompted after he lit the fire and fanned it to flaming, bright and hot.

No answer came.

A few moments later, Henry stumbled from his bed half asleep. His father's gaze flickered over him dressed in a haphazard manner, shirt buttoned askew, and suspenders hanging. More importantly, Hank Cross took his son's measure before returning his attention to the damned cooking implements—staring at the coffeepot, pan, and ladles like he'd never seen them before.

Worried, Hank knew the boy took in his mother's form prostrate in the bed. Of course, he'd heard Hank's question to her—there was no reason to assume that he hadn't—and more disturbingly he likely noted her lack of reply.

The boy appeared fearsome to his father's concerned eye and said nothing to his mother, unwilling to venture down that same silent, burdened path.

"Go fetch a bucket of water," his father told him, resigned.

Henry sidled over to him, standing far closer than usual. The boy jerked his head over in his mother's direction and whispered, "Is she sick?"

"In a way," Hank admitted, holding his cards close to his vest. "Now git. We ain't got all day."

That command snapped the boy out of whatever trance caught him. He snatched up the bucket and rushed out the door, headed for the river—pretty darn fast too. For his part, Hank didn't move an inch but remained staring at the fire, every now and again furtively glancing over at the shape of Polly laying in the bed, and puzzling over the events of the previous day.

When the boy returned carrying the water, Hank found his will to make coffee had ebbed away. "We can go eat with the men. You go on ahead and let them know that I'll be down to the bunkhouse directly."

The boy, needless to say, didn't tarry.

———

WHEN THE HEAVY DOOR CLOSED, Hank moved over to stand by the side of the bed. "Polly?"

With a visible effort, she opened her eyes but said nothing. Hank sat down on the edge of the bed. "I know you're taking this hard."

"My girl drowned," she croaked.

He stared at the chinking in the rough log wall, then turned his attention hard to his wife. "That's not exactly what you said last night."

That comment provoked her into sitting bolt upright in the bed, eyes blazing. "My girl drowned. She would never just run off like that. Do you hear me?"

Her thin hand and clawlike fingers grasped his forearm and grasped it hard.

Hank stared at his wife, who in that precise moment, appeared more akin to an apparition than to Polly Cross, his wife of twenty years. "I hear you, but what do you propose on doing?"

"Do?" She hissed. "*Do?* I don't propose on doing anything at all. She's dead to us. We will not go to the Coopers and drag her off, screaming and kicking and making a show of it. As far as anyone will ever know, she's dead. But don't you put up a grave marker."

"I don't follow you," Hank admitted in a low voice.

"She might come back, and that's a bad use of fate. How would you like to find your own grave marked if you weren't even dead?"

His wife hadn't loosened her grasp at all, and it seemed probable that the light in her eyes came from a fever.

"I'm not sure that I'd care, if I had run off," Hank replied.

"No. I'm not having it, do you hear me? If she comes home and finds we've put up a grave for her with her name on it, she'll think that we don't care."

"If she is alive and well and living with the Coopers,

we probably *don't* care any longer." Of course, that last part may have been a lie. "Besides, it will only be a matter of time before word gets out."

She tightened her grasp into steel. "That's why you must take care of this. You have to run them off. *All* of them. For now, and evermore."

Hank shook his head in a slow wag. What his wife wanted amounted to nothing short of a full-out range war.

He changed the conversation. "Are you feeling well enough to get up today?"

She considered it, having said her piece and having made her point. Clearly. "I don't believe so. Last night delivering that baby took more out of me than I thought." She chuckled without mirth. "Huh. One new life entering the world fresh with promise, and another gone wrong. If I feel up to it later, I'll cook supper. Otherwise, you two can take your meals with the men today."

"Do you want anything? I can bring a plate back for you."

Polly reclined back in the bed, weakened. "I want my girl back and the Coopers gone from here once and for all. That's what I want."

Hank rose to his feet and stared at his wife in their bed. That marked the point where Hank Cross started worrying about Polly's mind.

42

WHILE THE GIRLS ARE AWAY, THE BOYS JUST MIGHT SCREW UP

JUNE 2023

PURE AND SIMPLE, SHE WANTED TO FIND OUT IF SHE would catch the men napping on the job.

Emory turned off the county road with every intention of giving them hell, as simple as that. Congratulating herself on at least acting in a straightforward manner, she wouldn't even sneak in from the BLM land and through the back gate. No, the execution of her mission was meant to be straightforward and direct. Heading down the Lost Daughter's rutted ranch road she paused under their old, rotting steer skull—eyeballs withered and clearly visible from the county road for all the world to see. Without bothering to leave the confines of her truck, she eyed the talisman with a newfound perspective. Sticking her tongue inside of her cheek—its implied warning might have scared some, but it certainly didn't scare all.

Not to mention that Orran Cooper's display put theirs to shame.

Placing the truck back into gear, she rumbled down the rutted dirt road.

Her arrival plan amounted to pulling into the ranch yard unannounced and unexpected. Her actions were twofold and simple. First, she wanted to verify whether anyone noticed when someone—herself in this case— arrived out of the blue. Fairly certain of the answer, she still needed proof. Especially since Suhanna had made it all the way into the ranch yard and over to the paddock where the horses grazed with nary a challenge. A challenge coming from those three men who would assure her that "they had matters under control." Doubtful. If they had, Suhanna shouldn't have made it to the horses. She should have been cut off and turned around in the yard, plain and simple.

Emory's second reason was that the Lost Daughter remained her home until the day she died. She could come and go whenever she damn well pleased. Without calling ahead. Not that anyone ever said anything different, but a notion took hold a bit around the periphery of her mind. The three men built a type of cowboy fraternity that didn't exactly involve her.

Well, she would damn well push her way in.

Riling herself up into a fight, she chided herself— easing up a bit. There was no *real* reason to go in there with guns blazing unless she drove straight up with nary a notice. If that came to pass, they deserved whatever she shot out. She knew, if she barreled in acting like a complete bitch, her chances with Jace would likely die out, once and for all. Well, it might prove a gamble that had to be waged. In her heart of hearts, she wanted to see Jace.

She wanted him to tell her that he cared.

That, and she wanted to crash their damned cowboy fraternity and kick some common sense back into them.

As she and her pickup approached the house, she

caught the flicker of someone looking out from behind one of the old lace curtains. Gap-toothed and half rotted, they still provided a decent enough screen. Good.

Of course, once noted, she would be identified without problem. She pulled up and parked in her usual place.

Her father came out on the porch. "Checking up on us?"

"Something like that. And I need to talk to you."

"Normally you call," he commented as a matter of fact, not disturbed one way or another.

"Not this time." Climbing onto the porch she gave her father a hug. "Probably it would be best if we spoke in private."

Lance Cross frowned at that last part and allowed her to enter the house first, trailing behind.

Inside and in what served as the living room, she found Monty blinking behind those damned blue glasses. He didn't even address her directly.

Instead, he spoke to his cousin, which irritated her no end. "What's she doing here?"

Emory cut that nonsense off. "You can ask me yourself, you know."

Monty acted like he hadn't even heard.

"Don't know," Lance explained, perfectly willing to ignore his daughter in this particular instance. "She's going to tell me about it. In private."

"Private, huh? That can't be good," Monty replied.

"Don't figure it will be." Then Lance turned to his daughter. "Where do you want to have this top secret conversation?"

If they talked around her, she would talk around them. "Where's Jace?"

"On his nightly rounds." Monty sounded baffled. "He don't know that you're here either?"

"No. No offense to anyone, but this is family business."

"Monty is family," her father countered.

"Wait until you hear who else is."

Her father stiffened. "Out with it."

"Suhanna McIlroy."

"No, she's not. What are you talking about?"

"I'm talking about that buzzard who collects the skulls and mounts them on his fence posts, and his totem pole art project with the horns painted in blood red. But I'll tell you another thing, it puts our two skulls to shame."

Her father's jaw flexed. "Our skulls aren't for decoration."

"Well, I doubt his are either."

She eyed both men. "Sheriff Preston ran Suhanna's plates and learned the car is not registered to her, but to a man named Orran Cooper out past the sale barn. Dave and I went up to his door to ask him about the skulls, which bother Terry to a point neither of us understand. Anyhow, he claimed that Suhanna is his cousin's niece."

"So?"

"The long and the short of it is that Hapless Susan didn't drown. She married a Cooper."

Dead, stunned silence filled the room.

"You have got to be shitting me," her father said.

THE WHINE of their Kubota came humming into the yard, and not one of them moved.

Jace.

He killed the motor in front of the house, and a few seconds later, his bootheels marked his progress across their porch. Without knocking, he came in through the door.

A trace of a smile began when he saw Emory, then he took in the mood of the room and the two men. "What's happened?"

Monty hitched his pants upward. "Emory's dropped a bombshell. That's what's happened."

Jace's eyes sought out Emory's and she gave the slightest one-shouldered shrug in return.

Poised to learn far more about them than Emory had ever expected or wanted, events as they unfolded didn't go in accordance with her initial plan. In fact, as the drama played out, it confirmed her reasoning as to why she wanted to meet with her father privately in the first place.

"Should I leave?" Jace asked, halfway turned toward the door.

"It's up to you," Emory replied.

"You know this changes many things." Her father spoke to all of them, but that didn't stop him from heading back to the kitchen. "Let's eat before the chili burns. And Jace? You might as well stay. Emory's just being protective."

"Right. That's it," Emory replied, poker-faced.

Sure. About a century and a half too late.

BOWLS AND GLASSES FILLED, Emory almost felt sorry for Jace since no one did much talking. Questions flitted through his eyes, but he, like the other men, held his tongue.

Her father's and Monty's expressions closed down, but concern set into the crow's-feet around their eyes.

"Do we need to say grace?" Monty asked out of nowhere.

Her father's eyebrows shot up.

A defensive Monty lowered his head regardless of Lance's opinion on the matter. "Dear Lord, thank you for the food. Please let whatever dang thing Emory's come up with to be untrue. Amen."

Emory frowned at Monty. "It's not untrue. But OK, if you want solid proof we can take those DNA tests."

"I ain't doing it," Monty countered.

She turned to her father. "Dad?"

"Maybe. Now get on with whatever it is that you've got to say."

She toyed with her spoon for a second. "Suhanna McIlroy is one of the Coopers, and our ancestor, Hapless Susan didn't drown, contrary to family lore."

"The Coopers?" Jace asked.

"We had a range war with them, and they *lost*," her father growled.

Emory directed her recount to Jace. "Terry and Dave called me out to Greeley because of a concern about a man who keeps nailing cattle heads to his fence posts and other places. Fairly menacing, I must admit. Terry, specifically, worried about a producer selling beef illegally, who he assumed used those skulls as a strange advertisement. Anyhow, it turns out that the skulls are coming from their widely scattered family and that man doesn't have any livestock on his ranch. Hasn't, in fact, since about twelve years ago. I can tell you that their neighbors don't care much for the family or their decorations—"

"Get on with it." Her father's prompt came in abrupt and impatient.

"Suhanna McIlroy is driving, or drove, a car around Stampede—a car belonging to Orran Cooper. Orran Cooper says that she is his cousin's niece." Another shrug. "Anyhow, the other brand inspector is named Dave Worrell. One of his cousins does genealogy for a hobby. We asked her to run the Cooper family tree based on Orran and Suhanna."

Emory now pushed the chili around in her bowl. "You know, when Suhanna came out here with Linda, she made a strange comment that stuck with me. Obviously, she saw Susan's grave and said that they had a Susan in their family, and that she lasted 'a lot longer than ours.' Well according to the genealogy, Susan didn't drown. She went over to the Coopers. Worse for us, they know that she was a Cross. Remember that threat that we found? They're trying to fight for the Lost Daughter. Again."

"You mean we have one of our own locked up in the hoosegow?" Monty asked, shocked.

"Who cares about that part," Emory commented, although he was right. In truth, the notion didn't sit right. But neither did the fact of their possible Cooper relationship.

Lance took a few spoonfuls, and the others followed suit. As the head of the family, whatever he decided carried the most weight.

In time, Lance stopped chewing, focusing on the salt and pepper shakers before lifting his eyes to everyone seated around the table. "Legally, everything is now registered to us. Hank took care of that once the land registry office arrived. They haven't got a leg to stand on. Susan was a weak link. Nothing more."

"Possibly," Emory resumed, "Orran Cooper claims they were robbed of a large spread worth a lot of money."

"OK," Hank turned steely eyes upon his daughter. "What do they own or have now?"

"Meaning can they afford to lawyer up?" She shook her head. "They don't appear to have much money. But the smart thing to do would be to run that title stuff."

"Linda already has all of that," he admitted.

Wouldn't that just be the case? "Ah. Linda. Did she give you a copy?"

Her father's voice remained gruff. "I told her to keep it."

"Well," Emory smiled a bit wolfishly. "Let's give her a call."

Lance Cross didn't appear to think much of that idea, but Emory had her own opinions on that matter. "It's either that or you're going to have to pay to have it done again. Don't worry, Dad. I'll do the talking."

"Hello, Linda? It's Emory."

A surprised voice came through. "Why, Emory! How are you, and where are you?"

"I'm at the Lost Daughter. A lot has happened."

"Is everything all right?"

A dry laughed escaped from her. "I suppose that's dependent upon how you take it. I know this request is coming out of nowhere, but when you and Dad worked on that grant filing, did you run titles on all the Lost Daughter acreage?"

"Of course I did. What are you asking?"

"We're kind of having a family meeting. I don't

suppose you feel like driving out here with that paper-work, and we'll explain it to you."

Breathless with a pulsing excitement that Emory felt, Linda gushed, "I'll be right there!"

With that, the preservationist hung up the phone.

It took every ounce of self-discipline Emory had not to burst into laughter at her father's expense.

Her father frowned. "Don't you say goodbye anymore?"

"I do. It's you and Linda who apparently don't. Anyhow, she's on her way..." Emory sang, and Monty let loose with his lone wolf howl.

"Settle down, you muttonchops," Lance commanded, not that it did much good.

Jace simply appeared bemused.

LINDA CAME TEARING down that old ranch road in nothing flat.

She all but sprinted to the house, papers in hand.

Emory opened the door for her. "Hi, Linda, it's good to see you."

Lance and Linda exchanged uncertain silences.

Slowly he rose to his feet, looking a bit sheepish. "Thank you for coming out here," he offered at length, stiff and formal.

"What's happened?" Linda panted, breathless.

Emory waited for Lance to start the account, but he nodded at her. Again, Emory ventured forth. "Suhanna McIlroy is sitting in the Stampede jail, charged with tres-passing here. We also found a threatening note that we believe she placed in one of the outbuildings. It turns out that she's one of *those Coopers*...the ones we have fought with over the years."

"What does that title insurance shit do?" Lance stood, clearly opposed to legal process and custom.

"It's not shit, Lance..." Linda began, but Emory jumped in, cutting her off.

"Linda will know far more about this than I do, but title insurance is so we can prove that all of the Lost Daughter is really ours."

Linda puffed up a bit, and her father semiglowered.

Emory turned to the preservationist. "You see, I ran into another relative of hers, and I have this strange notion that he might want to drag our title through the courts."

Her father veered toward less ornery. He said for Linda's benefit, "Emory's leaving one part out."

Emory backed up in her account, filling in the gaps. "You remember Dave Worrell from the funeral? His cousin does genealogy. And we've received a bit of a shock. We always believed that our Susan drowned back in the 1880s. It turns out that evidence points to the fact that she married one of the Coopers instead...and that makes Suhanna there a distant relative. If everyone's got everything right."

Linda's eyebrows shot up and she held out the title report to Lance. "The title is clear on what is listed here —I would guess the only thing to do is to check and verify whether you are missing any parcels. The cemetery plot has a lien..."

That notion still pleased her father. Emory squirmed, and Jace came across as perplexed. Monty blinked and nodded, as if a mortgaged family burial ground amounted to the most natural thing in the world. "Yeah, we needed money for the fine for the underreporting, right about the point that Emory began her new career."

"What was your old career?" Jace asked.

"Mavericker," her father responded in a flat way. Emory for her part, didn't find much to laugh about there.

Jace quirked is head in response.

"I'll explain it to you later," Emory replied, giving her father the stink eye.

Lance, however, had moved on to more important considerations as he scanned the title report.

"Where's the box canyon?" he asked.

Linda moved over to his side, peering at the paper intently. "What box canyon?"

Emory's heart did a funny little hitch.

"Here we go," her father muttered under his breath. He also scratched behind his left ear twice—their family signal to stop talking in front of outsiders.

Linda, oblivious to that detail, kept going. "I didn't know anything about a box canyon."

"Well," Lance said with a smile designed to scare the shit out of anyone, "we don't use it all that much."

43

THE WASTING DISEASE

1887

THE LOSS OF SUSAN GRIEVED POLLY MOST FIERCE, AND SHE never did return to her former self. She fell into a type of melancholy from which she couldn't or wouldn't drive away, not that she tried all that hard, truth be told. All conversations with Polly took the inevitable return to the drowning of Susan, "her lost girl." She became so convincing in her steadfast determination that Hank even second-guessed himself at times. Every now and again he found himself buying into his wife's account that Susan drowned, vanishing without a trace.

It grew obvious to all that the loss of Susan played upon her mind. In matters of domestic life, Polly slowed down and her internal fire dimmed.

More and more often, she required rest, and remarked upon vague pains of no specific origin.

"You need to eat more, your dress is just hanging off of you," Hank commented more than once.

"If Susan were here, I could eat," she would murmur.

But that didn't hold true, and deep down, they both

knew it. Those listless days turned into listless nights as the pain inside of her grew, and the scent of shit trailed in Polly's wake, no matter how hard she tried to keep herself clean.

Meanwhile, a few more settlers and families straggled into the area, giving wide berth to the Cross family and the Coopers, but to a lesser extent. In fullness of time, a general store took hold and flourished halfway the distance to the county seat, and not long thereafter, a blacksmith set up shop nearby. Before long the tentacles of civilization stretched back into the hinterland of Colorado and took root. And with each new arrival, and each new public addition, the possibility and probability of Susan emerging and the true account coming out, grew. Her defection might be interpreted as a weakness in Hank Cross's iron hold. Then again, it might scare people off even further.

Regardless, her mother withered away into a ghost of her former self.

Then came the day when Polly, aged thirty-seven, could not rise from her bed.

Hank, taciturn with worry, grew of shorter temper as he struggled to determine the best course of action. One late afternoon, Hank came in from the range to find Polly feverish and moaning.

He stepped outside of the soddy and let loose with a sharp penetrating whistle that split the air as sharp as a knife and carried.

One of his men jogged up. "Boss?"

"Find Henry and send him back to me, will you?"

The man answered with the jut of his chin. "He's in the upper pasture. I'll go fetch him."

The man saddled up and rode. Rode fast.

Hank sat down in the chair by his wife's side of the bed, doing his best to ignore the sweet scent of shit and her ravings and moans.

He held her hand for a while, until she turned away with her back toward him, pained by the weak light filtering in through the soddy's mica window.

A COUPLE OF HOURS LATER, judging by how the sun traveled in the sky, Henry and the hired man rode back in. Hank, upon hearing their horse's hooves, rose from his chair and went outside to intercept them.

"I'll need my horse saddled and brought up here," he told his man. "And take care of these two but bring me mine first. Henry, you come with me for a moment."

When the hired hand hastened out of earshot, Hank explained in a low voice, "Your mother has taken poorly. I fear this is near to the end, and that she will die before much longer."

The boy swallowed. "What do you want me to do, Pa?"

"First, I want you to go in there and tell her that you love her. When that is done, the second step is what I want to talk to you about. I'm going to ride over to the Coopers' spread to tell Susan that her mother is dying and asking for her."

Hank put his hand on his son's shoulder and shook him lightly. "If I don't come back, you're the man of this operation. Do you understand me?"

Wide-eyed, and trying not to shed tears, the ten-year-old boy answered dutifully. "Yes, Pa."

"And don't trust the men we have hired too much

because they are riders, gun handlers, and cowboys, but they are also paid killers. I planned it that way, but they'll turn on you if they sense an opportunity. Not Stuart and not Sorensen. You should be able to trust them, but you're going to have to make your own decisions even there. You'll have to trust your instincts, but you'll have to develop them first. But as to the rest of the men...use trust with a strong measure of caution. And never fail to pay them. No matter how tight money might become, you *always* have to pay them and pay them on time. Understood?"

"Maybe I should ride instead," Henry offered.

"You seem to be forgetting how we took their son hostage."

"No," Henry replied, doubt and fear grappling. "I remember. But Susan wouldn't let anything happen to me."

The boy had a point. Hank mulled that over. Still, he wasn't old enough to handle the ranch. Not the way it stood—armed to the teeth. "People can change with time, and I don't know how much I would bank on that."

"Not Susan," Henry claimed, feeling strong about it at first, then backing down a notch. "I think."

The man came with Hank's horse. "Give it to the boy," he instructed. "That is, if you want to ride him."

The boy's eyes lit up.

"Make sure you shorten those stirrups." He eyed the operation as his man took one side of the saddle and his son the other. "I'm sorry to place you in this position," Hank said at length.

"Maybe Susan shouldn't have run off like she did," Henry countered as he turned his father's horse toward down the path.

It stood to reason that Henry had a better chance of emerging unscathed. But it gnawed at Hank something fierce, the fact that Old Man Cooper had ridden into their outfit, brave and unarmed, while he sent his boy to do what could only be considered a man's task.

44

THE STICKING POINT

JUNE 2023

WHEN THE OTHERS CLEARED OUT FROM THE HOUSE— Linda driving home and the men returning to the bunkhouse—Lance Cross held his daughter back from wandering off as well.

"This is serious," he admitted.

"No shit, Dad. That's why I wanted to tell you alone and not throw this into a circus ring. Anyhow, thank goodness for Linda or we'd be in a whole lot more trouble."

"The title is the title is the title. Linda has nothing to do with us holding the title. She just did the legwork so that we can prove it."

Emory eyed him. "Now you're just being difficult, but true. Now, what is the story behind the box canyon? The *real* one."

"I don't know," Lance admitted. "That's the problem."

Emory narrowed her eyes. "You've been making the loan payments on the cemetery, haven't you?"

He seemed to find her question funny. "Yep. But I don't see what one has to do with the other."

"What if you try to get a loan on the box canyon. Wouldn't they pull title insurance?"

"I like the way you're thinking, but it didn't work like that the last time. On the cemetery I already had the title reports beforehand. *From Linda.* Back in the 1950s a loan got taken out. Linda pulled that all together for the state grant, but nothing came through on the box canyon."

"Did you notice it at the time?"

"Hell yeah, I did. What do you take me for? Anyhow, I didn't want to be poking around under that rock too much."

"Then that must mean you figured that the Coopers hold title to it." Emory watched him closely.

"Figured that they held the title? Not so much. Questioned it? You bet. So don't talk about this to anyone."

Emory sat down in one of the chairs and hinged forward, elbows resting on her thighs. "Running the title insurance shouldn't hurt...would it?"

"I don't honestly know. The more we bring attention to it..."

"Linda would know the answer to that," Emory sparred.

A fact which bothered her father. "She might." He sighed.

"Do you want me to ask her to do it, or at least ask her how we would do it ourselves?"

"I'll sleep on it," her father replied. "Last time she had title searches done. Now, enough of this legal shit. I think there might be a cowboy who's waiting up to talk to you."

Her heart gave a tug. But first things first, and the ranch always came first. "Do you even use the canyon?"

"That's not the point."

Of course it wasn't. "No, what I'm asking is how bad

will it be if we lose it? I don't think the Coopers could cause that many problems."

"I disagree," Lance Cross replied, dead set upon the matter. "It's in their blood. We don't want them among us back here. Hell, it took enough to get rid of them the first time. We sure don't need to do that again."

"Fine. But just so that I know, how much do you figure that box canyon is worth?" Emory asked.

"Well, happily, the jet-setting crowd won't want it, because except for during the spring runoff, it's pretty much of a dry wash with a small spring. Enough for a small amount of stock, but it'll turn brackish in the late summer if rain doesn't come."

"Maybe I'll go riding out there tomorrow to see for myself what we are talking about," Emory said. "Just to get the lay of the land for myself."

"Sure," Lance replied, "and I'll even go with you. But we're also going to go into town to talk to Bob and try to scare that Suhanna away, once and for all if we go about it right. Now, why don't you go hang out with people your own age and let me go to bed?"

Emory stepped outside onto the porch and drank in the stars.

The crisp night air and the deepest of velvet night skies set her heart and soul to longing.

Jace must have felt the same way, for across the yard the door to the bunkhouse opened. A fall of interior light radiated outward before he closed the door gently behind. It would take him a moment for his eyes to adjust, but Emory found him in the blue shadows, and she cautioned herself not to scare him off.

She must have come into focus for him about that same time. He took a few steps forward into the center of the yard, causing the sensor light to go off, shattering the romance of the night into harsh fragments of white light.

"I guess I make pretty good target practice about now." He sounded guilty.

She took his words to mean bad combat memories from Afghanistan. "Why don't you come stand over here, and we can view the night sky together," she called out in a low voice. "Target practice is for suckers."

"That it is," he sounded a bit sad at the notion, but walked over. "Stars and the night sky are so much better."

Then he put his arm around her, and she leaned in.

THE NEXT MORNING, Emory hummed as she pulled breakfast together. The standard family rule ran along the lines that whoever rose first started the coffee. Next, unless extenuating circumstances or a serious problem intruded, meat and eggs never went amiss. If people were up to eat the food on time...and they usually were. Otherwise, leftovers and microwaves were made for each other.

Her father heard her rustling around and joined her.

"Coffee ready?" he asked, coming into the kitchen.

"Can't you smell it?"

"I can. I was just gauging your mood."

"*My mood*. Jace is stable and true, if that's what you're asking, and none of this mess seems to bother him overly much. So, my mood is fine where all of that is concerned. My mood is not so fine about Suhanna and the box canyon. Did you come up with a plan?"

"Yup. Well, part of one."

She made a face at him. "Feel like sharing?"

He listened for footsteps on the porch. Silence. "We're going to see the sheriff and maybe Suhanna. Then we can stop by the box canyon. Beyond that, your guess is as good as mine."

"What needs to be done around here?"

"The regular for now—and Monty and Jace can handle it. That's the plan so far, unless we learn something different in town."

EMORY AND LANCE CROSS drove into town and parked right in front of the sheriff's office for the entire world of Stampede to see and take note.

"Are you sure you don't want to pull around back?" Emory asked.

"And what—let people think that we're hiding?" Lance answered, aware of the fundamental change in his approach to law enforcement as a whole.

Entering straight through the glass double doors, they walked by the empty receptionist desk, passed by the ever-present black-and-white photos where only the names and occupations changed, and headed back to Sheriff Preston's office.

Lance displayed the rare courtesy of knocking on the door jamb.

The sheriff had an angry red scratch on his cheek. More noticeable than that was his shocked expression when he figured out the source of the knock.

"Well, hell." He rose to his feet and came out from behind his desk. "Now what's happened?"

Lance stuck out his hand, and they shook as Emory waited behind. The sheriff's eyes traveled over to her.

"Come on in and take a seat if you want." He moved

back behind his desk. "Nice to see you, Em. Staying long this time?"

"I don't think so," she replied, claiming a chair.

Remarkably, her father moved deeper into the interior of the 1960s nondescript office. Joining her he took off his hat, claimed a seat, and set his weathered Stetson on his knee.

"What's the status of that McIlroy woman?"

"She'll be staying here this weekend. At least."

"I want her to leave town and to stay away from Stampede, Bob."

Emory held her tongue, waiting to find out just how much her father would divulge.

Preston's gaze didn't waver. "Some of that falls beyond my control."

"Emory's found out some disturbing news that complicates matters," her father offered.

"Oh?" The sheriff's eyes traveled over to Emory.

Since her father did not appear inclined to explain further, Emory waded in. "Can this be off the record and held in the strictest of confidences?"

"That depends upon what you are going to tell me. If it involves a crime, the answer, frankly, is 'no.'"

"No crime," Emory claimed. At least nothing recent. "We think she's a distant relative. As a result, we also believe that her presence here is not a coincidence. This all stems back to the late 1880s, but we think they plan on coming after the Lost Daughter one way or another."

"So, the Old West rides again. Is that it?"

"Why not," Lance replied, but it wasn't a question. "We'd like to see her if we can. Once we get an idea of what you think might happen."

"What I think will happen is that the law will take its course. The bond will likely be six thousand dollars, but it may go up. I guess learning whether or not they can come up with that amount will let you know a bit more about their wherewithal. I figure, based upon her priors, that she'd skip out of state."

"Then you try to arrest her again?"

"Sure, if the authorities there catch her. Dependent upon whether they have anything on her in Arizona, they will either retain or extradite her."

"Has she lawyered up?"

"Public defender. But let me tell you what. She resisted arrest which wasn't a smart thing to do, no siree. How do you think I got this?" He pointed to the scratch. "Now that was not a smart thing to do...and I've got a few bruises to show for it. I took a picture of everything, just in case."

"Wildcat, huh?" Her father chuckled.

"One that's none too bright," the sheriff replied. "That should be up to a hundred and twenty days right there, and seven hundred fifty dollars."

"Then how do you figure she'll skip if she gets bail?"

"I'm playing devil's advocate. Look at the size of her and look at the size of me. The judge will likely go easy on her, but I can drag out the proceedings a bit if you like. Do you need time?"

All of them turned various scenarios over in their minds. "Did you find any weapons on her?" Emory asked. "Anything menacing?"

"Carrots," the sheriff replied.

Emory reared back a bit with that one. "To lure the horses. Do you still have them?"

"I'm one step ahead of you. I already sent them to the lab for processing. Just to make sure there's nothing to them."

"You're thinking poison?" Lance asked, unconcerned which answered.

"It's best not to take chances, but this is a strange one," the sheriff replied. "So that's why I guess I'd ask the reason why you want to talk with her. Yes, I can grant you supervised access, but that might muck up the water. Unless you have a real reason not to, I'd allow the law to take its course. That is, unless you're keeping something hidden from me."

Lance inhaled, debating how much to disclose. "Hell, since you've been on the level with me, I'll be on the level with you. Our box canyon is up for debate. I don't know why, but it didn't come back on the title report Linda Paulson ran. I never thought nothing of it, until we found a threatening note from Goldilocks back there."

"Threatening note?"

Lance fished around in his back pocket and pulled out his billfold. He rifled through the contents and extracted the note. "Here. It don't look like much, but it's notable."

"Yes, indeed. We'll take that as evidence." Preston pulled out an evidence bag from one of his drawers.

Lance dropped it in. "Hell, I've seen worse. That ain't nothin'."

"Doesn't matter," the sheriff replied.

"I planned on giving her a scare when we found this here," Lance admitted, much to Emory's initial shock.

"I'd think we'd best leave it now," Emory cut in.

"I'd listen to your daughter, Lance," the sheriff replied. "Let justice run its course, and if you're asking for advice, I'd tell you to get that title run, no matter the outcome. You likely hold squatter's right in worst case, but you'd want to get that all cleaned up, and cleaned up soon. Likely, if you haven't been paying all along, you'll owe plenty of back taxes. Do you go out there every year?"

Emory felt her father's reserve return and return strong. "I'd rather not answer that question. But we're headed out there today."

The sheriff nodded. "Let me know if you find anything that I ought to know about. I want your word on that, Lance."

The rancher held out his hand.

45

LIES TAKEN TO THE GRAVE

1887

AT THIRTY-SEVEN YEARS OLD, ADELE "POLLY" CROSS approached death.

The wasting disease had laid her low, and life out in the scrap and sage hadn't come easy. It never came easy.

Henry rode in the direction of the Coopers' and forded the river in the same exact location where Susan once crossed. The water ran lower this time around. Splashing through in the late summer, the water didn't run more than twelve inches high.

Henry judged the depth and the speed—figuring that it wouldn't be the water that did him in, but a bullet instead.

Riding at a fast pace and on account that he was a lone rider, he slowed when their outfit came into view. A far better house than their soddy, the Coopers' homestead boasted a white clapboard construction, it even had green painted trim that showed care and pride. Obvious even to the boy, it put their old soddy to shame.

He rode up to the door at a walk, and waited atop his horse until someone came out to meet him.

Victor Cooper himself stepped out onto the porch.

"I'm Henry Cross," he explained.

"You know, boy," the old man said, "I have two guns trained on you that can take you down at any time. What do you want here?"

Henry thought a curtain twitched in one of the upstairs windows. Real glass windows.

"I'm here looking for Susan, sir. Our ma is dying, and I've been sent to let her know as much."

The old man appraised him without sympathy, but he seemed to weigh the rights and the wrongs of the situation. "I don't know that she can travel if that's what you're asking. You'd have to ask her yourself, but she's in the family way and her time is near."

"May I dismount?"

"If you're so inclined."

The old man didn't leave the porch but shouted back through the screen door. "Ma! Susan's brother, Henry, is here."

His sister didn't come quickly, and the man just kept staring at him, watching his every move.

In time, it sounded as if someone approached with slow, ponderous steps. Susan emerged through the door, stomach leading the way.

Henry had to swallow a couple of times to keep from bursting into tears.

"It's Ma." He completely forgot the old man's presence. "If you want to see her before she dies, you've got to come and come now."

Susan pressed her lips together as if she might burst into tears as well, but slowly shook her head.

"I trust you, Henry. I always have. But I can't return home." She cast her glance over to the old man who showed no signs of moving. "I've built a life for myself here, and you can see the way it is with me."

"Can't they hitch a wagon for you?" Henry asked, near pleading.

She turned to the old man. "Do you mind if I have a word in private with my brother? He has nothing to do with any of this. As you can see, he's just a boy."

The old man softened a bit, holding an obvious soft spot for her. "If you like."

Susan made her way down the three porch steps, heavy and lumbering. She crossed over to her brother. She didn't hug him but grabbed his forearm instead. "I had to make a choice when I came here, a choice you might not understand. But it was either remain a Cross or become a Cooper. There is no point in between. That's the reason why I can't go with you. I've made my bed and will soon be in it delivering this baby. Tell Ma that I think of her every day, but I've carved my own path, like she did herself."

Henry nodded, feeling miserable.

"Now you'd best turn back while their hospitality holds." Susan gave him a quick hug before moving away.

"Are they treating you good? She'll want to know," he called out after her.

Facing the patriarch, she paused on the middle stair. Slowly and with effort, she turned to face Henry once she'd reached the top of the stairs. "Yes, Henry. They're treating me just fine."

HENRY RETURNED HOME at a near gallop, empty-handed and uncertain. Uncertain whether to tell the strict truth, or make the account something closer to what his mother would want to hear.

Hank Cross, hearing the horse's hooves, met him outside the soddy.

"Did you see her?" he asked.

"She's having a baby, and it looks like any day now," Henry replied. "She couldn't come."

"You told her that her ma is asking for her as she lays dying, correct?"

"Yes, sir. She said she had to make a choice as to where she belonged."

"And she chose them."

"Yes, sir…but maybe she had to." Hank Cross turned to walk away, disgusted. "But, Pa?"

His son's voice stopped him.

"She said to tell Ma that she thinks about her every day. She did. Honest."

And that would have to do.

POLLY'S thin and waxy parchment skin stretched over her bones scared the boy something fierce. But he sidled toward the bed as his father had told him to do.

"Ma?" he whispered.

Her eyes opened.

"I saw Susan. She's expecting a baby any time now and couldn't come. She said to tell you that she thinks of you every day."

With that, Polly closed her eyes, her clawlike fingers clutching the blanket. "Are they holding her hostage?"

"No, I don't think so. Their house is real nice with glass windows and all."

"Susan always got her head turned." With that, Polly fell silent.

And that marked the last time Susan's name was ever mentioned around Polly.

———

ADELE "POLLY" Cross died on a cold summer's day. The kind that came in the higher ranges that allowed summer snows. One morning, weighing next to nothing at all, the matriarch made of flint crumbled and died.

They carried her to the hill not far from the soddy and faced her body west toward the setting of the sun. No eastern promise for them, for the East meant a retreat from the West, and the West was where they would remain. If they ever turned eastward, it would mean that they had failed. And if there was one thing they never planned to do, it was to fail.

Polly's final resting place was dignified with a marker —and against the mother's wishes, so was Susan's. They marked them both with the same death year: 1887. For that proved the year she died to them, having drowned while crossing a river.

46

SHIFTING GROUND AND THERE AIN'T MUCH TO THAT

JUNE 2023

THE TRIP TO THE BOX CANYON TRAVERSED LAND SELDOM seen by most, and for once, that included Emory and her father. The canyon's hidden entrance, located about a third of the way up from the valley floor between two low hills, would be hard to find unless a person had an idea where to search. True, a few telltale cottonwoods punctuated the gap, but still. The trees rooted and grew where no one would take much notice unless for a particular reason, and that amounted to a fair part of the beauty concerning their hidden box canyon.

Of course, that box canyon which served a much greater purpose back in the settlement days when livestock possession ruled over the land.

Father and daughter trailered in their horses Kai and Draco, below the mouth of the canyon, where they parked the pickup in a turnout and unloaded their mounts, already saddled and ready to ride. They didn't mount up before retrieving their rifles and stowed them in their saddle scabbards, because one just never knew.

"Is there even a way to ride here from the house?"

Emory asked, scanning the rugged terrain, noting the scree slides and dense brush alongside the stream.

"Yeah, but you go through BLM land, and maybe cross over part of another spread. Frankly, with the ungated fences, you can easily end up riding more than it's worth. It's easier to trailer in the mounts and take it from there. In the old days without the fences, it was a different story."

Their turnout, located along an old seldom-used wagon track, appeared as a delineation between the centuries. The road itself had morphed into a county road that no one bothered, adding to the impression— whether true or not—that they abandoned the twenty-first century and headed back into the nineteenth. The canyon, guarded by a trickling stream feeding dense coyote willows, appeared nearly impenetrable, and should any modern passerby be curious enough to venture farther back, they'd have to fight with the bushes to get there.

As would the Crosses.

"Gosh, I haven't been here in years," Emory commented, looking around for tire tracks or other signs of people. "How do you suppose anyone ever found this in the first place?"

"They were on the lookout for this type of thing, especially if they needed a natural pen. Here are other tire tracks in this pullout beside ours...but no foot-prints," Lance commented. "Of course, it rained pretty good the other night."

"Bad timing. Still, it doesn't seem like a spot that many would go looking for. Not in this day and age."

She left unsaid what they both thought—*except for the Coopers.*

"True," her father agreed, turning Draco through the

scrub brush toward the willows and the stream. "It should open up once we get a stretch farther up the stream."

Lance pointed Draco into the water, walking the horse upstream against the slight current. Emory gave them a ten-yard head start before she and Kai waded in to follow. Judging the depth of the flowing water, their discovery trip, if taken earlier in the season, would prove a whole lot more difficult in the high spring runoff. But for now, the water ran a manageable nine inches or so deep.

A quarter of a mile in, the stream bed widened, allowing the willows and brush to give way, and the canyon fanned out before them, dry beyond the immediate streambanks. Boxed in by steep cliff walls and displaying the darker gray of a different geological footprint, the outcroppings retained the area's characteristic vertical cleft-rock formations. Both father and daughter took the measure at the top of the flats, land ringing around the hidden canyon like a lasso. True, places to take cover existed, but the standard rule always remained—chances were whoever controlled the high ground controlled the outcome.

"And the land at the top of the formations?" Emory asked.

"Probably old Cooper land, but then again, who knows then, and who knows now. Hell, for all I know, it might now belong to the BLM. No telling without a map and research."

A decrepit old log structure stood off to the side, with a few fence posts standing upright marking the remnants of an old stock pen. "That might be an old mustanger's cabin over there." Emory pointed to the structure, the roof long since caved in. An old, rusted stove listed, for some reason, outside in what might have once been their yard.

Together they rode over to the structure, gazing at it from their saddles.

"There might be footsteps," Emory said, walking Kai and peering down at the ground with intent. "There's a print. But no horseshoes or hooves to speak of. Small size. Probably a woman's."

"Looks like."

"Hikers?" Emory asked, but the question lacked merit and they both knew it. In her own way, she figured that she at least tried to be fair.

"Possibly, but that looks like a sneaker to me."

Again, both Crosses scanned their surroundings, shifting in their saddles.

"There isn't much to this unless dry washes are your thing. That, or you needed it to pen up horses or cattle. Still, easier said than done," Emory replied.

"Or you needed a place to hole up where you wouldn't be seen."

Of course, her father's words held the ring of unvarnished truth. Emory surveyed the ground. "Someone could come back here, if they really wanted to, but they would have to know enough to enter by wading in through the river or by repelling down from on top."

"Yes," Lance agreed. "And unless they are a random hermit wandering loose in search of a lair, it's probably something to do with our old friends."

HORSES RETRAILERED, the Crosses pulled out and headed back to the Lost Daughter.

"It seems to me that we are going about this the hard way," Emory said.

Her father side-eyed her.

"Now we're going back into town to get the title insurance," she complained. "We could have done that while we were there this morning. We both know that we were going to need that all along. Why can't you just call and give whoever your credit card number?"

"Because," he uttered the single word drawn out and slow. "I want to talk to that Suhanna…"

"*Dad.*"

"Don't Dad me nothin', and it's not what you think."

"Uh-huh." Emory stuck her boot square on the dashboard. Unlike Terry, her father said nothing. In all likelihood, he didn't even notice or care.

"Well, guess what? I'm coming with you," Emory announced, "so don't try to drop me off at home."

Lance Cross chuckled. "Wouldn't have it any other way."

"SHOULDN'T we call first to make sure we can see her?" Emory asked as they reached the outskirts of Stampede.

"No," her father answered decisively. "After all that talk about letting the law run its course, all we'd be doing is setting ourselves up for an argument."

"I'm with Sheriff Preston on this one."

Mind made up, her father didn't respond at all. He kept on driving.

Of course, as if to make a statement to both her and anyone else who might have cared within the larger populace, he pulled up right in front of the building's entrance as they did before. His statement being, this time around, the *Crosses are working with the law*. Of course—there was a caveat—they'd work with the law if it went their way.

Entering the building, this time the receptionist with the mile-high bouffant manned the desk.

"Hi there," Emory began. "I met you a couple of years ago, but I seem to have misplaced your name."

"I know you," the woman replied all snappy and bright. "You're Emory Cross. Bob takes great pride in you. I'm Louise Burney."

Emory leaned on the counter. "Nice to see you again, Louise. Say, we were already in here this morning but hoped we could bother Sheriff Preston one more time."

Louise, facing in that direction, looked past them and out into the parking lot. "You're in luck. He just drove up."

Sure enough, the sheriff made his way into the building—clearly surprised to see them again. "Did we miss something earlier?"

Lance stuck his hands in his back pocket. "I decided that I really want to talk to Suhanna, advisable or not."

"Shit," the sheriff replied, then turned to the woman. "Excuse my language, Louise."

"I've heard it before," she replied.

Father and daughter sat in the waiting room of the green Naugahyde chairs and fishing magazines while the sheriff went back to the holding cell. It took a while, but he eventually returned to retrieve them.

"That took a bit of convincing," Sheriff Preston told them. "She is within her rights not to talk to you, but boredom won out, sitting back in the cell alone. You might want to go easy on her."

Lance stretched as he rose to stand. "Sure."

Emory wondered what that fake lack of concern meant.

Nevertheless, they followed the sheriff down the hall into an interview room.

"I'm sure that you both understand that I'll have to stay with you at all times," the sheriff said.

"What if she asks you to leave?" Lance countered.

Bob Preston knitted his eyebrows together at that one. "We'll cross that bridge if we come to it, and the answer is still probably 'no.'"

Inside the room a handcuffed and sullen Suhanna McIlroy waited, seated.

She glared as they all filed in. Emory and her father took a seat, while the sheriff stood, his backside blocking the door.

"What do you want?" Suhanna demanded in a nasty voice.

Emory wondered that herself.

"Are they treating you OK?" Lance asked.

"What's it to you?" she countered.

Right. What was it to them?

"Nothing much," he responded, stretching out and taking up more space in that small room. "What if I told you that I sympathize somewhat with your position."

"I'd say you played me for a fool."

"No. Not at all. You've just picked up a fight that's lasted over a century, and I'd say the one who is being played is you."

Her eyes flashed, but she didn't disagree.

"What I don't understand," Lance continued, "is the 'why and what' you expect to gain from all of this. Someone is going to end up hurt in all of this, and that person could easily be you."

"Lance..." the sheriff cautioned.

"Don't misunderstand me," her father said, pulling himself together and leaning forward, staring into Suhanna's eyes. "Is someone making you do all of this? It seems an elaborate charade from where I'm sitting. Emory, tell her what you know."

The woman's eyes darted, uncertain and a few degrees less hostile.

"Suhanna, I met—I forget the exact relationship— your relative Orran Cooper. In fact, I've been up to his house to speak to him."

Suhanna grew very wary around the eyes. "You didn't go up there alone, did you?"

That question took Emory back. "No, I went with another brand inspector."

The woman tilted her head, a small enough movement that conveyed a lot. With a flash of insight, the realization hit Emory that the Arizonan might fear none other than Orran Cooper himself.

"Anyhow," Em continued, undecided and undeterred whether she cared about the woman's potential fear or not. "He said you fought on the side of right *but* he looked a whole lot less certain when we told him that his car's tags are expired. Not to mention that fines and tickets were likely coming his way. I came away with the feeling that he expected you to pay for those."

"That bastard! Why in the hell would I pay for his expired tags?"

Emory shook her head. "Why are you driving his car? But that's not really our concern here. What does he want, and what do you want? Maybe we should all just put our cards on the table."

Both her father and the sheriff listened, intent.

Suhanna weakened. "Well, I'm not going to pay his damned fines."

"I don't blame you," Emory agreed. "You could just take his car back to him when you get out."

Everyone in that small interview room felt the Arizonan's rising discomfort and saw her blanch. "Um, I'd rather not do that. I think I'd just leave the car here and go back to Arizona where I belong and leave this Colorado shit behind."

"Do you need help?" Lance Cross asked, puzzled for certain, but displaying a genuine concern.

Suhanna heard the concern as well and responded on a dime. Predictably her eyes teared up. "He's crazy—batshit crazy and for one, I'm sorry I got pulled into all of this."

"Pulled into what?" Emory, halfway toward feeling sorry for the blonde, stayed on her guard. Especially when she noticed the men turning a shade too sympathetic to whatever tale Suhanna prepared to unfurl.

"Righting past wrongs, reclaiming what is rightfully ours. Returning in glory. That type of shit. Not to mention all the money it would be worth. I sold my damn trailer down in Arizona to help pull this off."

Well, that explained where the booze money came from.

Both men pulled back a little.

Emory tried, somewhat, to appear sympathetic. "What's the deal with the boot hook?"

"That belonged to Susan," Suhanna explained. "I've always felt that she willed me along when I carry that with me. Then that dumb Linda picked it up. I'd like that back, by the way."

Her father most surely stiffened at the criticism flung at Linda.

The realization that Suhanna might communicate with family members the same as she herself did didn't sit well with Emory. She shuddered at what, on the surface, appeared a shared family trait.

Suhanna felt the sentiment in the room turning against her and tried to tamp that hostility down. It didn't exactly work.

"I meant," she muttered, "when I get out of here."

Lance chuckled, still pissed by her crack about Linda. "That might be a while."

"I didn't do anything wrong," the blonde wheedled.

"Yes, you did." Emory countered. "What about the threat?"

"That? That's just a silly note. Orran said to put it somewhere. According to what he knows, that's the same threat we used back in the day. He wanted to know if you'd be able to identify it. Kind of like a game."

"Whatever," Emory sang, leaning back in her chair. "The trespassing on agricultural land is what will most likely do you in."

"Well, folks," Sheriff Preston broke in, sensing the turning tide of civility. "Is there anything more you have to say before I take her back?"

Emory and Lance exchanged glances with a shrug.

"You ain't getting any part of the Lost Daughter, and that's the final word," Lance said.

Sheriff Preston helped the prisoner to her feet.

"You haven't dealt with Orran yet," she threatened with conviction. Without ceremony, the sheriff pulled her through the door.

47

AFTER THE AMBUSH

1889 (TWO YEARS LATER)

HANK CROSS WONDERED IF OLD MAN COOPER WOULD come riding in himself, like he did before, or whether he considered himself too damn old for such heroics. He thought he heard a muffled sob from the root cellar, but that didn't much matter to him.

In time, a sharp cutting whistle came from his look-out, meaning a rider approached.

Hank Cross stood in the middle of his yard and waited.

He'd be damned, but it was none other than the patri-arch again.

"I want my boy," he said, drawing to a stop. "I've left instructions with my men that if you've castrated him, you'll pay. It doesn't matter if it takes every last red penny that I own, you'll swing for it. And," he offered with a nasty sneer, "how do you think your daughter, Susan, would take the news?"

"You leave Susan out of it." Hank spat in the dirt. "She's birthing your lot's babies and she's not involved in any of this."

He called over to one of his men. "Get the boy out of there so his father can get a good look at him."

Two of his men pulled the young man out of the darkness and into the light. Dried blood streaked his face, and bruises formed.

"Are you whole, boy?"

"Yeah," he said sullenly. His white shirt turned a dirt gray—blood streaks turned dark to a reddish brown.

His father eyed him. Eyed Cross. "What do you want? You killed three of my men, and wounded another who made it back."

"You didn't stick to your part of the bargain we made the last time around. I found this whelp helping himself to some of my cattle, branded with my brand. We had agreed to knock that shit off, if you recalled."

"Is that true, boy?"

He shuffled and kept silent.

"Answer me," his father's voice cut across the distance. Harsh. Unyielding.

"Yes."

"There you have it then. From his own mouth. Now the question becomes, how are you going to make this right?"

"Like I asked before. What do you want?"

"If you wanted to know the truth, I want you and your family gone. I don't ever want to hear your flea-bitten name again, but I'll settle for the box canyon. Written out on paper and legal. I heard that you filed for it a couple of years back. Well, I want it signed over."

"And if I tell you no?"

"Well then. The first bullet goes through your boy, and the second goes through you." He called over his shoulder. "Men!"

The sound of hammers cocking from various locations around the compound carried.

"What'll it be?" Hank pressed.

"I'll sign," he said. "And I hope you rot in hell."

GREEN SKY MEANS ONE HELL OF A STORM IS COMING

JUNE 2023

"Well, hell," Lance Cross said, long legging it back out to the pickup. "All of this shit for a sand wash canyon. Not to mention that she's drinking up her trailer money."

Emory ignored it. "Anyhow, we need that lab result from the carrots. Are we dealing with that title report now?"

"Might as well since we're here. Linda told us we go to the Rimrock Clerk and Recorder's Office for that. Apparently, record of that box canyon is too old to be found anywhere else."

They pulled up in front of that office and hopped out.

Not a damn thing transpired inside, so they had the clerk's full and undivided attention, for better or for worse.

"Howdy, Lance," the clerk greeted them, wary about the eyes.

Obviously, he and this woman knew each other.

He spoke for Emory's benefit. "Glenda here helped me with the cemetery loan."

Now she understood the woman's hesitation and nodded her greeting or sympathy.

"This time," her father said, walking up and leaning on the counter like he owned the place, "we need to find what there is on the box canyon off of county road twenty-eight."

The woman's eyes narrowed. "You'd have to point that out for me."

Underneath a protective hard plastic sheet, on the counter a mounted large county map waited for just the occasion.

"Here." He tapped at the location, the first joint in his index finger crooked with hard work and the beginnings of arthritis.

However doubtful, she wrote down whatever coordinates she needed. "This is going to take a bit. *If* we have anything, it'll be in the old records in the basement. You might as well go get yourself a beer, or a cup of coffee."

"I appreciate it, Glenda."

"It's all full of dust and spiders," she muttered.

Truthfully, Lance could have cared less, but he tried to convey sympathy, and he almost succeeded. He turned to Emory. "How about you let your old man buy you a beer—and Glenda, can I bring you back one?"

The woman's ringing laugh had a lovely bell-like quality to it. "No drinking on the job," she replied, "but I might just take you up on that later."

THE ACE HIGH, the broad daylight version, offered a completely different experience than its nighttime version. Bent old men lamenting the state of the nation lingered over whiskey with beer shooters to young men with nary a job prospect in sight. The thin old lady with the beehive hairdo shellacked in place sat at one end of the bar smoking a cigarette despite the "no smoking laws" and nursing a cocktail.

Emory lifted her eyebrows in that woman's direction.

"Leave 'er be," Lance Cross said. "Are you carrying?"

That got Emory's attention right quick. "No. Should I be?"

"Don't know. I kind of feel a fight coming on," Lance said, just as an older man came around the corner behind the bar. "Hi, Henry."

"Hey, Lance. I haven't seen you in ages. Where've you been?"

"Working out at the ranch and keeping on the straight and narrow. I'll have one of them nonalcoholic beers, and Emory, what would you like?"

"Diet Coke, please."

"It's flat," the old man said, completely unconcerned.

"Coors Light, then."

The man nodded his approval. "You can never go wrong with a bottle."

Meanwhile, Lance tipped his hat to the beehive at the end of the bar who nodded back, blinking her false eyelashes in some weird replica of a 1968 seduction movie move.

"What are you flirting with her for?" Emory muttered the accusation under her breath.

"You'll see," he replied, then louder. "Now, why don't we sit at the bar and be sociable. Henry? How is everything in your world?"

"Nothing much changes in here, as you can see for yourself. I just work the day shift to keep up with what's current. The night shift's getting too late for these old bones."

Lance nodded. "I hear you. What is the word around town?"

"That ex-ranch hand of yours, Cade Timmons, has got a new baby. But if you ask me, he's getting himself into trouble. He's gone a lot, that's for sure. Cade Timmons and fatherhood don't strike me as a natural pair."

Her father just offered a soundless chuckle and a slow, hanging wag of his head. Emory's stomach turned a bit cold, as her cell mercifully rang and gave her something specific to do.

Sheriff Preston. "Hello?"

"Hi, Emory. I didn't know whether to call you or your dad. The phone record's come in, and Suhanna's one call went to a number belonging to Orran Cooper."

"You don't say. Don't suppose you have the lab reports back, do you?"

"Nope. It'll take a few days."

"I'll let Dad know. We're at the Ace High..." She turned her back away from the patrons and lowered her voice. "...waiting for the county clerk."

"Let me know what you find out. Is your dad drinking again?"

"No. O'Doul's or whatever in the hell they call it. I am having a Coors Light. Don't worry, I can still shoot straight."

"Not funny, Em."

"I'm just pulling your leg," she replied. But she truly wasn't.

TURNING BACK TO HER FATHER, she held up her phone in

a way that let him know that she needed to tell him about the call.

"Just a minute, Henry," he said, turning to his daughter.

She whispered into his ear. "So much bullshit. Suhanna called Orran for her one call."

He called over at the bartender. "Say, haven't run across that lady from Arizona—Suhanna...Suhanna..."

"McIlroy," the bartender provided. "Don't tell me that she's got her hooks into you too. Anyhow, my revenue's going to take a hit when she leaves town."

"Monty was interested in her or something."

"Oh? Don't know about that. Old dogs and new tricks, I guess."

"Right." Lance acted as if he agreed. "What's she doing here, anyhow?"

"No idea, but she's not staying at a guest ranch. She's gotta get bored, sooner or later. Let's face it, there's not all that much to do here, unless she's big into fishing."

"Doubtful," Lance replied, then turned to Emory. "Are you about ready?"

"Sure." As the pair of them prepared to leave, the beehive at the end of the bar spoke in a raspy voice, rough from too many cigarettes.

"She feels her family has a claim to the area. Failing that, she's hoping to marry for money. Her words, not mine." The woman took a drag off her cigarette and exhaled, the smoke hanging in a cloud in front of her. "Probably it's all a load of bull. But get this. If she figures out how to get what she feels she's owed, she must pay half to some uncle of hers. I wonder why that would ever be. Families and legacies get complicated, I guess."

Emory and Lance locked eyes.

"Why, thank you for letting us know. The Lost Daughter isn't on the market."

The beehive took a drag off her cigarette and offered a sage-like nod.

———

BACK AT THE county clerk's office, Glenda met them with a shake of her head. "I'm sorry, but I didn't find anything about that title at all."

"Now what?" Emory sighed to either her father or the clerk, it really didn't matter which.

The woman didn't appear overly concerned. Then again, she probably dealt with matters like this, if not every day, every week. "Well, you say that you believe you own it, correct?"

"Correct," Lance replied without the trace of a doubt.

"But you haven't paid taxes on it?"

Lance shook his head. "That I don't know. I just pay the bill when it comes. That's the assessor's office, right?"

"Yes." The woman removed a binder from a shelf filled with them of different shapes and sizes and flicked through a couple of pages. "You could pursue squatter's rights by staying out there, or somehow occupying the land. Or you could pursue something called a quiet title. Here is says, 'A quiet title can be pursued by anyone holding a legitimate stake in the property. Sometimes there are multigenerational issues where title is not clear.'"

"Yeah." Hank sounded relieved. "I think that's what we're talking about here."

She nodded—a slow, thoughtful nod. "You didn't hear it from me, but if someone was to stay out there camping, or you built an improvement like a stock tank for example, *and* you filed the quiet claim, I'd say you'd have a jump on the situation."

Emory thought back to the Lost Daughter. "You know, Dad, there is an old ledger I found poking around in the soddy. Maybe we'd best go locate it and take another look."

"Fine," he replied, although his mind ventured elsewhere. "So how do I go about the quiet title, and how much would it cost?"

"It says here that a complex quiet title to remedy multiple defects, meaning it wasn't deeded or recorded correctly, at multiple generations might exceed five thousand dollars in costs, even if no one contests it. You'd need a property lawyer it seems."

"Shit. I don't like dealing with lawyers."

Most certainly he didn't like the cash outlay. "You've never dealt with a lawyer," Emory corrected.

"And I know I won't like it," he replied testily, then turned his attention back to the clerk. "Now, what happens if it turns out to be contested?"

"I'm sure the costs would go up from there."

"Wonderful." Lance tipped his hat, concluding the conversation.

For the moment.

BACK AT THE LOST DAUGHTER, Jace jogged up to the pickup when they pulled in.

"How'd everything go?"

"Strange," Emory answered. "We saw Suhanna—who had us all going, by the way—but then Sheriff Preston called a bit later and said that she made her one call, and that call was to Orran Cooper, the owner of the car she's driving."

"Warning him?"

Lance shook his head, uncertain. "Maybe she's looking for reinforcements."

Emory physically turned to stare at him. "You know, Dad, for a man who thought she was pretty cute, you sure seem to take a dim view of her now."

He found that funny. "I just wanted to see if I could get you going."

"Uh-huh."

"Anyhow, where'd you say you found that ledger?"

"In the soddy. I put it off to the side for a later date."

Her father hefted himself from the pickup truck. "I guess that date is now. And Jace? How do you feel about camping and packing in supplies to build a stock tank?"

"Fine," he replied.

"Before you agree to anything," Emory cautioned, "let's see what we can figure out here. Besides, it might not be safe."

"Hell, little girl, life ain't safe," her father lectured, heading toward the old soddy bunkhouse.

———

THE THREE OF them walked up to the soddy, the door stuck again, and her father gave it one hell of a whack with his kick. "If we're going to keep coming out back here, we might as well fix that door."

"And put a lock on it. Anymore we're getting too much traffic back here, and there're things in here that we don't want anyone messing with."

"Yeah," Jace admitted. "I told Em I'd fix it, but just haven't made it that far."

"Welcome to the club," her father lamented. "Emory never forgets a damn thing along those lines."

Monty, at that point, stood in the doorway. "What is this, a convention?"

"We're looking for a ledger I found a couple of weeks ago." Emory moved around the castoffs to the old desk where the ledger lay face down. "Here it is."

She picked it up and flicked through the pages and pulled out one of the loose sheets stuck inside. "This is what I wanted you to see."

She held it out for her father.

"Want to ride back into town?" Her father joked, but he really wasn't kidding. "Why don't the two of you have lunch in town after you show this to Glenda. Now, everyone get your phones and take a picture of this. I don't *ever* want to hear that that slip went missing and with it any proof in our favor."

"Do you want me to go back to the clerk's office and start that quiet transfer deed?"

"Not yet," he cautioned. "No sense on paying out money that might not need to be paid unless it is for the lower price. Still, I've got one thousand five hundred or two thousand dollars so that this doesn't follow you around for the next fifty years."

He thought about it. "You might as well stop back in. When you do, ask Glenda if you need to give this paper to Bob to be entered into evidence."

49

PICKUP CONFESSIONS

JUNE 2023

"JACE, DO YOU WANT TO DRIVE?"

Lance Cross heard his daughter's question and smothered a smile as he hustled away.

Jace, not noticing anything amiss at all provided the standard answer, "Sure, no problem," and headed for his truck.

Emory, for her part, bit back a smile as she congratulated herself on letting Jace take the lead. Of course, she was perfectly able to drive...but that wasn't the point. She climbed into the passenger's side, and he claimed the driver's seat. She couldn't help but admire his profile and his groomed beard.

He glanced over at her and caught her staring. "What?"

"Nothing," Emory replied, sinking down a little into the seat and looking out the side window, so that he wouldn't catch her smile.

"I've got a question for you."

"What's that?"

"Since I've been around, there's been basically the

threat of a range war sparking off, I've learned that you killed a man—"

"In self-defense," she interrupted.

"That Monty has warrants out for him, but under different names and your father makes slow-elk jokes. You started out as a mavericker, a historical preservationist is heartbroken over your father, and you talk to ghosts." He paused.

"I didn't hear the question."

He glanced at her while trying to keep his eyes on the road.

"That was more of a statement," Emory murmured.

"Is that how things go around here as a rule?"

"Pretty much." She felt she had to come up with something to add a positive spin. "Anyhow, you're leaving one part out. I have a whale of a scar on my leg, so there goes my modeling career."

He titled his head and did his best not to laugh. "Shoot. I'll keep that in mind."

"Seriously, there's less drama if people leave us alone." She thumped her hand on her thigh. "Wanna turn on the radio?"

He caught her actions and considered her words. "Not really, we're talking."

Emory, uncomfortable, pressed ahead. "Now it's my turn to ask you a question. What do you think about all of what you've just said?"

"That's your question?"

"That's my question." She refused to embellish.

Jace rubbed his jawline as he thought. "OK. I feel *OK* about all of that."

She looked at him through narrowed eyes. "Are you sure?"

"Yeah." He nodded, gripping the steering wheel and

looking over at her. "I am, but here's why. From what I can tell, people come to you and your family for help, or else they try to take what you have. In a way, you're only defending your community and way of life. Kind of like my tour in Afghanistan."

Emory nodded. "Do you want to talk about that?"

"Not right now." He fell silent, and she didn't know what to say. "Sometimes I have nightmares and wake up screaming, but beyond that…and that doesn't happen so much now. That hasn't happened much since I moved out here."

Monty hadn't said a thing about that. That old buzzard was loyal to Jace too.

"Why do you think that might be?"

"I guess it's because I've felt accepted by everyone—that I don't have to pretend or make myself out to be something that I'm not."

Tension released from Emory's shoulders. "Yeah, we're pretty much just ourselves. There's nothing else really to be. My family likes you, and I do too."

"And I like all of you, but some more than others." He reached his hand out and covered her hand resting on her thigh with his. "Do you mind?"

She smiled and turned over her hand to hold his. "Not at all."

———

WHETHER EMORY FELT WELL on the way to falling in love or not, they had Lost Daughter business to attend to. Accordingly, they went to the clerk and recorder's office, although they kept bumping shoulders and coming in contact on the way in, where they found Glenda predictably behind the counter.

"We found at least a record, signed and dated." Emory heard both the pride and the relief in her own voice. "Dad also said I should ask you whether I should take this original to the sheriff's office as evidence. You both probably need it…"

Glenda looked it over. "Wow, that is old, isn't it? Let me make a copy for our records. Maybe I'll make two while I'm at it. I'd say since that is original, you'd want to be very careful with it."

Emory nodded.

Glenda made two quick copies. "Does this all mean that Lance wants to go ahead with the quiet title?"

"He does, as long as it costs him something in the region of one thousand five hundred dollars."

"I can't guarantee that…but you do have a promising start."

Emory looked at Jace, who shrugged. "Let me call him to double-check." She pulled out her cell. "Hey, Dad? Glenda wants to know if you want to get started on that quiet title. She says we have a promising start."

"You might as well go ahead. If it goes to a property attorney. We'll have to argue or bargain with him when the time comes. Anything else?"

"No. We're going to the sheriff's next, and then we're going to lunch."

The call ended, and Emory nodded. "He said to get everything started. We don't need to limp around with this for another century."

"I think that sounds like a good decision."

"How and when do we pay?"

"Let me get started, and I'll file and register this. That'll cost about one hundred dollars. Then it goes over to an attorney. We can probably use Sam Thompson, who's local enough. He'll contact your father, and

334 | RANDI SAMUELSON-BROWN

they'll likely have a meeting and come to an arrangement."

"So, for today, I just pay the filing and recording, correct?"

"That's the size of it."

"Do you take credit cards?"

"Honey," Glenda replied, "everyone takes credit cards these days."

NEXT, they headed for the sheriff's office.

Louise was manning the reception desk. "Well howdy, stranger," she said upon catching sight of Emory.

"Hi there. This is Jace Scott. Say, we're here again to see Sheriff Preston."

"You better watch her," she said to Jace. "The sheriff's going to think she's developed a crush on him."

"Very funny."

"You can go on back."

"We found an old receipt," Emory said from the doorway, all business. "which we just filed at the clerk and recorder's office." Then she remembered her manners. "This is…my friend…Jace Scott."

The sheriff stood halfway up, and they shook hands. "Friend, huh?"

"Works for me." Jace cracked a grin and Emory colored.

Breaking up the tide against her, Emory handed the sheriff the paper. "Dad wants to know if you should keep this as evidence."

"It couldn't hurt," he said. "We'll return it once we get everything straightened out. You know, the lab results came in. Suhanna attempted to feed the horses plain old carrots. Not a trace of poison or tampering to be seen."

Shit. "Now I feel stupid, getting worked up like that."

"Not so fast," the sheriff said, reclaiming his chair. For what it's worth, I don't think this matter is resolved, and it's something beyond a woman coming onto your property and feeding your horses carrots. Her actions could have been a dry run for something worse. You know horses. Feed 'em once, feed 'em again, and you've become a trusted snack machine."

"Pretty much. What do you think will happen next?"

"Call it a sixth sense or call it what you will, but this ain't over. That woman is nowhere near as talkative as she was when you and Lance paid her a visit. Ever since she made her call to that Cooper person…"

Emory took that in. "We're getting the box canyon title cleaned up as best we can. Other than that, I guess it's business as usual."

A twinkle lit the sheriff's eyes. "This one is pure trouble," he said to Jace, "but she sure has made something of herself."

"He likes you," Jace said as they left the building.

"Of course he does. I like him as well. He's the one who always took an interest in what I was doing. I wouldn't be surprised to learn that when it comes down to it, he brokered the brand inspector internship. He told me something to the effect that if I wanted a hardscrabble life, I was well on my way, and to just keep going how I went. He suggested that I apply myself—which turned out to be the kick in the pants that Dad needed as well."

Jace grimaced. "I would have guessed that your father was the one who did the kicking."

Emory laughed. "True, but Sheriff Preston cares about his constituency. Deep down, Dad knew we both could do better too."

50

THINGS THAT GO BANG IN THE NIGHT

JUNE 2023

EMORY AND JACE RETURNED TO FIND LANCE AND MONTY saddling up.

"Going somewhere?" Emory called over to the pair of them, climbing out of Jace's pickup truck.

"We've got a plan," her father replied. "I'm going to attempt to ride to the box canyon from here, while Monty will trailer up and try to find the way from the valley floor to the canyon's rim."

"I understand trying to find the route from here, but what's Monty supposed to discover?"

Her father shrugged. "We're just covering the angles."

"Sounds like a plan. Say, a couple of things. The lab report on the carrots came back clean. *But*, and I want to emphasize that, the sheriff said he felt Suhanna's attempted feeding could have been a dry run. He also said that he didn't trust the situation as we now have it."

"Yep," Monty's voice came across loud and clear. "That's why we're riding. Oh, sorry, Lance."

"Monty's right. And what are you sorry about?"

"You're the boss. I shouldn't steal your thunder like that."

Jace rubbed his forehead to hide his smirk.

"No problem," Lance replied, eyebrow cocked at the outlandishness. "Anyhow, I still think, after we get it all checked out, that someone needs to go back into the canyon. Armed, of course." A pause as he tightened the cinch and checked the tightness. "I don't suppose Bob gave any particulars on what he expected might happen."

Emory shook her head. "He said he's developed a sixth sense on these types of things. When you two go riding, I hope you're careful."

Jace stepped forward a few paces. "I can come as well to look for decent sniping locations if you want."

"That might come in handy," her father said. "However, I want you to stay back here with Em for the time being. I don't mean to pry about your service record, but what exactly were you—that is, if you don't mind me asking."

"United States Marine Corps scout sniper."

"Hot damn," Monty replied, gushing. "Boy, you are *hired*."

Jace blushed. "I hear they're doing away with that division now, but it had its uses."

"Her father scanned the outfit, pleased. "That sure will come in handy. Maybe you could look this place over and see what you think. We've had our share of trouble back here."

"I already have, sir."

Emory felt so proud, she thought she might burst into tears. And that would have been completely uncalled for, not to mention ridiculous.

"Maybe we'll just get some chores done," she said, covering up her admiration.

THE TWO COUSINS returned a few hours later, both horses trailered back, and the men pensive.

"Someone's been in the canyon since us," Lance told them.

Emory frowned. "How can you tell?"

"Monty found a man's footprints that ain't mine. Anyhow, I found the canyon's overland route...it's a bit convoluted, but it's doable. No one will be coming from the canyon to the Lost Daughter via that route. That's one possibility put to rest. Monty, however, found something else."

Of course, he spat before speaking.

"Trail dust get in your lungs, cowboy?" Emory snarked.

Monty ignored her. "There's a way up to the rim from the road. It's fairly hard to find, but it's there. What's worse, a man's footprints were there as well. Now, he didn't climb up or anything, but he knows it's there."

"So, the question to you, Em—since you're the only one who's seen or met that skull man—what do *you* think?"

"I think I'm calling Torrie to see if she can do a welfare check. There's no sense in us going all spooky about Orran Cooper, if he's sitting in his living room one hundred miles away as the crow flies."

She found the deputy's number, and the call went through.

"Hey, Torrie, now I think I could use some help. Could you go do a welfare check on Orran Cooper? For the record, we don't think he's there, but out in Stampede instead. We need you to lay eyes on him, one way or another."

Emory hung up. "She's on it. Now I guess we wait until she calls back."

Again, her father scanned the ridges. "Call Terry and Dave as well. Let them know what you're up to, and what we're likely facing. But, Em? Make it the G-rated version."

———

EXACTLY TWENTY-THREE MINUTES LATER, the sheriff's deputy called back.

"He's not here. But guess who is staying out at his place? None other than that guy we arrested out at the processing plant and who got tossed in the psych ward. He ended up getting released—the doctors said he suffered from a psychotic episode. But check it out. He said he remembered me and had better things to do than stand around talking to a government pawn, but that he liked a woman with a bit of beef on her.

"I told him to shove it or I'd put him in another arm lock. Anyhow, he went on to say that his cousin was in Rimrock County. I told him the fishing was good up there. Then the cousin kind of laughed, and said, and I quote, 'That's what he was doing. Fishing with dynamite.' I told him, of course, that was wildly illegal. Then I booked it out of there. Weirdo."

"Thanks, Torrie, I've got to run." Emory clicked off and turned back to the men. "We've got trouble coming. Orran Cooper is up somewhere in Rimrock County. And I'll bet his footprints will match those that you saw. Not to mention that Suhanna's ex is at Orran's house while he's away."

"Shit." Her father spat. "Lock and load time."

No doubt.

"The question remains," Emory said, "where's the fight going to be? Here, in town via the law, or out in the canyon? Keep in mind that Suhanna claimed that Orran Cooper was batshit crazy."

"Maybe she's the crazy one," her father said, although he didn't sound convinced.

None of them had any way of telling.

"Dad, I'm going to call Sheriff Preston about this."

"Fine," he replied. "No one's stopping you. If Orran Cooper is in town, I want to know it."

She placed the call. "Hey. I just got off the phone with a deputy friend, and Suhanna's ex-husband says Orran is up here fishing with dynamite. He hasn't been by trying to visit Suhanna, has he?"

"No." The sheriff still processed all the information she gave. "I haven't heard anything about any idiot dynamiting ponds either."

"We've been checking the box canyon—Dad and Monty found a man's footprints."

"Not enough to go on," the sheriff replied, firm and clear. "Put me on speaker if you've got people who need to hear standing nearby."

"Dad, Monty, and Jace." She pressed the speaker button and held it out for everyone to hear.

"I received the docket, and Suhanna's arraignment is Tuesday, the day after next. I dragged it out as best as I could. If I were you all, I'd keep in mind that she isn't going to get free from here. Not to mention, you're well on your way to establishing legal title to the box canyon. That wouldn't be a place to take a stand. So, it holds to reason that if something is going to break out, it would likely be on your spread."

Emory clicked off. "It doesn't feel right."

"No," Lance replied. "It doesn't. But something is coming. I can feel it in my bones."

"It's too quiet, and something's wrong," Emory said. Everyone was seated around the kitchen table as she served up a weak version of dinner.

"I agree," Lance said, taking a bite of his roll, before tossing it back on his plate. "I can't eat. This isn't sitting right."

"I don't think the fight's coming back here," Emory said.

"I think it's going to happen in town," Jace offered intently. "If Suhanna's ex is really batshit crazy and there's really only the two of them in on this, well, judging from what I experienced in Afghanistan, it seems the strike hits where the greatest amount of damage can be inflicted—and that is where the people are."

Four sets of eyes locked into each other as they sat at their plates.

"Remember that killdozer guy in Granby?" Monty asked.

"Vaguely," Lance replied.

"He went nuts, started bulldozing the buildings. No one got killed, but it sure came close," Monty drawled. "How many deputies does your Sheriff Preston have exactly?"

"Don't know the number, but I'll bet you all are right," Lance said, sounding dead convinced on the matter. "Em, you wanna make that call, or should I?"

"Either way," she answered, staring at him.

"Maybe you better do it. Just in case I'm wrong." That damned twinkle again.

If he wasn't her father, she would have flipped him off.

"Let's ride," Emory said. "I think we better leave one of us behind."

"Today that's Monty," her father decided.

"Yep," he drawled. "I'd say that me and the spur can handle it."

51

CALL IN THE CAVALRY

JUNE 2023

The explosion shook Stampede.

Even the bar patrons at the Ace High heard the noise over the jukebox and their respective whiskey fogs.

"What in the hell was that?" people asked, streaming out from the bar to determine the source. It wasn't like they had a grain silo to explode, or anything understandable. Far louder than a transformer blowing, the lights remained on.

Everyone looked up and down the street, not noticing a damn thing.

"Should we call 9-1-1?" someone asked, distrustful of the entire concept.

"Might as well," another person answered. "Report the loud bang and see what they have to say."

Before they dialed, the first wail of a siren came flying down the main street, headed for the sheriff's office.

The siren pulled up right out in front of the sheriff's office. The gathering waited for an ambulance to follow, but none came—so matters must have not been that serious. Everything in the street and in the town turned back to quiet, and the bar patrons drifted back inside. The general consensus bantered back and forth, running from a gas tank exploding in the garage after hours to a meth lab blowing to smithereens. The fact remained that no one saw any sign of smoke or flames or smelled burning. The incident was shrugged off after ten minutes passed, the customers drifting back in to drink their drinks, and to resume their conversations or pool games.

Just another night in Stampede.

***

EMORY CALLED the sheriff as she and Jace loaded into her father's pickup, thudding down the rutted ranch road and barreling toward town. Her father drove far faster than usual, knuckles white on the steering wheel.

"He's not answering." The line kept on ringing until it switched into voice mail.

She left a message. "Sheriff Preston? Please call me when you get this. We think if there's a problem regarding Suhanna, it's going to be in town. *Not* out at the ranch."

She hung up. Her father drove even faster.

***

AS THEY SPED INTO TOWN, nothing looked outwardly different. The main street was near vacant, except for the Ace High drawing in the loose change in town. They sped right on by, heading straight for the sheriff's office. In front, they saw a deputy's car, lights still flashing and no one inside.

Jace sat at the passenger's window. "Why don't you

drive straight on by like nothing's happening, circle around the building as best as you can, and we'll see what we've got."

"We won't have coverage if we're all driving around," Emory said.

"True. Em, you jump out at that dark corner there. Wait for us if you can. I'm dialing your number and you put your phone on speaker, but low volume. Leave your phone on at all times so that we can keep in contact."

Jace pulled out his phone, hit her contact, it rang. She accepted the call and stuck the phone in her shirt pocket. "Fine. And if the sheriff calls?"

Jace came across as strictly military. "He can wait."

"Maybe," Emory replied.

Her father pulled up to the dark corner out of the reach of the few streetlights, and Jace hopped out, followed by Emory. He grabbed her rifle from the rack and held it out for her. "Don't give away your position unless you have no other choice."

"I already knew that" she said. To her surprise, he winked at her as he hopped back into the cab. Her father killed his headlights and drove around the corner.

Her phone beeped for a call waiting. She pulled it out. Sheriff Preston.

"Shit." She hissed into the night.

Torn and wanting to answer, she let it go to voice mail.

She could hear her father say, "What in the hell…"

"Keep driving," Jace's voice told him. "We want to check out the full perimeter."

Her father's voice continued from the distance. "The whole damn back corner of the holding cells is missing."

Emory hissed into her cell. "The sheriff just tried to call me."

Silence on the other end. "Do you have a message?" her father asked.

"Yes."

"Listen to it," Jace conceded. "We've almost done the entire perimeter. Wait. There's a car there. In the parking lot by the door. And the sheriff's pickup."

Emory pushed the voice mail button. "Attempted jailbreak in progress." The line went dead.

She switched lines. "He said an attempted jailbreak is in progress, but the line went dead. He didn't say anything else but that. Now what?"

Jace came through. "We know there's the sheriff, a deputy, Suhanna, and whoever is trying to spring her. That's four of them against three of us. Em, do you have a pocketknife?"

"Yes."

"Go slash that car's tires but be careful."

Emory hurried toward the parking lot, keeping to the shadows, and skimming along buildings where she could. She crossed the street, keeping out of the streetlight's reaches as best as she could, racing toward the outer wall of the sheriff's building. She crouched down as she crossed underneath the windows. She held the car in her sights when she heard the front entry door open.

She froze.

"Someone's coming out the front," she whispered low. "Where are you two?"

From her phone she could hear scuffling sounds.

"Hang on, Em." Her father's voice came through. "Jace is going on the roof."

Wedged between a juniper bush and the brick wall, she waited, her rifle leveled and using the scope for a better view.

Into the darkened parking lot, Suhanna struggled

within the grip of the sheriff, all but dragging her to the car. The deputy trailed behind them, handcuffed and his hands on his head. None other than Orran Cooper followed behind the procession carrying what appeared to be an AK-47.

From up above, a beam of light landed dead center between Orran's shoulder blades.

"Halt!" Jace shouted.

Orran paused, then kept walking.

Emory had them all within her sights. "I've got a bead on him."

A shot rang out from the side. Her father. "That ought to stop him."

Instead, Orran pushed the deputy headfirst into both the sheriff and Suhanna, and the three of them went sprawling forward.

Two simultaneous shots rang out, and Orran crumpled to the asphalt.

"Everyone OK?" her father's voice shouted.

"Yes," the sheriff called out.

Suhanna peeled herself up off the pavement and started to run. Again, that deadly beam of light.

"Don't make me do it," Jace called out. "Hands up high!"

The Arizonan stopped, turned toward the light, and looked exactly like a deer in the headlights before it met its Maker.

When she hesitated, Sheriff Preston sprang forward and grabbed her—wrenching her arm behind her body.

Emory called out. "I've got you covered."

"Could someone help Walter up?" the sheriff called out, his hands full. "He's cuffed."

"I've got it, Bob." Her father jogged across the parking lot to help the deputy. "Are you OK, son?"

The deputy was pretty banged up, in all honesty.

Emory walked over toward Orran. She looked back up at the roof where Jace still stood and held up her hand in a wave. "I'm calling an ambulance. Dad—maybe you should go in the office just to make sure."

"I shot him in the arm," she said, calling up to Jace.

"I got him worse than that. I'm not coming down until the situation is resolved. It's always best to have the advantage of height."

Ah. A man after their own hearts.

EMORY PUNCHED IN 9-1-1, and within moments the ambulance approached from the hospital about six blocks away. It whizzed by the crowd forming outside the bar. Some of the more intrepid customers streamed toward the sheriff's office, lured by the excitement and the spectacle's aftermath. Meanwhile another off-duty deputy tore up in a private vehicle and skidded to a stop.

He bolted from his seat, using the car door as a shield.

"Identify yourself," he shouted at Emory, gun drawn and pointed right at her.

She knew the voice from what she could see of his face belonging to Michael Henry, who she went to high school with. "Emory Cross, Michael. And you're late. You missed all the action. Dad's inside with the sheriff, and he has a rifle. Do you have keys to the handcuffs? Walter needs to be released and checked over."

His gun lowered. "Who's that on the rooftop?"

"Jace Scott. He was in Afghanistan."

The deputy kept a wary eye on Jace as he sidled over

to the cuffed deputy. He stared at the body of Orran, face down and unmoving.

"He's bleeding," Michael said.

"Stay out of his reach," Emory replied. "We think he's dead, but we don't know for certain."

The deputy edged around him as the ambulance pulled up and the paramedics, uncertain, still hopped out.

Michael flashed his badge. "The man on the roof has you both covered, but I'd be really careful in case he tries to pull something."

But the body on the ground didn't move. Orran Cooper appeared most likely dead, felled by two bullets shot at the same time.

Then the quiet mountain town lit up with the approach of lights and sirens coming in different directions. The law reinforcements had all arrived.

Remarkably, Orran Cooper had the faintest thread of a pulse as they loaded him into the ambulance.

52

AFTERMATH

JUNE 2023

TWO HOURS LATER WHEN MOST, BUT NOT ALL, OF THE visiting law enforcement left Stampede much more subdued than when they came tearing in all lights and glory and after the fact, the Cross faction and Sheriff Preston sat in his office.

"We tried to call you to warn you," Emory told him.

The sheriff shook his head. "I was on my way out for the night when it sounded like a cannon went off in the back. I never thought someone would attack the sheriff's office in Stampede, Colorado. Dynamite, of all things. That lunatic set off a charge and blew off the back corner—it crumbled. He could have killed his relative, but I guess he didn't care all that much."

"Where's Suhanna now?" Emory folded her arms, her adrenaline fading.

The sheriff sounded subdued. "Transported to a more secure facility in Georgetown. That one is underground, would you believe. Anyhow, we've got an awful lot of reports to fill out."

"I owe you a debt of gratitude," Preston said to all of them, "and to you, Jace. Thank you for taking charge."

Jace sat back in his chair, ran his fingers through his hair. "I don't know that I took charge, it's just that my training kicked in. Lance and Emory figured out a lot of it. Without them, this would have been far worse."

"We'll wait for the hospital to update us or for the autopsy report to come back, but I have both of your statements. There won't be a problem. You all gave him fair warning."

Lance rose to his feet. "I've had about enough for one night."

Emory considered the sheriff. "Do you suppose that Suhanna knew he was coming?"

"That was my overall impression. But now, I'm not so certain. He blew off the corner of the building when she was in that very same cell. To make matters even worse, I'm not sure what he planned on doing with any of us. I distinctly got the impression that she was as much of a hostage as we were."

"But back to what happened here. You said there was the explosion—"

"And I went running back, but thankfully, not before I reported the incident. I called it in, thinking maybe the hot water heater blew up, or who knows what. To be honest, I let my guard down, however. I rushed back to the holding cells, and that weasel already made his way in the building through the hole he made. He had a gun to her head and said he would shoot." The sheriff looked sad. "Some family," he muttered.

THE RIDE back to the Lost Daughter passed in a subdued manner of a bad experience survived. Emory laid her head on Jace's shoulder, and her father looked as pleased as anything at that development. Every once in a while, he looked at the pair of them. When he couldn't stand it any longer, he belted out with a guffaw.

"You know that you two both shot at exactly the same moment, don't you?"

Emory and Jace didn't respond, not that it bothered Lance. "Well, I'd say that is quite a remarkable coincidence."

He elbowed Em in the ribs.

"Please don't say something embarrassing," she said, tired and content and saddened all at the same time. Now she had two men whose deaths she found herself involved in.

"Wouldn't dream of it," Lance said, smiling straight ahead, as he saluted the skull hanging from the Lost Daughter's crossbar.

They would all live to fight another day. And with luck, for the rest of the century.

A LOOK AT:

ON THE FRINGES

From Award Winning author Randi Samuelson-Brown, a gritty tale about one woman's stark determination to create her own destiny.

Maude Montgomery, gifted with the second-sight, is trapped in a bad marriage to a confidence man who doesn't inspire too much confidence in her. Yearning for a better existence, she gets more than she bargained for when her husband abandons her in a remote outpost of Nebraska.

Alone for the first time in her life, Maude has a decision to make–return back East to nothingness and mediocrity, or head deeper into the West to find her fortune. She chooses to take her chances in the west, and lands in Cripple Creek where she learns gold is *not* scattered about in the streets.

Armed with little more than an untested belief she can sense gold ore deposits, Maude becomes tangled up in the gold camp's underworld and is instrumental in the makings of a mining swindle. Uncertain where to turn, or who to trust, she's about to learn first-hand that all that glitters might not be gold, and freedom demands a hefty price.

AVAILABLE NOW

ABOUT THE AUTHOR

Randi Samuelson-Brown is originally from Golden, Colorado, but now lives in Denver. A passion for Colorado history was instilled in her by her father from early on, and she latched on to the most notorious aspects of life in the West. She was even a finalist in the 2021 Colorado Book Awards.

When not writing in her free time, Randi is often riding horses and traveling around Colorado and the West, finding inspiration from people, places, and open spaces. She loves speaking at museums and organizations, and especially loves meeting readers.